I0662787

Skyfire

An historical novel

Arthur W. Johnson

BIG WORLD NETWORK.COM

COPYRIGHTS

Copyright © 2020 Arthur W. Johnson

All Rights Reserved

Cover Design by Ahnasariah Larsen

Cover Art from Pixabay.com

All rights reserved. No part of this publication may be reproduced, distributed, or transmitted in any form or by any means, including photocopying, recording, or other electronic or mechanical methods, without the prior written permission of the publisher and the author, except in the case of brief quotations embodied in critical reviews and certain other noncommercial uses permitted by copyright law. For permission requests, contact Big World Network at ceobwn@gmail.com.

This is a work of historical fiction. Any references to historical events, real people, or real places are used fictitiously. Names, characters, and places are products of the author's imagination.

Distributed by Big World Network.

ISBN: 978-0-578-68175-7

Second Edition 2020.

Managing Editor: Ahnasariah Larsen

Interior Design by Ahnasariah Larsen

For June,
My super wife of 52 years.

Table of Contents

Skyfire

An historical novel

Prologue

The band of thirty cloaked figures stood on the bare hilltop, silhouetted against the great ball of the sun as it neared the western horizon. In unison, their cloaks swayed as the chilly wind swept undaunted over the treeless crest. The silence gravitated between fear of the unknown darkness as it approached and an almost holy respect for the sun as it lay down to rest beyond the trees on the far hill.

As the upper rim of the sun disappeared, the old man, who was considered the spiritual leader of the band, turned and the wind whipped his long, white beard past his shoulder. The light from the sun seemed to shine from his eyes as he raised his arms and spoke.

"Tan y'n cunys lemmyn gor uskys," he said, almost as if speaking a prayer. The little band of Celts gathered around and lit the pyre just as he had commanded.

Chapter 1

"The ship was cheered, the harbour cleared,
Merrily did we drop
Below the kirk, below the hill,
Below the lighthouse top.[1]

Seamus felt refreshed. He enjoyed the sea. Captain Fowler had marveled at how quickly he had learned to shift his weight from foot to foot to compensate for the roll and pitch of the deck. But it seemed like such a natural thing to Seamus, rhythmic and poetic, and he had always been comfortable with lilting phrases.

A fortnight had passed since they had weighed anchor and let the sails take their first big gulp of air. During that time, they had all worked day and night, eating and sleeping whenever time permitted. The *Irish Lassie* had tacked crosswise and at times into the wind to prevent them from being blown into the Norwegian Sea. But now, the winds had shifted and were from behind. Captain Fowler had told all hands to stand down as he turned the helm over to his first mate and gone below for some much-needed sleep.

Seamus stood at the railing by the bowsprit with one hand on a shroud line. As his red hair blew in the wind, he watched the deep blue waters part around the graceful prow of the snow. He had laughed when he first heard

---

[1] The Rime of the Ancient Mariner, by Samuel Coleridge

the term for this type of ship. His new friend, Kyle, had explained that she was called a snow. She had a trysail mast abaft of the main mast, making it different from a brig, although they were alike in most other ways.

"So, what do you think," asked the voice from behind him.

Seamus turned to face the blonde-haired Kyle and leaned his back against the white railing, one arm extended along its rolled edge to brace himself against the gentle pitch of the ship.

Kyle Owens had been talking to him during the various lulls about the town called New York, with its bustle and busy air. He said he was excited to be returning. He hoped to find work on the wharves where he could become a rich man in a short time, at least that's how he had put it to Seamus.

"It sounds good," Seamus said to the young man who was around his own age. "I can't imagine what it would be like to be rich, though." He looked at Kyle for a moment before asking, "What will you do with all your money?"

Kyle smiled and looked dreamily across the gently rolling waves. He was the same height as Seamus but of a sturdier build. He laid a powerful arm on the railing as he said casually, "I will buy a whole fleet. That's what I'll be doin'. I'll have ships sailin' from Crow's Head Cove in Ireland to Long Island Sound in New York in a steady stream. Why, they'll be passin' each other goin' back and forth." He looked Seamus square in the eye to add as much sincerity as he could to his next phrase. "You can do whatever you want in America and become a wealthy man at the same time."

Seamus turned back to the sea and leaned both elbows on the railing, lacing his fingers together as he said, "I don't know if I care to become too wealthy." His mind flashed back to a sitting room in Ireland with fine paintings and tapestries on the walls. He almost feared wealth for what it did to a man's soul. "I think I just want to be comfortable."

"You can have that too, if it's what you want," Kyle said. "For me, that's not enough. I want to live like a prince, and I'm going to do it! You'll see."

The two stood staring toward the western horizon, unbroken and empty, yet full of hope. Each saw hope in a different way, but it was in the same general direction for both of them.

Finally, Kyle broke the silence. "We'd better get some rest. There's no telling how long this lull will last."

"I'll be along shortly," Seamus said as Kyle walked to the hatch.

Why, Seamus wondered, did he have such an aversion to wealth? Was it all due to Lord Mayfair's attitude or character? Did he fear becoming like him? But there was Mike Darcy, owner of the End-O-Lough back in his home town of Athlone on the River Shannon. Mike could be considered wealthy, yet he knew every man in that part of Westmeath by his first name. He treated every man in town as a friend. Then there was the captain of this very ship. Granted he had only known him for a couple of weeks, but he seemed amiable. He owned the ship, paid cash for the cargo and seemed to have wealth, but he treated his crew well. They seemed to enjoy working for him. He seemed like a decent human being.

Another thought occurred to Seamus. Both men had begun poor and built what they had themselves. He had heard them say so. With poor beginnings, he reasoned, they would be able to feel a kinship with those less fortunate, unlike Lord Mayfair who had been born to wealth and had never experienced a hole in his trousers. Maybe that was the key, he thought. As long as he earned his wealth and remembered where he began, he would never be like Lord Mayfair.

As he lowered his hand from the railing, it brushed across his jacket pocket and he felt the round bowl of the pipe. Then there were people like Jamie McFee, the wee man in the woods, who had left the pipe behind. He never quite understood why he left the pipe. But he had given Seamus back the hope he needed when he was in his worst despair. They were complete strangers until that unusual meeting. The priest at the monastery was another odd experience.

They offset the Lord Mayfair's of the world, he thought. Those were people with noble souls who truly wished to help others.

He caught sight of something on the distant horizon, small, yet alarming. As he watched the speck grow at a snail's pace, it seemed to take on the shape of a pile of sails, reminding him of the agonizing wait he had been forced to endure at Crow's Head Cove.

When he had come to the edge of the sandy bluff overlooking the scattered thatched roofs that climbed down the slope toward the beach, he had seen a mountain of canvas entering the still, blue waters of the hidden crescent. He had stopped and ducked behind a clump of hardy broom weed growing in the sand, for the Union Jack was flying from the mast. At first, he had wondered how the English had known to look for him here before realizing that they would not have sent a fully fitted man-o-war after one man. No, that ship was not after him. Their prize was to be far more valuable. They wanted the illegal whiskey ships.

A young lad had puffed his way up the hill and passed Seamus without taking notice of him. He had watched as the lad grew smaller to the south, where a little spit of land was clearly visible. Then Seamus had descended the hill to the town. The English presence made him nervous but he felt he could blend with the town folk well enough to escape special notice.

The people in the little village at the end of Slieve Miskish had been a-bustle from the moment the canvas had first been sighted. Hoping to make himself welcome, Seamus had offered his help to the first man he saw working. The man with auburn whiskers fringing his chin gave him a quick glance then nodded toward a pile of sacks, saying, "Take those ta' the back o' the cottage and dump them down the chute, lad."

As Seamus returned to retrieve his own bag after dumping the last of the pile, the man patted him on the shoulder and said, "I see you're no stranger to work. Will you join the lads and me for a pint?"

"I would be proud to," Seamus replied. "But is there no more to do?"

"Nay, 'tis done, lad. Leave your bag inside the door and come with me."

As they walked to the pub, the man introduced himself as Jack and explained that the life of the village was centered on the whiskey trade, the smaller part being authorized by the British. Each villager played a part in the vaster plan of sending the whiskey off to America, so each had a given duty in a time of need such as this. Hiding the extra grain was his duty, for if the British were to find it, they would know that the village was producing far above their allotment. "There are even those whose duty it is to wet the fishing nets that are never used and hang them by the wharf to give us the appearance of a sleepy fishing village," he said.

"And the lad running up the path," Seamus asked, pointing toward the hill he had descended, "what is his job?"

"His task is to warn off any ships coming in. He'll cross over to the other side of Crow's Head and flash by sun reflection off a mirror a signal to stand away. When it's cloudy, he uses pennants. When it's all clear he will flash a safe signal and they will proceed into the cove. His father held that job before him."

Seamus was surprised by the highly organized system with which these people worked. "Do you have to do this often," he asked. "I mean, do the British call in here frequently?"

"Nay, hardly ever," Jack answered. "But I think they were pointed in this direction this time."

"What do you mean?"

"We should have had more warning of their coming. But that part of the system seems to have failed this time." He eyed Seamus suspiciously for a moment, then seemed to think better of it and laughed. "Those fools think they will catch a ship by lying to inside the cove. But they're empty coming in. It's going out that they are fully loaded."

Seamus laughed with him at the stupidity of the Captain of the war ship as they entered the pub. Even he, with no knowledge of the world, could see the lack of logic in the Captain's thinking.

Seamus came out of his daydreamed remembrances long enough to see that the speck he had been watching was only a cloud. It had been joined by many others to create a line across the far strip where ocean and sky met. He could see that the snow and her crew were in for some heavy weather in a few hours. As he went below for a bit of sleep, his mind drifted back to the cove again.

He had waited in the little village for a fortnight before the man-o-war set sail in search of other trophies. Jack had been kind in providing him with food and shelter instead of sending him off to the caves as Jamie McFee had predicted. Of course, Seamus had earned his keep. He had mentioned Jamie's name in the pub that first day and been accepted almost as one of the villagers. He had taken his place and worked hard for his new friends in return for their kindness. There were never any questions about his reason for leaving Ireland. He supposed that they all felt that he was just one of the many young men going to America in search of a better life. He never offered another reason, for the fewer people who knew, the fewer who could be hurt by the information. How could he have told them that there was a murderer in their midst, and that it was himself? They had been too kind to him to return their kindness with the burden of that knowledge. Secrets are hard to keep and the more people who know them increase the risk of exposure manifold.

Eventually, the British ship set sail on a northeasterly course out of the cove. Once word was sent back from Cod's Head that she had rounded the point, the clear and safe signals were sent off the other side of Crow's Head and two sets of sails appeared in front of the cove in a matter of hours.

The sight of all that white spanking above the two wooden hulls caused a lump to form in Seamus' throat. His new fate was cast now for certain and the size of the venture lay before him in the form of those two small ships bobbing on the surface of the unending sea beyond.

The loading of casks, whiskey and fresh water, took only a few hours. The larger, converted galley had no room for him, already being fully manned. But he was welcomed aboard the little snow called the *Irish Lassie* as had been foretold to him. As he clambered aboard, he had doubts as to her ability to withstand the rough seas he had heard about because she was so small. But his doubts were put to rest by the young man named Kyle, who Captain Fowler had assigned to literally show him the ropes. Kyle had indeed shown him the ropes and was now teaching him about hope, though Seamus thought Kyle's hopes were a bit too pretentious.

They had quickly set sail before the man-o-war could trap them in the cove and were plying a course for Reykjavik, Iceland, for the first of many stops for provisions; for the snow, fully loaded, had little room left for those necessities.

Seamus laid his head on the neatly coiled rope and pulled his jacket tight to ward off the North Atlantic chill. As his eyes closed, a smile crossed his face, for he had left his ghosts behind and knew he would rest peacefully.

He dreamt of days gone by when he and his father would net salmon at the southern end of Lough Ree, just where it flows into the Shannon River. He could see Fahey sitting in his coracle, holding his end of the net with himself not thirty meters away, doing the same. He could almost feel the tug of the current on the net and the bobbing of his own coracle. The bobbing became fiercer. He didn't remember this. What was happening to his dream? He was being heaved about, as if by some gigantic hand. His father was no longer there and he was being pitched about unmercifully. But he held fast to the end of the net with one hand and to the coracle with the other. Until now, the little boat had not tipped, but as a wave of extraordinary size took him aloft and dropped him, he was jarred awake.

The dream was gone and he lay on his side on the deck with the coil of rope in one hand and the loose end in the other. Suddenly he was pitched on top of the coil and knew it was no dream. It was the nightmare all sailors feared. It was a tremendous storm at sea and he was caught below decks in its fury.

With his cap pulled tight, he made a dash for the ladder, but it seemed to move sideways and he was slammed against the bulkhead. He would not trust his legs this time and crawled to the base of the ladder. As he climbed, he felt as he had when he was a boy and the wind blew the trees as he neared the tops. It was exhilarating and frightening at the same time. The ladder swayed to and fro at an alarming speed. He reached the top and crawled out onto the deck, tasting the salt spray as it blew in his face.

He reached the capstan and got a firm grip before the briny waves again broke over the rail, engulfing him and all went momentarily black. As the wave receded, he heard a shout along the deck. It was Kyle's voice that yelled in the stormy night, "I can't hold!"

Seamus crawled and rolled in the direction of the voice and found him slid halfway through the railing, elbows jammed between neighboring balusters to anchor himself, legs and feet exposed to the ocean's violence. The receding wave had washed him overboard but luck had provided him with this last purchase on his life.

Seamus took the loose end of a dangling shroud line and stripped the lanyard off the lower end of the deadeye. He looped it under Kyle's arms and back through the upper deadeye, tying it firmly before the next wave broke and he had to find something firm to grab onto.

As the deluge subsided, he looked to where Kyle had been; by the flash of lightning overhead, he saw a jagged void. The torn railing flipped and bobbed on a passing wave. Kyle was not to be seen. He heard the captain shouting commands from the helm, but he did not respond. All he could think was, Kyle's missing. But in another flash of lightening he spotted Kyle's limp body, swaying away from the hull as the ship listed. The shroud line had held. The next wave pitched the ship the other way, and he imagined that he heard him hit the hull with a wet thump.

Quickly, he located a boat hook and crawled to the edge of the deck where, after several tries, he was able to snag the taut line that held his new friend. With all the strength he could muster, he dragged Kyle's inert body onto the deck and pulled him over to the base of the mast, where he lashed him securely before racing for the helm ahead of the next breaking wave. He felt he was starting to understand the rhythms of the sea.

"Tie yourself down, lad," Captain Fowler bellowed above the roar of the sea. Before he could respond, he felt himself being tugged across the slippery deck by the salty hand. What worried him most was the feeling of falling. He kept expecting the splash as he hit the waves but was surprised by the painful crunch as he slammed into something hard. As lightning streaked the sky, he looked up and saw the square opening of the hatch above his head. He said a silent prayer of thanks for forgetting to close the cover on his first trip up the ladder. Now he would have to do it again. But at least he was alive to make the climb.

Half way up he looked back during another lightening flash and spotted the rope, no longer in a neat coil. He went back down and tied the loose end around his waist, then dug the other end out from under the heap and dragged it up to tie to the top rung of the ladder. He looked aloft and lines from The Rime of the Ancient Mariner went through his mind.

With sloping mast and dipping prow . . .[2]

Odd to think of poetry at a time such as this, he thought. But then, *I wonder who killed the albatross.* A chill possessed him as his mind flew back to Mayfield Manor, and he said to himself, "I did. But this ghost is supposed to be gone."

He set his jaw and crawled out onto the deck with resolve. The deck heaved and dropped and pitched to port as he slid the cover into place. He would weather this storm and so would the ship. The masts groaned in agreement and he made his way to the helm. The leech lines and halyards sang under the strain as the wind and waves roared around the ship. And the last stanza came to mind . . .

> *'He went like one that hath been stunned*
> *And is of sense forlorn.*
> *A sadder and a wiser man*
> *He rose the morrow morn.'*[3]

Such a sad and lonely epic, he thought, *but what else could Samuel Coleridge be expected to write, with all that opium influencing his mind? I shall write cheerful poetry*, he mused, *to counter all the grays and the blacks in this life.*

Just as with the Ancient Mariner, when he began to see the beauty of life, it began to improve. The gale winds weakened from a shriek to a low howl and the mountainous waves contented themselves to buffet the ship rather than bury it.

---

[2] The Rime of the Ancient Mariner, by Samuel Coleridge

[3] The Rime of the Ancient Mariner, by Samuel Coleridge

He stooped to pick up the small creature lying at his feet. It made a rippling sound of popping noises as the cups on its many arms lost their suction on the smooth teak deck. And it writhed about his hands as he carried it to the edge of the deck and dropped it to its life.

Seamus made his way to the base of the mast with a warm feeling growing in his breast. Kyle grinned up at him and said, "Am I a prisoner, or will you untie me now?"

"Are you fit to stand against the pitching yet," he asked.

"Ha! I can stand against anything," Kyle said.

Seamus smiled down at his new friend, himself a sadder but wiser man. He was amused by Kyle's bold front. "Do you remember the railing that you were holding onto?"

When Kyle nodded, he pointed at the empty space where the rail had been. He saw horror cross Kyle's face at the thought of what could have been.

"But how . . ." Kyle stammered. "Everything went black. How did I get here?"

"I'll tell you about it later," he said as he untied the lashings. "Right now, Captain Fowler needs our help."

As they approached him, Captain Fowler pointed at the hatch and yelled over the wailing wind, "See that the bilge pumps are being manned!"

Seamus slid the cover back and Kyle stepped down onto the polished ladder. He slipped his feet to the sides of the rails and slid down the ladder, bouncing on his toes on the deck below. Seamus smiled at the way he did that and decided that if he were to become a seasoned seaman by the end of the voyage, he had better learn to do it as well. He started out right but somehow when he reached the bottom, his posterior hit the deck and he rolled over backward. Kyle slapped his thigh and laughed.

"It takes practice." He laughed again and raced off in the direction of the pumps with Seamus close on his heels.

They found a lone seaman standing by the pump with one hand resting on the lever. He looked exhausted as they approached. They knew him as Mickey O'Roarke.

"It's jammed," he said. "Norris has gone below to see what's in it."

Kyle gave a shudder and Seamus knew why. *Below* was barely high enough for a man to crawl through, since the lower deck had been added to provide a flat place to stow cargo. It was best known as the rat deck for the population that inhabited it.

Kyle yelled down through the narrow opening, "You alright down there, Norris?"

"Aye. It's one of them furry fellows what's sucked part way up the pipe. I'll have 'em out in a shake, I will."

He splashed his way back through the foot of water and flung the soggy carcass onto the deck, causing Kyle to jump back as it slid against his boot.

"There's naught to worry 'bout now, lad," said the bearded Norris as he poked his head up through the hatch. "'E's drowned now."

He clambered out and slid the cover into place to keep the beady eyed population from following, then added, "but, there's plenty more down there that ain't. They're swimmin' around and grabbin' on to whatever they can." He looked at the others and added with a shudder, "includin' me."

Seamus also shuddered at the thought.

"Let's get that pump going again, Seamus," Kyle said. The two of them relieved the original pumpers. As the two tired men slid down the bulkhead to rest, Kyle added,

"The worst of the blow is over, lads. Soon it will be clear sailing again." As they worked the pump handles up and down, Seamus, at Kyle's urging, told the tale of how he had been washed overboard and rescued. Seamus was proud of his courage but tried to sound humble as he told the story.

"Now there's a handy lad to have around," Kyle said to the two resting seamen.

"I'm grateful to the captain for bringing him aboard."

After a while, the pump began to wheeze.

"That's it then. We're sucking air, now."

The four tired men walked slowly back to the hatch, not noticing how little the deck was moving. Seamus was the first to emerge on deck to the glorious sight of the sky aflame above the western horizon. Seamus thought once again of Father O'Conner.

II

Westward bound below the coast
Of Iceland's southern end we sailed.
The night was brief as we bore on
With breeze from stern that never failed.

Seamus sat on the railing near the bow where he spent most of his free time searching for the future. He had written those lines in keeping his promise of writing cheerful poetry. He stared to the west where the sun had set only a few hours earlier and was amazed that the sky had never grown dark. It was nearly daybreak as he continued to stare west before writing,

And yet the sky in bright red flame
To west where sun has long since gone
The sun now rises to the east
What spark it left to oppose the dawn.

He was interrupted as Captain Fowler looked over his shoulder and asked, "What are you writing, lad?"

He felt his face warm with a blush as he answered, "A few lines of verse, Captain."

"That's noble. It's not often we have a man of letters aboard. What university did you attend?"

"I'm no man of letters," Seamus admitted, half turning. "My village priest, God rest his soul, taught me all I know."

"He died, then?"

"He was killed by . . ." Seamus stopped. The facts were coming dangerously near to the surface. Kyle had told him that the captain liked to get close to the members of his crew, but that was one secret he would not learn. He changed the subject, referring to the last stanza he had written. "Why, with the sun rising in the east, is the sunset still visible to the west?"

"'Tis not the sunset you see," he replied, laying a fatherly hand on his shoulder.

"That, my young friend, is the birth of new lands."

His voice had a dreamy quality that sent a shiver up Seamus' spine. He looked into the Captain's steady brown eyes for a clue to the meaning of his words.

"This is one of the most unique places on the face of the earth," Captain Fowler continued, "where fire and ice exist side by side. Volcanoes and steam holes come right up through the glaciers. I can never resist spending an extra day or two here." Waving an arm to encompass the whole ship, he added, "though this trip we may be here even longer to make a few repairs."

Seamus said, "I've heard of volcanoes but I've never seen one. Will we go near enough for a good look?"

"Aye. They're all over the mainland of Iceland, but what you see ahead is a chain of small islands called the Westmanns. They're forming out in the ocean. We should be close enough for your good look in a few hours." He patted Seamus' shoulder. "Then you'll really have something to write about."

He swaggered away, leaving Seamus to his solitude and thoughts. *The birth of new lands*, he thought. Seamus had always thought of a volcano as a destructive force, yet the Captain had called it a birth. He wondered how such a phenomenon could be both, considering what he had read about whole cities being buried by lava and ash. That was death. How could there also be birth in such a thing?

As the sun rose from the sea, the light played in strange patterns across the distant cliffs that made up the southern coast of Iceland. Seamus marveled at the unusual and sometimes grotesque shapes formed by the alternating shadowed and lighted areas. He could easily understand how the Norsemen, with their lack of education, saw gods and demons lurking among the pitted portals where sea and land battled for dominance.

As the sun spread its warmth across Seamus' back, he watched a gannet with its wide spread of wings reel and plummet at a high rate of speed, only to disappear beneath the waves with hardly a splash. He watched the spot for a moment only to be surprised by the gannet's reappearance some twenty feet away. It broke water and leapt into the sky with a fish in its beak in a single motion. He watched as it grew smaller and blended with the sky in a course set for the coast.

He looked over toward the Westmanns and saw the columns of smoke and steam billowing high above the islands. It looked like thousands of downy pillows piled high above the sea, ready to topple at any moment. As though in answer to his thoughts, he felt a rumble growing up through the ship into the soles of his feet as the deck quaked beneath him. The vision of the Norsemen again crossed his mind: Norsemen trembling in fear of the monster growling within the bowels of the earth. The downy pile was surmounted by more pillowing billows, seemingly tossed up from within the heap.

The rumble had brought the Captain back to the bow for another look. "You should be able to see the eruptions soon," he said. "That's just the steam and smoke. The real excitement is the huge chunks of rock that come flying out of the mountain top and the fiery sparks that spread over the land."

Seamus looked at the Captain for a moment, taking notice of the excitement on his face. He seemed more the child with a new discovery than the manager of a ship. For the first time since they had weighed anchor, Seamus saw the Captain to be only in his early thirties rather than an aged and wise sea Captain. The dark hair in front of his ears ran to the bottom of his rounded chin before pointing the way up through its cleft to his lower lip. The mustaches stopped before rejoining the side-whiskers. The brown eyes peered at the billowing steam with a sense of adventure from under dark brows that were striving to become bushy. His eyes belied the appearance given by his leathery cheeks, brown and weathered by countless years exposed to punishing salt spray and reflected sunlight. Seamus realized that no matter how abused the exterior became, youthful joys could be locked safely inside, to be brought out and cherished from time to time. He decided that he liked Captain Fowler, even though he ran an illegal ship.

A jolly pop on the back took him by surprise as Kyle's voice boomed in his ear,

"Well, lad, what d'ya think of that?"

He looked around to find that the entire ship's company was at the rails. Although they had all been this way before, they gaped as if seeing the spectacle for the first time. It was an awe-inspiring sight, impossible to ignore, even if it were an everyday occurrence.

"It's something different, alright," Seamus said, "as if—". He stopped and waited for the words to finish forming in his mind before writing more of the poem.

And God breathed again
Into the morning sky
A huger vapor plume
Than made by you or I.
E'en the birds, in awe
Ceased to fly
Fearing, lest He hear
Their hungry screech and cry.

"As if what," Kyle asked, peering over his shoulder. "I can't read, you know."

After Seamus read him the lines he'd just written, Kyle glanced up at the sky and said, "I hadn't realized that the birds weren't there. You seem to notice everything, don't you?"

Seamus shrugged. He didn't think it unusual to notice such details.

Captain Fowler turned to them and said, "What's more unusual is that he should see the steam from the volcano as the breath of God." He eyed Seamus for a moment, then asked, "Have you ever heard of Surtur, lad?"

Seamus thought for a moment before replying, "No, I don't believe I have."

The Captain turned back toward the plume and leaned on the railing, a thoughtful look coming over his face.

"There is Surtur," he said, tilting his head toward the eruption. "The Norsemen called him that. I've done a bit of reading myself," he said, glancing at Seamus. "In a story called 'Ragnarök, World Doom,' it states, 'Surtur rides first, and both before and behind him flames burning fire. His sword outshines the sun itself.' The Norsemen believed that he was both First Cause and World Destroyer."

Kyle shook his head, signifying that he didn't understand. Seamus' eyes lit up as the significance came clear to him.

"Sure," he said, "first cause being the building of an island, and world destroyer would refer to incidents such as the destruction of cities, like Pompeii."

"Aye," the Captain said. He looked again at Seamus curiously. "You are well read, then, aren't you?"

Kyle stood silently by for a moment, then turned and walked away saying, "I don't understand any of this."

Seamus watched him as a parent would a child who was upset with himself over some inadequacy. He felt that he needed to take him under his wing and help him over this little upset. When he turned back to the Captain, he realized that he also had been under scrutiny. He wondered what tales his own eyes had told as he diverted them to the paper in his hands.

"I know how you're feeling, lad. I've been that route myself. My own brother refused his schooling and missed out on so much. I tried to explain how he could see the world from an armchair but he wouldn't listen. He's a thatcher in County Cork, and a good one, too. But he'll never leave Cork by travel, or by reading."

"I've got to help Kyle, though," Seamus said, "and I think I know how to get his attention. You see, he wants to one day own his own . . ."

The ocean suddenly came alive with the explosive force of Surtur's wrath. The waves danced and leapt as they had not done before, and the deck vibrated as though Surtur had laid hands on the ship and shook it violently. Every man on deck clasped hands over his ears to protect them from Surtur's bellow.

As it softened to a rumble, the Captain yelled to the crew to brace for a tidal wave and raced to the helm.

Chapter 2

I can't sleep at night.
I am restless, toss and turn.
I have a new friend, you see
Who makes my heart burn!

It was not often on this voyage that Seamus had time to think about the past, but it was a slow day with the ship doing all the work in a trailing wind. He sat at the bow and gazed toward his destiny as his mind wandered back to meeting the woman he had so dearly loved. They had known each other as children all their short lives. But there was a gap in their teen years until that chance meeting as adults, a gap caused by his constant work on his father's farm.

Seamus had rebelled, in his mind at least, when he reached his early teens, not against his father, whom he loved as well as any son could, but against the land. His town friends had plenty of time to play around and just be boys, so why couldn't he? They weren't working from sunrise to sunset, but he certainly was. He stewed silently but did the work anyway. He was his father's son.

When he was sixteen years of age, Seamus had stopped rebelling. He had also stopped attending studies. He had given over his whole life to the farm and his father. He rarely saw his friends unless they stopped by to urge him to loaf with them, for which he no longer had the time nor the desire.

He seldom saw anyone, in fact, and was rapidly forgetting and being forgotten outside the farm.

Now he was nineteen and another three years had passed. He was completely married to the land and the care of his father, Fahey, the King of Potatoes, whose joints were so swollen that he probably would never plow again. Thus the Prince of Potatoes became the regent.

He divided his days between the fields and the chores to keep the aged cottage that he had grown to love from tumbling down around them. His father had taken over what he considered to be the wifely duties, such as the cleaning and the cooking. He would never do it as well as Lorna could. He didn't have her talent. Seamus constantly told him that it was alright if it wasn't up to her standards, and that she could see from where she sat in Heaven that he was ailing.

Finally, in late spring after all the planting was done and the chores were finished, Seamus said, "I think I'll go into Athlone for a change and maybe have a pint and a pie. Would you like to come along, Da'?"

"I think I'll just stay here and rest in the sun if you don't mind, Son."

"I understand. Can I bring anything back from the town for you?"

"Nay. I have all I need, thank you, Son."

So off he took himself and hiked into Athlone whistling as he went. He was so wrapped up in the beauty of the day that he wasn't paying attention when he rounded a corner and walked right into . . .

"Patricia?"

"Aye. 'Tis Seamus as I recall," she said, as though it had been more than a few years since she had last seen him.

"Aye."

"This is embarrassing," she said.

"Are you hurt?"

"Nay, Lad. What about you?"

"I am fine." He was stunned when the sun caught a glint of lavender in her eye as she turned her head.

She smiled at his expression and broke the spell when she said, "You've become something of a hermit out there on your father's farm."

"Nay, just busy with the work. I'm taking some time off now that the crop is in the ground. I'm going to the End O' Lough for a pint and a pie. Would you like to join me?"

"I think I would. Besides, you owe me for all the times you pulled my braids when we were little." She laughed and took his arm, turning with him toward her Uncle Mike's pub down the street.

"I suppose I do, don't I," he said lightly.

Seamus' step was suddenly a little lighter, as though the muddy boots from the fields were replaced by dancing shoes. He realized it and laughed inwardly at the thought of himself dancing.

"What are you smiling about," Patricia asked as she squinted up at him in the sunlight.

He told her and they both laughed. Then they looked at each other with a new realization. They both felt something they had never felt as children. It was a tingling sensation and an inner warmth, almost like a glow. There must have been an aura about them as they entered the pub because conversations ceased and the four other occupants eyed them. Even her uncle, Mike Darcy, who owned the pub, was staring at them. They didn't notice as they sat at a table near the window.

They were so wrapped up in each other that they were startled when Mike, now standing over them, said, "What will it be, then?"

"Hello, Uncle Mike," Patricia said as she looked up.

"What . . . oh. Could we have two pints and two pies please," Seamus managed to ask. As Mike turned away, Seamus whispered to Patricia, "I don't know what has come over me."

"I believe I do, Lad. It has happened to me, also."

"What would that be?"

"We have fallen in love."

He looked at her in disbelief. "I've never been in love before."

"Nor have I," she whispered. "It feels . . . good, doesn't it?"

"Oh, aye . . ." he replied bashfully.

Whatever he was about to say was interrupted as Mike plunked down their order and said, "My customers generally come to the bar and collect their own food and drink, but I suppose I can serve royalty at their table in your case."

"I'm sorry," Seamus said. "We got caught up in conversation."

"Oh, aye, I can see that," he snickered. "You and my niece look more like a couple of love birds."

Patricia reddened and lowered her gaze. Seamus stammered.

"It's alright, Lad." He smiled down at them. "But you missed my jest about royalty."

"What do you mean," Seamus asked.

"After all, you are the Prince of Potatoes, aren't you, Lad?"

"Oh, aye," he said. "I've gotten so busy with the work, I had forgotten that old jest."

"'Tis no jest, Lad. You should be proud of the title."

"Oh, but I am."

"Enjoy your lunch," Mike said as he turned away.

They spoke of many things that had transpired in the last few years.

" . . . and Da's arthritis has gotten so bad that he can't do very much anymore. Now the thatching on the roof needs mending. I've never done that and I'm not sure how to go about it."

"Let me tell my Father," Patricia said. "He is the best thatcher around Athlone, you know."

"I had forgotten, but yes, I did know. I will do the work if he will just show me what to do."

"I'll tell him as soon as I see him."

"Perhaps I should call on him and ask his permission to see you before we continue to meet each other."

"That is the proper thing to do," she said encouragingly. She glanced at those staring from the bar and added, "the rumors are about to begin as it is."

"Then I shall walk you home and ask him now. The Lord knows, I want to do things the right way around."

They rose from the table and Seamus went to the bar to pay for their meal, but Mike refused to accept his money this time. "It's on the house today. After all, she is my niece."

They walked not quite hand in hand, for that would not be proper on a 'first outing', but close enough that the backs of their hands occasionally brushed together, sending tingling sensations up both their spines. They were enjoying the new feelings and were playing them for all they were worth. They arrived at the Darcy cottage and Patricia called out to her father, but he did not respond.

"He must be repairing someone's roof. Would you care to come in and wait for him?"

"We shouldn't be here alone together. Someone may stop by and then the rumors would really fly."

"I suppose you are right." She looked up and down the lane and when she was sure no one was in sight, she held his cheeks in both her hands and kissed him full on the mouth before dashing inside and closing the door.

He stood there, stunned by the unexpected kiss, not knowing whether to go in after her or go home. Discretion finally won and he turned toward the realm of the potato with a new lightness to his step.

As he approached their cottage, he noticed his father sitting on the bench with his head leaning against the warm stucco wall. He turned his head as Seamus scuffed some pebbles in the road.

"How was your pint and pie then, Lad," he asked as Seamus sat down and leaned against the wall.

"It was fine," he said with a contented sigh, "but it was the company that made it so, Da'."

Fahey smiled knowingly as he tilted his head forward. "Who is she, then?"

"Is it that obvious?" As Fahey nodded, Seamus rocked forward, laced his fingers together, and rested his elbows on his knees. "Do you remember Patricia Darcy, the little girl whose sleek black hair I was always in trouble for pulling?"

"Aye, I do."

"I ran into her on my way into town. Literally!" Seamus paused for effect. "We shared a pint and a pie at the End O' Lough. But we shared more than that, Da'. We've fallen in love."

Fahey smiled and again leaned his head back against the wall. "I knew the day wasn't far off, when you would take your final step as a boy and become a man." He turned his head toward his son. "What does John Darcy say about it, then?"

"He wasn't at home so I wasn't able to speak with him. But I will ask him if I can call on her."

"You are doing the right thing, Lad."

"She is so beautiful, Da'."

"I know how you feel about her, Lad. It's how I felt about our Lorna from the day we discovered each other until the day she died. I still feel that way and I look forward to the day I see her again."

"Oh Da', don't get morbid."

"I'm not being morbid. When you get old and tired, you look forward to that which you miss the most. So tell me about Patricia," he said to deflect any more comments about his own feelings.

They sat in the sun until it was ready to set, and Seamus poured out his newly found feelings to his father. Then they discussed the correct customs of courting for the sake of their neighbor's sensibilities and propriety. Finally, as the chill of the evening fell, they went inside for the night.

II

The morning sun was just breaking over the horizon as Seamus and Fahey were sitting down to breakfast. Seamus got out of his chair to answer the knock at the door.

"Mr. Darcy! Won't you come in and join us for breakfast," Seamus asked.

"Nay, Lad." He said as he removed the cap from his balding head. "Patricia fed me well this morning. But I will have a cup of that fine smelling coffee."

Fahey rose and offered a gnarled hand. "Good morning, John."

"And a fine good morning to you, Fahey." He said as he offered his own callused hand. "'Twill be the third day of sunshine in a row. It can't last too long for my old bones," he groaned.

"I feel the same. What brings you out so early?" Fahey asked. He thought it a bit early in the morning to be calling about his daughter's welfare.

As John sat his lithe, bird like frame on the chair, Seamus interrupted. "I forgot to tell you, Da', Mr. Darcy is going to teach me how to mend the thatch. At least, Patricia said she would ask him," he said hopefully as he set a full cup in front of Patricia's father.

"Aye, she did, Lad. She couldn't stop talking about you last night after I got home," he said with a smile and a wink.

Seamus colored as he sat down. He cleared his suddenly clogged throat and asked, "Would you mind if I called upon her, Sir?"

"I would deem it an honor, Lad."

"Thank you, thank you," Seamus said in obvious relief. "I was afraid you would say no."

"Why would you think that?"

"Some people think of us," he nodded toward his father, "as dirt farmers."

"I find what you do as noble as thatching. And you," he also nodded to include Fahey, "are the most noble. After all, what do people call the two of you?"

"You're referring to the King and the Prince of Potatoes," Seamus interjected. John Darcy nodded agreement.

"We appreciate that," Fahey interjected. He looked at Seamus and asked, "How were you intending to pay Mr. Darcy?"

Seamus turned back to John Darcy. "If you will trust us for it, we will have the money in the fall when we harvest the potatoes."

"That will be fine, Lad. I trust you."

"Thank you. You are very generous, Sir." He paused for a moment, then asked, "What tools do I need for the roof?"

"I've brought enough for the both of us. After you've finished your breakfast, we'll get a start."

Seamus learned the fine art of thatching on a warm spring day in the year of 1831 and enjoyed the company of his future father-in-law. Fahey fed them lunch, and by nightfall they had become fast friends as they finished the job.

III

Seamus was glad that the potatoes grew on their own with very little help from him. He would occasionally hoe out a few weeds and take care of the chores that needed doing, but over the next few months he seemed to find more free time than he ever had for his boyhood friends. He often found himself at the Darcy cottage, escorting Patricia here and there and being seen together as young couples were meant to do universally.

They often walked for miles in the countryside, admiring the flowers at the various cottage doors or the young lambs or calves cavorting in the pastures. Their favorite haunt became the banks of the River Shannon. They had found a willow that hung out over the water where they would sit for hours talking about the future. When no one was looking, they would dart out of their secret place and go to the pub for lunch before returning to their respective chores.

They managed to spend a great deal of time together, and life had become as idyllic as either of them could have hoped. The summer was passing quickly with so much to do when they were apart.

IV

Patricia had for some time had tomboy tendencies, probably because her mother had died when she was ten years old. She lacked the feminine touch in her upbringing. More than once her father had apologized for not being able to guide her in that area. She would come in from play with a skinned knee that she had not noticed and he would worry over her and wish he could provide a mother's touch.

"It's alright Da'," she would tell him, "I'm big enough to take care of myself, now. I don't need a mother to dote over me."

She grew to the ripe age of nineteen with an occasional feminine insight from a female cousin or an aunt and didn't feel that she was lacking any of the knowledge she needed. At nineteen she was in love for the first time and was groping for all the information she had never been given regarding relationships between the sexes. Of course, there were some things that were only discussed between mother and daughter that she would never learn from an aunt or a cousin. Now there were times when she felt cheated, but she had a determination within herself and would never let that stop her. Suddenly Seamus was the most important person in her world.

She would figure out what she had to do to make him happy. She had confessed these facts to him on one of their outings, and been surprised that he showed no concern over her lack of knowledge or experience.

"I don't know any of that either," he had replied. "So, we'll learn all about it together, won't we?"

He thought they were off to a good start. Their long discussions under the willow by the river were an excellent beginning. He admired her spunk and her quickness. Patricia had a way of looking at things logically and coming out with the right solution every time. He liked that about her.

The waves grew larger and the snow's bow began to rise and fall in the troughs, shaking Seamus out of his reverie. He held on to the railing and rode with the movement, enjoying it like a child riding up and down hills in a cart, the wind a constant on the back of his head.

Chapter 3

And yet, ye shall again depart
And conquer lands both high and dry
But stay ye near the many streams
That flow to me 'neath one vast sky

Seamus thought it was odd to have dreams within his dreams, but that is indeed what was happening to him. He was reliving his journey and the dreams that accompanied him along the way. Once again, he dreamt as he slept during the voyage to the New World.

He dreamt first of rain, drizzling for hours before turning into a cold, steady downpour. The weather had reflected his mood. He kept going back and forth between reliving the rage he felt for the Monster when he pulled the trigger, to the futile feeling of total loss when he thought about Patricia's rape and death. Seamus paddled his coracle to the bank of the river Shannon and climbed out. He pulled the little hide boat out after him and lifted his hastily assembled pack after him onto the soggy grass. Grasping the seat board, he upended the willow-framed craft over himself and his bundle to ward off the rain.

He was accustomed to being caught out in the rain. That didn't bother him much. But he was tired and had been wet for so long that he thought a rest wouldn't hurt.

Besides, he thought, *I have a pretty good head start if they are after me.*

As he began to doze, the memory of the look on his father's face as he told him what he had done came flooding back. Or should he say the looks on his face, for there were several competing for dominance. That aged face had looked sorrowful when he told about Patricia being taken by Lord Mayfair. Then he had looked worried as Seamus told about how he had confronted the man. He looked proud when he thought about it some more. The corners of that toothless mouth between the hooked nose and the upturned chin appeared to smile as Seamus told about the final outcome. But then the worry and sorrow were again clear in his brown eyes as he thought about the consequences.

Then the loss of Patricia came crashing down on his soul as he shivered under the little hide boat, and he wept uncontrollably until he fell into a fitful sleep.

Seamus had known the instant he pulled the trigger that he would have to leave Athlone forever. The laws were clear and harsh. Killing an Englishman, let alone a lord, was punishable by instant death. He hoped and prayed that his father would not be punished in his stead.

Perhaps, he thought, *that was the reason for the look of worry on his face.* No, that couldn't be right. He knew his father better than that. His only concern would be for Seamus. He felt the love that his father held for him, and with that thought, he had finally fallen into a deep sleep under the coracle.

This could not be a dream. He could feel the warmth on his face. But there was Father O'Conner, beckoning him to follow. The old man had a look of contentment on his face and for the first time in Seamus' memory, his hair was neatly parted to one side. But was the sunset such a warm thing that he could feel it so intensely? He had never been close to the fire in the sky, so he couldn't say. But if it felt this good, he would gladly follow.

"I'm coming, Father," he said as he sat up. The motion stirred him back to reality. It was still the dark of night, but there was enough light to see his coracle leaning against a tree several feet away. The light danced across the hide bottom and he jumped to his feet, swinging around. "A fire. But who . . . ?" The little man sitting on the stump pulled his stubby pipe from his teeth and raised a hand in a show of peace.

"You were moanin' somethin' awful, Lad," he said, nodding toward the tree,

"Underneath that coracle you were. Did ya' have a mishap?"

Seamus scratched his head, looked at the boat and back at the round-faced man. He was still in a state of bewilderment but the memory was coming back. "The rain," he said. "I was on the river in the rain. When it got too hard, I landed and covered myself with the boat."

"Aye, wise thing to do," the little man said. "I don't mean ta' pry, Lad, but what were ya' doin' on the river in the rain, and in a craft seldom seen in these parts anymore?"

Seamus hedged on the first part and hoped that he could distract the little man with the rest of his answer.

"My Father taught me to build the coracle," he said with pride. "He said it was an ancient design mostly used in Wales now."

"Aye, 'tis true," the little man agreed, inviting Seamus to continue.

"He helped me build it just last week," Seamus lied, for in truth, he had made it himself the day before only a few miles south of Athlone. He knew that the quickest escape would be down the river and that the coracle was easy for one man to handle both in and out of the water with its light, willow frame. His father had taught him to build the coracle many years before. Fahey had given him the hide as he left the cottage.

He continued the lie. "I told Da' that I wanted to try it out and that I'd be gone for a few days. I'm on the way home now, you see."

The little man slapped his thigh and said, "Ah. That explains what you said in your sleep then."

Seamus looked at him quizzically and asked, "What was that?"

"You said, and in somewhat of a fit like you were late, I might add, you said, 'I'm coming, Father,' just before you awoke."

The phrase had stuck in his mind from the dream. With the phrase was the memory of Father O'Conner standing among the fiery clouds, beckoning him to follow. He wondered if Heaven was as wonderful as he said the Celts believed it to be. If so, then his friend and mentor was truly content. He suddenly realized that the little man was speaking to him. It occurred to him that he would have to be careful about daydreaming because his expressions often gave away his thoughts.

"Forgive me," he said, "I didn't hear what you said."

"I asked where you were from," the man repeated, his pixyish face showing concern.

Seamus had been afraid of that question. He'd never been out of County Westmeath before. He had to search his memory. Surely there was someplace his Father had told him he had traveled. Guarding his expression, he recalled a trip Fahey said he had made long ago.

"Castleconnell, to the South," he said. He recalled that it was on the banks of the River Shannon, a logical place for this trip to start and end. He appreciated the soft-spoken man's aid with the fire and friendly conversation. But he was becoming agitated with the questions. He wasn't sure how long he could continue without making some sort of slip.

The stranger tapped the loose ash from his pipe and tamped the rest of the half used dottle with a stubby, darkened finger. As he re-lit it with an ember from the fire, he peered at Seamus from under his shaggy brows. Seamus could see that he was doing some serious thinking. He began to doubt the wisdom of choosing Castleconnell, when the man bent forward and laid the ember back on the fire.

Seamus thought of Patricia. Their love had been like the ember on the end of that twig, growing with each passing breeze, ready to burst into a blaze of passion. But it had suddenly been snuffed out in the cold, uncaring sands of life.

As the stranger squared himself on the stump, he said, "I'm from Limerick, myself." He cleared his throat, crossed his legs, put the pipe to his lips and waited for Seamus to speak. When he didn't, he blew out a wad of smoke and continued, "It's just a short stretch o' the legs from Castleconnell, ya' know?"

He sat, puffing and staring through the smoke. Seamus knew there was a message in what the little man had said, but he didn't understand what it could be. He seemed to be playing cat and mouse with Seamus and it was working, for he was shifting uneasily as the little man said, "I know everyone in Castleconnell, Lad."

Seamus' spine tingled. He had been caught in a very ingenious trap with no escape.

"If you've not committed a crime, Lad, there's no reason ta' worry."

Seamus discovered a few hairs on the nape of his neck that hadn't stood up with the man's previous statement. His mind was racing. What could he say that wouldn't trap him further? How much did this little man know? The thought of Lord Mayfair slumped, cross-eyed and lifeless flashed through his mind. Committed a crime? Yes, he'd done so, and with good cause. But would this man agree with his reasoning? Was he a British sympathizer or a true Irishman? How could he broach the subject without convicting himself?

The firelight danced across the little man's face as Seamus studied his features, looking for a hint of his loyalty. The man's silence made him feel rushed. He had to say something soon or the mere silence would be his judge. *Test the water,* he thought. That's what Father O'Conner had taught him. "If you're not sure of an Irishman's loyalties, test the water. Ask him in Gaelic if he's Irish. The young ones might not know the phrase but the older ones will. If they're true, they'll answer in Gaelic. If they're not, they may caution you. If they're not sure about you, they may look around to see if anyone heard, then reply."

Seamus cleared his throat as he summoned his courage. He bared a verbal toe and dipped it into the surface. "Are you Irish?" he asked in Gaelic.

The little man seemed to be enjoying the nerve game. He defied the three possibilities, for he did not immediately answer, caution, or look around. He just stared at Seamus through the smoke in the same level stare.

Seamus sat cross-legged, pulling at a tuft of grass, waiting, staring back at the face that was finally starting to show some humor. The corners of his mouth turned up in a smile and Seamus felt a huge relief.

Finally, he replied in Gaelic, "Of course I'm Irish, more than most. I long for the good old days and the old ways before the English ruined them." In English he asked,

"Why do you ask?"

Seamus lay back in the damp grass and looked up at the fire's light playing among the oak leaves, thankful, or at least hopeful, for an ally. "Because," he quietly said as he hefted himself onto an elbow, "last night I killed an English Lord."

There was something about the man's look that was akin to triumph as his eyes sparkled in the firelight. Then his expression changed to doubt. As Seamus watched the features change with the light, he made up his mind to never be caught without a plan or a ready answer again. He realized how lucky he had been this time.

"I should say that you have plenty to worry about, then, Lad," the man said as he knocked the remaining ashes from his pipe. He looked at Seamus with a furrow plowed deep into his brow. "What will you do, and where will you go?" he asked, and pocketed his pipe.

Seamus looked at him forlornly and replied, "While you were talking and asking questions, it occurred to me that I hadn't given it any thought. I just took to the river for speed. But it'll run out soon."

The little man scratched the underside of his chin with the back of his fingertips. Seamus could see that he cared about him, at least as a fellow Irishman. He realized how many other people had cared over the years, and that he'd repaid their kindness by having to run away. He could never do the deeds that ought to be done as special thanks for their kindness. A door was closing behind him and the draft it caused sent a chill along his whole being. He caught a mental glimpse of a girl in a pale blue dress with white lace at collar and cuffs that made her violet eyes stand out like cornflower on a clear day, and the feeling of remorse intensified.

"Lad, are you listening?"

"I'm sorry. I was thinking of home."

"I could see that you were leagues away. I asked if you've given any thought to the New World."

"I can't afford the passage," Seamus replied, "and I'm not prepared to swim that far."

"Aye Lad, but you could work for your passage." He looked at Seamus with a wry smile. "It's done all the time. When I was in my younger days, I did it just to see the coast of France. And I learned something else, too. You needn't go to a busy port to do it."

Seamus' head snapped up at that, since he didn't care to be seen by too many people.

"Aye, you can believe that. When I was young, lads were sneaking away to seminaries in France because the laws wouldn't let them go freely. And you're going in the right direction, too." He caught the smile playing at the corner of Seamus' mouth and continued, "You follow the Shannon to Limerick, then head south by south west to the Kenmare River. It widens out to a great huge bay where ships come and go at will. Stay to the south side 'til you can see Dursey Island." He had retrieved and filled his pipe and again had a burning twig in his hand. "There, you'll . . .," he puffed twice on the pipe, ". . . see a small . . .," again he puffed twice, ". . . cove."

Seamus had rocked forward on his toes in anticipation. "Aye? And?"

The little man's eyes twinkled through the smoke.

"Once a week a ship stops in for cargo bound for the New World. They're always shorthanded, Lad."

"But what if they have no use for me? I know nothing about sailing a ship. Or, what if they're fully manned?"

"First of all, Lad, don't ask too many questions of them. They're carrying illegal whiskey to America. But it'll get you there. The point is that they can't hire like normal ships or they'll be caught. So they're willing to take on novices and train them. The second thing is that if you can't get aboard one ship, you wait and go on the next."

Seamus' uneasiness must have shown, because he was quick to add, "You need not worry. The folk around there don't like the English either. There are plenty of caves to hide in and the people will be glad to feed you since you've cut the ranks of the English down by one." He thought that statement over and added, "But of course you might not want to mention that."

Seamus sat back in the damp grass, pleased with the plan the little man had devised. He noticed that the moon had broken through the clouds and sent a silvery path across the Shannon right up to his feet. He wondered if this was a sign that the path he was about to take was the right one.

No matter, he thought, *it was the only one on offer.* He heard a voice off in the woods and turned away from the fire.

"Tell them Jamie McFee sent you, Lad."

He turned back to the stump, but it was empty except for the well-used pipe with a curl of smoke rising from the bowl. He sprang for the pipe with the intention of catching the little man, but was caught up in another thought.

Wasn't it ironic to stop on a riverbank, cold, wet, lonely and despondent, and to leave with hope in his heart, and a direction in mind? He doused the fire, dropped the coracle in the water and started to climb in with his pack. *But what of my father's safety,* he thought. Maybe he should go back and face what he had done so that Fahey wouldn't lose what little he had left. On the other hand, if he went back, he would be executed and his father would have even less to live for. He stood with one foot on land and the other in the little craft for a moment, weighing his decision. What he chose to do would determine the course of the rest of his life.

It was then that he realized what Jamie McFee had really done. Besides giving him a plan, he had revived his sense of hope, the hope that had died with Patricia. That was the most important ingredient in his escape. He suddenly felt buoyant enough to sail the Shannon without the coracle.

And who knows, maybe the ocean without a ship, he thought as he paddled out to the center of the river to catch the current. The eastern sky was growing light and it was a clear azure. "No more clouds," he whispered as he pointed his little craft south. But how was he to forget Patricia? That cloud would be with him for a while.

III

As Seamus entered Limerick by the east gate, he couldn't help the feeling that people were looking at him suspiciously. He had to remind himself that a guilty look would bring those stares a lot quicker than a cheerful composure. He spotted a sign reading Platter and Pint, rubbed his hollow belly, and set off for a meal.

Just outside the pub, he dropped his pack, now heavier with the hide from the coracle rolled up inside. He hoped someone would find the willow frame in a few weeks and get some use from it, but not too soon. He had hidden it pretty well in the brush about a half mile upstream and walked the remaining distance into Limerick. He pulled the coins from his pocket and counted them. He had not checked to see how much Fahey had given him, but he didn't want to ask for food and not have enough money to pay.

Satisfied, he entered and ate his fill, anxious to be on his way. He hadn't taken time to notice the other occupants of the pub before going to the out building. As the back door closed behind him, the portly man asked his neighbor, "Did ya' see how fast he put that stew away?"

"Aye. In a bit in a hurry, if ya' ask me."

"And without a pint ta' wash it with," the larger man said. "Ya'd think someone was after him, ya' would."

His friend nodded and sipped his pint. He wiped his mouth and asked, "By the by, did ya' hear about the young Lord Mayfair?"

"No. What did he do now?"

"Then ya' haven't heard! It's not what he's done but what was done to him!"

"What, did someone finally flog him?"

"Worse! Killed him! And it was a lass what done it, too!"

"You don't say. Where?"

As he opened the door on the way back from the necessary, Seamus heard the reply.

"'Twas at Mayfield Manor up in Athlone, it was!"

They looked up and watched as Seamus quietly pulled the door shut and walked straight through to the front door, glad that he had paid for his meal before he ate. Outside, he picked up his bundle and with longer than usual strides made tracks for the south gate. The tale of his deed had already overtaken him and he could almost feel the pursuit of those appointed to capture him and bring him back. He felt the hot burn of hemp on his neck and raised his hand to rub away the thought. He couldn't believe that an Irishman, true and noble of soul, as Father O'Conner would have put it, should have to swing from a rope for ridding the world of the scum off the privy.

The feeling of being alone outran him again as he walked toward the Kenmare, and for the first time in years he longed to see his mother's gentle face again. Life had been so cruel to her. The loss of his older brother in childbirth, and then his own hard birth, were bad enough. But to lose the last child and her life together was too much. He wondered if he would ever visit those three graves again. He wondered if he would ever visit Patricia's final resting place.

IV

The midmorning sun was warm on his face as he walked through the streets of Kilgarvan. He stopped for a late breakfast in the pub where the people were cheerful. While he was there, he asked one of the locals for directions to the Kenmare.

"Why Lad, you're about ta' fall into it as you swallow that meal. It's just down the track a hop or two."

"How far, then, is it to Dursey Island," Seamus asked.

"Off ta' the New World then, are ya', Lad," another man asked. "A couple of days should see ya' there. Do ya' know the cove?"

Seamus was surprised. Apparently a lot of young men came this route, for it seemed to be a routine matter to point the way.

"I've heard of it, but I've not seen it."

"Of course, of course. Why else would ya' be asking. When ya' get ta Eyeries, steer a course away from the bank, toward the south, and follow the track across country to Allihies and you'll save yourself miles of walking. That's the end of your journey, then, Lad. Or should I say, the beginning."

Seamus realized the vastness of the adventure unfolding before him. He was excited about the prospect but at the same time, longed for the security of home, a home he would never again see. He knew that loss would niggle at him but he would just have to invent his own kind of security.

As he approached the bridge, he looked back and waved a final thank you to the innkeeper and the other gentleman, who were standing in the doorway. He crossed over and headed downstream along the slowly moving ribbon of water. He wondered how many young men those two had watched over the bridge with a farewell wave.

He covered a lot of ground that day, wondering all the while how many young men would be waiting for a ship out of Ireland. Perhaps he would make a friend to cut through the loneliness of the trek. The empty road wound gracefully through a thicket and around the base of a hill, leading into another glade. He was paying little attention to what lay ahead until he saw the stonework.

Like a ghost from the past, the old Norman castle loomed above the trees, its ramparts crumbling away under the voracious appetite of father time. The ivy climbing the south wall was taking part in the feast by devouring the mortar between the stones all the way to the top of the walls. Most of the tower above the northeast corner had plunged from existence, leaving the naked stone steps to bear the brunt of the storms yet to come. Sunlight played across the inner walls in such profusion that it was obvious there was no roof. He doubted that anyone occupied this place, but all had abandoned it to its ghosts who skulked about the halls and battlements where they had fallen and long since rotted away.

He found a message chiseled roughly into the stone by the entrance and touched the coarse chips as he read,

The ghosts of men ye must confess
If peaceful sleep ye desire to possess
For o'er the ramparts they shall roam
Lost and cold, in search of home.
That ye disturb their earthly quest
Shall prey upon thy peaceful rest.
And Thou shall see the crimson blade
In every restful, shaded glade
Where thou wouldst dare to lay thy head
And make thy soft and slumbering bed.
Confess thy sins and thou shall rest
Thy spirits locked within this keep.

A chill possessed him as he read the last line. He eyed the massive oak door, which seemed to be rotting as he watched. He didn't trust it to keep the ghosts from all the previous confessions of murder left on this doorstep. He resolved to find a priest and make his confession, sending his own ghost back here to molder. The clouds certainly formed quickly enough to make him feel morbid. He felt the weight of his albatross.

As the gray sky began to darken, he came upon a willow overhanging the bank of the Kenmare. It made him think of Patricia. He decided that this would be his lodging for the night. As he curled up to sleep, he wished that she were alive. She would get such joy out of an adventure like this. But if she were alive, would any of this have happened? He had only intended to scare Mayfair into releasing her. He lost control when the lord had said she was dead and then taunted him.

Perhaps sleeping here would bring happy dreams for a change. He was getting tired of the sleepless nights. As he dozed, he briefly saw her violet eyes.

"... *won't kill me. Not for a dead gi ...*"

"Not again," Seamus yelled as he sat up.

The eyes had changed to that horrid red pair that were looking at themselves and at him at the same time. "Not again," he sobbed as he dropped his forehead onto his knees. "I'll lock you in that keep soon, Mayfair!"

He paced beneath the willow until he was calmed and worn out enough to try sleep again. His sleep was fitful at best. Morning found him sitting on the bank of the Kenmare, thoughtlessly throwing pebbles into the water.

He wondered why he hadn't dreamt of Patricia. He was sure it would be more peaceful. Lord Mayfair was there and he was dead. Father O'Conner was a regular visitor to his dreams and he was dead. His mother even put in an appearance occasionally, and she too was gone. But not Patricia, the one he most longed to see.

As the sun climbed the eastern clouds, he ate some of the bread from his pouch, then continued his journey to the sea.

This time he woke gently and had trouble remembering where he was, since the seas were so calm they didn't rock the boat. He looked around at the trappings below deck and it all came back. He supposed he should go on deck and see what he could do to help.

Chapter 4

The threads unraveled
And the knit fell away.
No substance remained
To warm the day.

I have a ghost," Seamus said to the black figure bent over the book.

The priest looked up in wonder at the phrase and replied sadly, "Why Lad, don't we all?"

"Not like mine, I fear, Father."

"Would you like to confess something, then Lad," the priest asked dutifully.

"Aye, Father, if you wouldn't mind listening."

The memory dream continued.

As he stood, the gaunt figure of the old priest blended into the monastery. His peaked cap fit into the pointed arches of the windows and the gray in his hair and eyes seemed to become part of the stone work. "Come this way, then," he said simply.

Seamus retold his story from start to finish, omitting nothing. The confessor listened in interest, then sat in silent thoughtfulness as though he was the jury, weighing the evidence. Finally, he looked at Seamus and asked almost in disbelief, "He rode your priest to the ground and killed him, you say?"

"Aye Father, he did."

"And he laughed as he rode away?"

"Aye."

"And I thought St Patrick had rid these islands of snakes," he said in disgust.

"This is difficult, Lad. There are two phrases in the Good Book at odds with each other here. 'Vengeance is mine, sayeth the Lord', and 'an eye for an eye'." He scratched his whiskers and looked at Seamus in a way that made him feel his soul being examined by those gray eyes. Heaven knew how deeply he had examined it himself lately.

"I felt that he deserved it, Father," he blurted out as if he could defend his actions to God Himself. "And I feel that I, of all people, had just cause. The Lass I was to wed is gone. The Priest who taught me the meaning of life is gone. And now I am gone from the home of my Forefathers. I may never be able to return, Father." The gravity of his situation finally caught up with him and he began to sob.

"There now, Lad, have it out at last," the priest said as he put his hand on the back of Seamus' bent head. "You need not carry such a heavy burden with you. I absolve you in the Name of the Father, the Son, and the Holy Ghost, Amen."

Seamus caught his breath and wiped his eyes. "Can it be that simple, Father?"

"No indeed, Lad," he replied. "You have just listed your own penance with your losses, and it is a far heavier burden than any I could give you. Mind you, I do not condone what you have done, but neither do I condone the murder of a fellow Priest or the abduction of your lass. It all evens out, though, and you will one day find peace again."

Seamus looked down at his hands and wondered if he would ever truly be at peace with his thoughts. "Father," but he paused for a moment, rephrasing the question in his mind before continuing, "Will this spirit haunt me for the rest of my days?"

The priest rose to his feet as he removed the banded purple sash from his shoulders. Straightening his cassock, he said, "Only if you allow him to, Lad." He looked at Seamus with a wisdom that only comes with years and said, "I assume that you are off to the New World?" When Seamus nodded, he continued, "I thought as much. When you board your ship, you make up your mind that the ghosts of the dead remain in Ireland. You are starting a new life and the ghosts of the past must remain in the past."

Seamus could feel a new resolve growing inside him. They walked to the door together, and as the priest turned the handle, he gave Seamus another look of wisdom.

"The right thing to do is to go back and face the music, you know." When he got no response he said, "So be it then," and opened the door. "I can't blame you considering the circumstances. Go to your new life, then, and may God go with you."

As the outer gate creaked shut, Seamus looked back at the gaunt figure as he began blending into the masonry again, and the priest raised his hand in the sign of the cross.

II

As Seamus continued on his travels, his mind played back over that last few days with Patricia. On the day of the fair, as they walked along the lakeshore, he had said to her,

> *"I do not love thee for love's sake.*
> *There is a kindred spirit here*
> *That has taken long to make,*
> *Far too long to count in years."*

The breeze was soft as Seamus and Patricia walked hand in hand along the bank of Lough Ree. Seamus kept admiring her shiny black hair and the way the sunlight reflected off the water into her violet eyes. He had felt something for her for as long as he had known her, but the feelings had changed as they got older. He had teased her when they were children, but they were fast approaching twenty and the days of braid pulling were well past. Now he just wanted to hold her and caress her. She was warm and soft and her eyes spoke volumes about her feelings for him. He looked forward to the day they would wed.

They had literally bumped into each on the village street a few months back. After the initial embarrassment, they both admitted to similar feelings and had begun seeing each other regularly. Here they were on Fair Day near the end of summer, alone by the lake, the passion growing within the secrecy of yet another willow overhanging the shore. They were sitting on the grass and it all began as a kiss and grew from there. They broke off at the same time.

"We can't do this," he said. "It wouldn't be proper."

"I know, Seamus. We must wait or we'll be shamed forever."

"We'd best be getting back to the fair before we're missed."

Perhaps it was the old Celtic love of revelry that returned each year with the fair that caused young men to feel strong and old men to feel young, young girls to feel beautiful and old ladies to feel like girls. Whatever it was, there were no sad faces to be found in Athlone. They were greeted by many well-wishers, who also looked forward expectantly to their wedding day. They made their way along the rows of booths and stalls set up by local and traveling merchants and stopped at a booth that sold baubles.

He looked at her with a twinkle and began making up rhyme,

"A stall with baubles, trinkets and beads
Of gems from Venus' and Neptune's seas
I shall buy for thee my lass
A gift that none shall e'er surpass
One as rich as are thine eyes,
As is the morning's bright sunrise."

"Sometimes you can be such a romantic," she said as she admired the wares.

He gently touched her shoulder and spoke softly near her ear, "There has never been a love such as I have for you."

She turned and smiled at him and said, "Nor than I have for you, my love."

Suddenly, there was a commotion in the street. They turned in time to see the newly instated Lord Mayfair galloping his frothing horse into the square, the steed's eyes bulging from over-exertion. The horse's flaring nostrils snorted in Patricia's other ear as its hooves threw up a cloud of dust, obeying the reins and stopping beside her.

"What have we here," Mayfair sneered, "a wench for the taking." He reached down and drew her up toward his saddle. She screamed and kicked, frantically trying to free herself. Seamus reached up and began pulling her back down. He was rewarded with a blast of rummy breath and Mayfair was forced to let go of her to avoid falling from the saddle in his drunken state. But not before forcing a sloppy kiss on her tender young lips.

As Lord Mayfair was righting himself in the saddle, Seamus started to leap at him, but Patricia held him back.

"No! He'll beat you in the end, Seamus," she cried before she wiped her mouth with the back of her sleeve.

"Not before I've gotten in a few good licks," he said.

"You'd best listen to the girl," Mayfair snorted as he steadied himself.

"What right do you have to take that kind of liberties," Seamus yelled.

"Why, the right of the Lord of Mayfield and Lord of this county, of course," He slurred. "As the Master, I have pick of the litter, and she is such a fine-looking bitch." He ended with a laugh of such superiority that it made Seamus' blood boil. He made another attempt to charge the Lord, but was again held back by Patricia's wise hands.

"Go back to your lowly dirt farmer, then, wench. I'll have you anytime I want you," Lord Mayfair roared as he rode away, his laugh loud and sinister.

Seamus broke free and picked up a stone from the street. He yelled the local version of the lord's title, 'Monster of Mayfield,' as he flung the stone and hit the horse's rump, causing it to rear up. The crowd in the square gave a concerted 'awe' as Mayfair managed to stay in the saddle, each privately hoping that he would fall, but glad for Seamus' sake that he did not. It was fortunate that Lord Mayfair was too drunk to know what had caused his horse to rear.

"Are you hurt," Seamus asked, turning back to Patricia, who had tears welling in her violet eyes.

"No," she replied. "But I am afraid of what he may do to you when he sobers up."

"Let him try. I'll deal with him then. Besides, what if he comes back for you later?"

"He's too drunk to remember me. Be careful, my love. I want a whole man to wed."

The story had gotten around later how Robin Clancy, Seamus' boyhood friend, and Robin's friend Will Brandon had been causing trouble at the fair the day Mayfair had stolen the kiss from Patricia. After Mayfair's horse had reared and settled, he had given Will a hand up onto his horse, trampled pottery and vegetables, and stopped beside Robin. Robin had been laughing as Mayfair's horse stumbled about, but then Mayfair pulled his booted foot from the stirrup and kicked Robin full in the mouth. As Robin lay bleeding on the cobbles, Mayfair said, "You're nothing but an Irish dog fit for my boot." Will, sitting behind the 'monster' on his horse, was laughing as the two of them rode away.

III

A week after the fair, Fahey stepped through the cottage door, cane in hand, to see who was calling Seamus' name. The rheumatism in his legs had eased in the last couple of days and he thought he could relieve Seamus behind the plow soon.

He squinted up at the afternoon sun peeking between the clouds, then back at the young man running down the road.

He held his cupped hands to his mouth and yelled back, "Robin, he's in the field out back." He watched as the lad changed course and marveled at how much the lad had changed the course of his life in a few days.

"Da'! He's taken her, Da'." Seamus later yelled, as he raced around the corner of the cottage.

"Who's taken whom," Fahey asked as Robin, puffing through still swollen lips with new blood on his cheek, came to a stop beside Seamus.

"Lord Mayfair has taken Patricia, Da'. Patch up Robin's face where Mayfair hit him with his riding crop when he tried to stop him, will you, Da'? I'm going after them."

"Be careful, Lad. You know how dangerous he is," Fahey said, his voice rising to catch up with Seamus as he raced away.

"That's twice the Mayfair treachery has hit me in the face in the last week," Robin said as Fahey dabbed at the cut with a wet rag. "There won't be a third time."

Robin left after Fahey tended to him. Fahey chose to occupy himself the only way he knew how and hobbled out to the field where the last row Seamus was plowing up for harvest ended in a zigzag. He would just straighten that up, then go on with the plowing and potato bagging, rheumatism or not.

IV

As Robin raced down the road, trying to catch up with Seamus, he kept remembering the maniacal look on Mayfair's face. The Monster had laughed and ridden away with Patricia across his lap. She was struggling but that was hard to do when belly down over a moving horse's shoulders. Robin had seen her mouth open and come down on Mayfair's thigh with her teeth, followed by his bellow of pain.

The only solution Robin could see was to do away with Lord Mayfair altogether. He began thinking about a plan that he could present to Seamus when he did catch up with him. He saw a lone figure coming toward him. When he got closer, he could see that it was Will Brandon. Will was smiling and waving and Robin wondered if there truly was something mentally wrong with him.

As they neared each other, Will asked, "Did ya' hear? Lord Mayfair kept his promise and took Patricia off to Mayfield Manor. Wait 'til Seamus finds out. I wish I could see the look on his face when he hears. That would be so much fun . . ."

Robin laid a fist into the rest of the words before they could emerge. The anger he felt for Mayfair had found an outlet in Mayfair's bastard brother. He could only see the maniacal face above the horse as he punched and pummeled the one beneath him. He fell back exhausted, and stared at Will's bruised and bloody face until the latter came back to the world of the living. Will groaned and looked at Robin, staggered to his feet, and stumbled into the grove to lick his wounds.

V

Father O'Conner stepped through the gate in front of the O'Lachlan cottage in time to see Seamus racing up the street in his direction. He leaned against the post and waited. As Seamus neared, he put his hands on his hips and asked, "Where would you be going in such a fit, Lad?"

He fell into step as Seamus answered, "To Mayfield, Father."

The priest took Seamus' arm and spun him to a halt, facing him. "If the rumors I heard are true, you have every right to be angry. But Lad," he said as he laid a caring hand on the nape of Seamus' neck, "remember who you are dealing with. He is capable of any kind of wickedness."

"Father, I know all that. I have seen the evils he's done in the past. But he has stepped too far beyond the boundaries this time," he hissed. "I don't want Patricia hurt, Father."

"I know you don't, Lad. Neither do I, but she is young, and the law is on Lord Mayfair's side. I don't like it any more than you, but he has a right to any lass before she is wed."

"I don't accept their law! She is innocent, Father."

"Seamus, Lad, listen to me." Seamus could once more see the look of the teacher in the good father's eyes as he lowered his voice and said, "You and Patricia have your entire lives before you. By now Lord Mayfair has already had his way with her and it is over." He tightened his fingers on Seamus' neck, as the Lad became more agitated. "Don't let that damage your love for her. She will still be the same person as before. She will love you no less, and if you are gentle and understanding, she will love you even more. At first she will feel soiled and unworthy of your attention. But if she sees that you care, she will return your devotion. Always remember, you get out of a relationship what you put into it."

"Aye, Father, I know. But I must do something to free her now."

Father O'Conner's reply was halted by the sound of a horse approaching at full gallop. Lord Mayfair pulled up beside them and looked back and forth between the two before commenting, "Nothing like a gallop in the countryside after an afternoon's tussle with a beautiful girl."

Seamus started forward, but Father O'Conner's hand, still on the back of his neck, stopped him.

"What right do you have, to abduct this man's betrothed and drag her to Mayfield for your foul use?"

"Ha! As the Lord of Mayfield, I have the right to do as I please. I have the right to any virgin prior to wedlock. And, Lad, she was a virgin," he sneered as he looked into Seamus' eyes. Looking back at the priest, he asked, "What right do you have to question me?"

"As the spiritual and moral leader of these people, I claim that right and, in that capacity, I demand that you set her free." Father O'Conner's eyes again locked in fierce combat with the unfeeling eyes of the young lord.

"Was it in that same sacrosanct capacity that you desired to strike me a few years ago in the End O' Lough pub?" Father O'Conner shifted slightly. The Monster had remembered as he said he would. Mayfair continued, "I told you I wouldn't forget."

His horse, anxious to be in his stall, began to prance and canter sideways, fighting the reins. He brought the animal under control several paces away and turned its head back toward the two men.

"Besides, I don't recognize your faith, Sir." With that he spurred the horse's flanks, causing it to rear and bolt straight for Seamus and Father O'Conner.

Seamus pushed the priest sideways and dove toward the gate, but it was too late. The sharp hooves caught the good Father in the neck and chest as he hit the ground. Lord Mayfair galloped away, oblivious to the damage he had done.

"She'll be better when I'm through with her, dirt farmer," he yelled over his shoulder as he rode away. The well-known, fiendish laugh died away as he rode on.

Seamus scrambled over to the fallen Priest, who was gasping and spitting blood. Crouching beside his Priest, Seamus raised his gray head onto his own outstretched leg. As he cradled the old man's head, the good Father raised a feeble finger to the gathering sunset and with his dying breath, said, "Tan y'n cummys lemmyn gor uskys."

Seamus looked down at the still face and wept the bitter tears of loss mingled with those of hatred. His watery eyes went back to the brightly-lit clouds, where he was sure he saw a darkly clad figure moving away from him.

IV

Patricia sat up dazed. She looked around the room with eyes that did not see the rich appointments. It was a man's room, boasting of silk tapestries of a boar hunt on one wall, faced by a foxhunt on the opposite. The wainscot around the fireplace spoke of one who chose perfection in craftsmanship, for each plank was indeed perfectly matched in grain. But her unseeing eyes cared nothing for the implication; her heart ached so badly.

She sobbed into her hands. "Oh Seamus, you'll not be wanting me now." But her words faded away, unheard by anyone but herself. After the monster had beaten her into submission, she had shown no emotion except for loathing him the entire time Lord Mayfair was using her. The deep fear she felt remained locked far from his reach. She would not grant him that desire, which he most wanted. She did not cry or scream. He had tried every form of torture his evil mind knew, but she had stared past him blindly. Finally, he had tired of the game and gone off riding.

As he stomped from the room, she had pulled her camisole over her head and felt a little better. She fretted with the dress, noticing a small rip he had made in his haste to remove it. She was about to lace the bodice when she heard the massive front door slam shut.

With a rush of relief, she let the tears flow until they cleansed her soul. She knew she should get out while she could, but she had become so exhausted that she finally welcomed the peace that only sleep could bring. But now another door had closed somewhere, startling her awake.

The hidden fear was also reawakened. She began to search the room for a weapon, her mind racing. Could she use a weapon on Lord Mayfair if he came for her again? She didn't know. She toyed with the poker beside the hearth, but decided that was too obvious. The man was no fool, only cruel. Her eyes fastened on the line of bottles on the serving cart. Broken, they would be sharp and small enough to hide in the folds of her dress.

She had moved within reach of the cart when a second door banged shut, causing her to jump and back away from the door by the cart. Her heart raced as she listened for footsteps, but she heard none. Instead, there was the drone of two male voices. She crept to the door that led to the sitting room.

VII

As he made his way through the woods of Mayfield Manor, Seamus thought about the irony of a loaded pistol being kept next to the chalice in the sacristy. He was probably the only person in Athlone who knew about it, and silently thanked Father O'Conner for his foresight. He hoped he would know what to do with it, having never fired a pistol before. He rubbed the muzzle for reassurance as he crept toward the great front terrace. He felt as though every eye of every stone lion support was watching as he crept along below the banister. He reached the French window and shuddered as his fingers wrapped around the lever. Slowly, he pulled down and could not believe his luck, for it moved with ease.

He stepped in and moved behind the heavy brocaded drape that hung the twenty feet between ceiling and floor. Motes of dust danced in the light shining through the crack in the drapes and he nearly sneezed, giving himself away. He avoided touching the cloth again.

He put an eye to the crack but saw no one in the room. What he did see were paintings on the walls in ornate frames, finely made furniture with curved legs, and decorative rugs on the floor in front of the furniture.

As he laid his hand on the edge of the red and gold drapes to part them, he heard voices saying good evening beyond the door and stayed where he was. He heard the front door close as the sitting room door opened. He watched Lord Mayfair stride boldly into the room, giving the paintings a sneer. He closed the door and went to the wing back chair near the hearth. After he sat down with his back to the room, Seamus slid out of his hiding place and over to the door. He turned the key left in the lock, and as it clicked Lord Mayfair waved toward the side table and said, "Leave it, John."

Seamus had worried about his accuracy from across the room, but this was more luck than he had expected. He crossed the room and aimed the pistol at Lord Mayfair's head.

"Where is she?" He had a look in his eyes of pure fire as brilliant as that in the hearth. His arms were extended and he held the pistol with both hands.

Lord Mayfair spoke and the words were clear. "Well if it isn't the lowly dirt farmer." He wore a testy grin on his face that made one loathe him. "Aren't you the one they call the prince of potatoes?"

Seamus shifted from foot to foot like a bird cornered by a snake. He barked again, "Where is she?" He shifted around so he could see Mayfair's face better.

The grin on Mayfair's face turned to scorn as he lied, "She couldn't take it so she killed herself." He waved his hand nonchalantly, and said, "But that's alright. The only good Irish are dead ones."

Mayfair made a sudden move, causing Seamus to back away. He caught his heel on the claw and ball foot of a Queen Ann's chair and fell backward. As he spun to catch himself, the priming charge sprayed from the pistol in an arc. But he was not aware of that, for he raised the pistol and said, "Then you too shall die." He pulled the trigger and the flint drove home with a resounding click as Lord Mayfair broke into a hideous laugh that made Seamus' spine crawl.

"You lose, dirt farmer," he said as he calmly rose and walked to another table. "You lost your priming powder and now you lose all." He casually removed a dueling pistol and a bag of powder from a beautifully engraved box. Seamus dove across the table, knocking Mayfair against the wall. Seamus scrambled to his feet, grabbed up the powder and re-primed his own pistol as Mayfair staggered to his feet. Lord Mayfair was inches from Seamus' pistol when the explosion ripped through the room. Mayfair seemed to watch the bullet as it entered his head between his eyes.

Both pistols sank into the deep pile of the carpet. Seamus turned back to the curtained French window and left the manor house.

Startled by the blast of the gunshot in the adjoining room, Patricia got up the nerve to open the door a crack and peaked around the edge in time to see the curtain fall back over the opening in the opposite wall. She opened the sitting room door wider and entered to find the 'Monster' lying on the floor with a pool of his own blood spreading outward from his head. The locked door to the hallway rattled. She stooped and retrieved the gun she had kicked and was about to go to the window to see who had done this when the hall door burst open, wood shards flying, to admit her captors. She had a fair idea who had gone through the curtained window.

VIII

For the first time since all this began, Seamus dreamt of Patricia and basked in her glow anew. He wondered when he woke why she had not come to him before. Maybe her trek to Heaven had taken longer than the others. Kyle was watching him when he woke.

"What were you dreaming about, Lad? I've never seen anyone smile in their sleep before."

"I dreamt of Patricia, the woman I loved."

"You never told me about a lady love. How could you leave a lady love, Lad?"

"It's a long story and I'm not ready to tell it yet. Maybe I will someday."

Chapter 5

He is only a babe
But a man to be.
I shall give him all
The good that is in me.

H e wondered what it was about sleeping aboard ship that brought on all the vivid dreams. Once again, Seamus' dreams harkened back to events he had actually experienced. This time they reached back to when he was seven years old.

The sky was a brilliant blaze of glory seldom seen in that part of County Westmeath. The mass of gray clouds was often too heavy for the sun to penetrate, as though the weather was conspiring to oppress the hearts of the Irish while the English whittled away at their souls. But moments like this spoke proudly of many times in the past, and many more to come, when these suppressed people would shine none the less.

Seamus O'Flarity gave no thought to such glories as his skinny seven-year-old legs carried him and his freckled face as fast as they could around the corner of the rectory. He was looking over his shoulder at his pursuers when he ran into the solid posterior mass of Father O'Conner, bent over the rose bushes.

"Is it the devil that's chasing you, then, Seamus, or are you racing someone?"

"The devil, I think, Father," he puffed, "with names like Robin Clancy and Will Brandon."

"When they come around the corner, you just act casual and look at the roses. I'll deal with the two of them."

There was no need to wait, for no sooner had he said it, that the two slightly older boys appeared around the same corner at full charge, kicking up dust as they backpedaled to avoid running head long into the middle-aged Priest.

"Will you be having foot races through my garden now, boys," he asked them sternly in his deep bass voice.

The boys looked at each other with that maybe-he-doesn't-know look, then back at him as Robin said, "We're sorry, Father. We won't do it again."

Seamus breathed a sigh of relief and kept his gaze averted.

The gray-haired Priest looked at them in mock severity and said, "I'd appreciate it if you'd find someplace else to race, so you won't trample the flowers; otherwise, there won't be any for the altar at Mass time."

"Aye Father," Robin said, "we'll not be botherin' you any more then."

As the boys strode out of earshot, the good father turned back to Seamus and for the first time noticed the evening glow in the clouds. He threw up his hands in a gesture of awe and said, "Lord be praised, what a magnificent sunset we're blessed with this day." He looked back at Seamus and asked, "Do you know what the ancients used to say about the sunset?"

Seamus had no opportunity to answer, because Father O'Conner said, "Well, Lad, 'tis a story with some length to it, so if you don't mind, I'll walk with you a bit." He turned and began walking in the direction of the O'Flarity farm, disguising the fact that he was acting as Seamus' protector.

"Our ancestors were the Celts of old. They were a warring people, you know. They were so fond of fighting that, if they didn't have a common enemy, they would fight among themselves. It was not unusual for a brawl to break out over the best portion of meat, sometimes to the death. There was no fear of death. In fact, the thought of going to the Celtic heaven was inviting. It was believed that heaven was much like earth, only better. There were no ills of the body. No one was ever hungry, for food would appear as if by magic. And the people were all beautiful, especially the women." He winked at Seamus and the lad saw the glint of a once-young hell-raiser that he thought should not have been there, even if he did not know why. They walked on in silence for a while. Seamus was thinking of the number of times he had playfully pulled Patricia's long plaits of hair or played other jokes on her. He wondered what thoughts were going through the good Father's mind to make him smile so.

The priest came back to the present and continued, "Anyway, as I was saying, a beautiful goddess had as her sole task that of luring men on to heaven. Each evening she would run along the horizon with a torch, setting fire to a string of bonfires in the clouds. This was, so it was said, to show man that the sun never set in the heavens and to point the way for those who cared to follow."

Seamus looked up at Father O'Conner with his nose wrinkled in a look of not quite understanding and scratched his head. The priest did not notice. Seamus kept silent and walked along with the priest, curious about the outcome of the story.

"Now, the Celts were not to be outdone by the fire in the sky. They built great pyres all across the land that could be seen from hilltop to hilltop;

and as the sunset reached its finest glory, the druid leaders could be heard to say, 'Tan y'n cunys lemmys gor uskys.'"

Seamus stopped and snapped his head up to stare at the Priest in wonder. He knew that the 'old language' had been outlawed by the English, and he was surprised to hear it from those lips. He was even more surprised to hear those barbaric words from the same lips that read the Christian text and spoke the Catholic Mass. He was still looking at the lined face, capped off with graying hair, when the good Father saw the look of curiosity and thought he was asking for a translation.

"Do you not know the 'old tongue,' then, Lad?"

Seamus shook his head. He had heard it spoken occasionally, but did not know the meaning of the words.

"What I said means, 'Now set the pyre at once on fire.'" Seamus took a step back as Father O'Conner raised his hands heavenward, fingers extended, "and the flames would leap up to consume the darkness and challenge the very sunset."

Seamus was surprised by the passion coming from this man, who was usually quiet although not necessarily soft spoken. As they hiked along the road, Seamus asked questions and began to relax. He had always seen this man as the leader of the faith, someone to fear. Now he was seeing a different man, a man full of emotion. This was a man, other than his father who he could look up to and learn from. He was oddly curious about his ancestry, even though the law said he was not to be taught its history or language. The English did not want them to be a separate people. The irony was that they refused to accept them as equals.

They stopped to watch the last of the fading color, and Seamus hopped up easily to sit on the wall. The walls were built of the stones cleared from the fields, not to separate the fields as much as to make the fields more useable. The walls zigged and zagged down through the valley for as far as the eye could see. He was starting to love the land as much as his father did. A gentle breeze ruffled his hair as he looked across the valley.

"Come, Lad, we'd best be getting you home before your Father misses you and you get no supper." He laid his hand on the cold stone and sighed. "You must remind me to tell you about the standing stones sometime. Oh, the tales there are about those."

II

"Aye, he's a good Lad," Father O'Conner was saying to Fahey as Lorna set a dish of mutton and potatoes before him. She straightened her apron over her swollen belly and smiled at her son. Seamus blushed. He was not accustomed to being complimented by the village Priest. "And curious and quick of mind, too," he continued. "I'd like your permission to give him a little extra tutelage if he's of a mind."

Three sets of eyes were trained on Seamus as he looked up from his plate. He stammered for a moment, not sure what his parents wanted him to say. "I'd like that, Father," he finally said. "Do you mind, Da'," he asked, turning to Fahey.

"I'm glad for you," he said. "I would not have expected any other answer."

Seamus turned back to the Priest. "And thank you, Father, for stopping the devils that were chasing me."

"Aye Lad, but you didn't have to bring it up again. Since you have, would you care to be telling me what it was all about?"

Fahey and Lorna stared at Seamus as he looked between them and Father O'Conner. He thought for a moment before answering. "I don't mind being called the 'Prince of Potatoes' by my friends. If anything, it's a mark of honor to Da' and me. But those two fellows, Robin Clancy and Will Brandon, have a way of making it sound mean and dirty to be a potato farmer. Robin was pushing me while he chanted 'Prince of Potatoes' over and over. Finally, I got mad and punched him on the chin. Then I realized how much bigger he was and that he had Will to help him, so I ran. That's when I came into your garden."

"The Celtic heritage does live on," the Priest said, "though it seems to be tempered by discretion. You did the right thing, Lad. Robin Clancy would be a good Catholic if Will Brandon were not constantly leading him astray. I know you were friends until recently. Will, on the other hand, was fathered by Lord Mayfair out of wedlock, and he rather looks to his older half-brother as a model. That isn't good for any of us, as the next Lord Mayfair looks down on the Irish as so many cattle, to be used as he sees fit." There was anger in the good Father's voice. "I dread the day when his father dies and he takes control of the district," Father O'Conner added.

"Aye, that'll be a sad day," Fahey agreed. "If my own Father had not left me the farm, I'd think of leaving the county."

"Leave Westmeath?" Father O'Conner looked stunned. "And here I thought you were a fightin' man."

"But only a moment ago, you yourself were sayin' how Seamus had used discretion when the odds were against him. Does that not apply to me?"

"Aye, it would if it were the same situation. But we are talking about your land and the home of your ancestors."

"I agree, and that is why I said, 'if my Father had not left it to me, I'd leave.'"

"That you did now, that you did. Then you are a good man, Fahey O'Flarity." He tamped a fresh load of tobacco into his pipe and leaned back in the chair as Lorna stepped to the hearth and lit a twig for him to light his tobacco. "That was a fine meal," he said to Lorna as she handed the ember to him.

"Thank you, Father. I'm glad you enjoyed it," she said with a nervous smile.

"I'll be heading back to Athlone shortly," he said. "Seamus Lad, you come to the rectory when you have some free time and I'll teach you all I know. Fahey, would you care to join me in a pint at the pub?"

"I think I'll take you up on that, Father."

As they left, Lorna sighed in relief. She was by nature an immaculate housekeeper, but she was more concerned about the appearance of the cottage and herself when the good Father was around than at other times. She took Seamus into her warm embrace and said, "You should be counting yourself among the lucky ones. It's not every Lad who has a chance to learn from such a gifted man as that one."

"Aye, Mother, 'tis true. At first I feared him, but the more he talked the more I could see how wise he is."

"Aye. Your own Father was lucky enough for some tutoring by the priest we had when he was a lad." She ruffled his flaming red hair playfully. He had inherited her hair and his father's slight build and good looks. "Well

Seamus, me lad, 'tis getting late. You should be getting yourself off to bed now."

As he climbed into his pallet of straw, he could only imagine all the things he hoped to learn from the good Father. Sleep was a long time coming that night.

III

The End-O-Lough was the only pub in Athlone boasting of a means for any passerby to know who was drinking without having to enter. Customer-specific mugs occupied the cubby-hole cabinet in the front window frame; if a mug was missing, its customer was inside. The thatched roof overhung the door and window by a couple of feet diminishing the light inside further. The inside was originally white stucco above dark wood paneling, but the white had yellowed from years of tobacco smoke.

"Would that be old Sean Clancy I'm standing behind, then?"

"Aye, and that sounds like the good Father askin'. May I treat ya' to a pint, then Father?"

"I'd be hurt if you didn't." He and Fahey went to the front window and took their mugs down from the hooks.

As he handed his mug across to Mike to be filled, Father O'Conner said to Sean,

"I must have a word with you about your Grandson, Robin."

"That young scamp, what has he done now, Father?"

"He's becoming a hellion, you know."

"That I've noticed. Since his father died last year, I've not had enough time to spend with him and keep him away from that lad Will Brandon."

"There lies your trouble, all right. I wasn't sure you knew. Can't you tell him to stay clear of the Lad?"

"I have. But the more he's around him, the more disobedient he becomes. I haven't the youth in me to chase him down, Father."

"I can see what you mean. And it doesn't help that Will and his mother get an allowance from Lord Mayfair. It makes him think he's a cut above the rest of us."

"Aye. Now there's another problem. The younger Mayfair thinks the same thing and it worries me what will happen when he inherits Mayfield Manor."

Fahey had been standing by without a word, but he could keep quiet no longer.

"That pile of rubble should be torn down brick by brick." He slammed his mug down on the bar, sloshing ale over the rim. "I've held my peace for a number of years now, since Seamus was born, in fact. But it still angers me that he got half my property before I could sign it over to the Lad." A law had been passed allowing a man to till twice his allotment of land provided half of it was in his son's name. Fahey had not gotten half his allotment transferred to Seamus after his birth fast enough and had lost it.

The door burst open just then, and the younger Mayfair entered as if he owned the pub and the whole town, which, in a manner of speaking, he did. He was a tall, handsome young man with flowing blonde hair and the beginnings of a goatee and mustaches. Unfortunately, his appearance was ruined by the sneer he wore and the haughty attitude he presented.

"Innkeeper, I'll have a pint of your best," he bellowed to make sure his presence was known.

85

"Did you bring your mug?" Mike asked sarcastically.

"Now, do I look like the sort who would carry a mug about with me," Mayfair asked with equal sarcasm.

"Nay, your Lordship," Mike said in the same tone, "But my regulars each have their own and I have no spares."

"Right. Well then, I'll have this one," he said, snatching Father O'Conner's as he was putting it to his lips. The contents splashed onto the priest's face and down his front. He forgot himself for a moment and aimed a fist at Mayfair's nose, but Fahey stopped him in a nick of time. Young Mayfair swung back to face the Priest squarely. His dead brown eyes and the vivid blue ones of the Priest locked in mortal combat as tension in the pub mounted. A brawl in the pub was not unusual, but for a Lord or a Priest to be involved was unheard of. Those near at hand could taste the electricity as the two stared at each other with loathing.

Mayfair broke the silence with a barely audible whisper. "I'll remember that." He slammed Father O'Conner's mug down on the bar, sloshing more of the frothy brew up onto the Priest. Fahey steadied his Priest as the young man wisely stomped out of the pub.

IV

Seamus came up to his Mother as she worked in her flower garden along the sunny front side of the cottage, beneath the overhanging thatch.

"Aren't they lovely when they first bloom," Lorna asked as she delicately moved the blossoms aside to reach a single weed. She was due to have the baby soon. This would be her third. Seamus had heard the stories about how the first one, an older brother, had been still born. It had taken his parents a long time to get up the courage to try again.

Seamus was the fruit of that attempt and he was very glad that they had tried. He loved life and his parents immensely. They told him that he was very difficult and didn't seem to want to come into this world. As a matter of fact, they said he was breach, whatever that was. They said something about refusing to come out and trying to crawl back in. He didn't know how that could be, considering how much he loved being here.

Seamus stood beside his Mother in the warm spring sunshine that made her hair shine, almost like the Virgin Mary's halo painted on the wall in the church. She was so beautiful when she was like this. He hadn't the heart to tell her that Fahey would be in from the fields soon for his lunch. She loved her garden so much that it seemed a sin to take her away from it to face the heat of the hearth. The colors in her garden were as varied as any he'd seen in town. His favorites were the pale blue pansies. He couldn't decide whether it was the muted color or the comical expressions they wore that he liked the best. He smiled at the back of his Mother's head as she reached toward them.

She gave a sharp yelp.

Seamus didn't know what to think. He stepped to the side and watched her round face. Her pointed chin quivered for a moment then stopped. Her usually red lips were pale and drawn tight. Her eyes widened then narrowed then widened again.

"Seamus," she whispered, almost like it hurt to speak. "Go and tell your Father to come".

As he started to turn, she grabbed his hand. She looked at him with glazed eyes.

"Then go and get Maggie as quickly as you can." But she held onto his hand. He felt strange as she stared at him, before she finally said, "I love you, lad."

She released his hand and he raced as fast as he could toward the fields. He met Fahey as he was coming in and told him what had happened.

"Go then and get the Midwife, Lad, and be quick," Fahey said as he set off at a dead run for the cottage.

As Seamus ran toward town and the midwife's cottage, he marveled at how fast his Father could move. The thought that he would soon have a brother to play with put wings on his feet and he was at Maggie's gate before he knew it.

He rapped sharply on the arched door and waited, prancing from foot to foot, but it did not open. He hammered with the side of his fist and still no one came. Realizing that the Midwife must be out, he vaulted the low wall into the neighbor's yard and knocked on their door.

It opened quickly as Mrs. Mac Dough asked, "What is this commotion?"

Seamus puffed breathlessly, "Maggie Thatcher, where is she?"

"Gone off ta' visit her sister, Lad. It's but a few miles along the road ta' Ballinasloe," she said pointing in the opposite direction from the O'Flarity farm.

Seamus was sure that Mrs. Mac Dough would forgive him for being brief, for everyone knew that fetching the Midwife was a time of urgent need. He ran so hard that his chest tightened and he could hear his heart beating in his ears. He thought he would collapse by the time he reached the sister's cottage. It was, indeed a few miles out of town, quite a few, he thought.

Maggie and her sister both came to the door.

"Come," he panted. "Quick . . . please!"

"You poor lad," the sister cooed. "That's a long way to run."

He nodded his head, unable to speak for lack of air. He wheezed and coughed and the overhanging thatch work began to spin above him before it all went black. He felt himself swimming, reaching for the surface, wet. As his eyes fluttered open, he discovered Maggie's sister bending over him, wiping his face with a damp cloth.

"There you are, then," she quipped as a smile broke across her face. "I thought you had gone on to join the Saints, lad."

Seamus remembered his mission and started to leap up, but she stayed him with a firm but gentle hand. "Relax now; Maggie's gone off to help. You need not run any more today." She dipped the rag into the pail of water beside the bed. "You're a brave young lad to run so far."

Seamus felt proud as he looked around the low room at the things collected over a lifetime. He had never been called brave before. He'd never had cause for bravery before and this was a feeling he rather enjoyed. He sat up slowly and this time she didn't try to stop him.

"I should be getting back, all the same," he said.

"I suppose you must," she said. "You're probably anxious to see your new brother." She smiled at him, then added, "or sister."

He hadn't thought of that possibility. For months, since his Mother had explained why she was growing fatter, he had only thought in terms of a brother.

"You need not run now, Seamus," she said as he raced to the gate. "She's in good hands."

He waved farewell as he walked a respectful distance down the road before breaking into a trot. He couldn't help himself. This was something new to him and he wanted to see the little creature, boy or girl, before anyone else, except of course for his parents and Maggie Fletcher. He trotted for a while, and then walked as he caught his breath before trotting some more. While he walked, he had time to admire the green pastures of the rising and falling landscape and the way the stone walls followed the contours.

He slowed to a walk again as he approached Mayfield Manor, with its three floors of windows and white marble pediments. The high stone terrace by the front door was large enough to hold his Father's cottage within the massive stone banister, balanced on the heads of so many leaping stone lions. The white quoins at the corners and white shutters at each of the many windows set off the yellow brick. His father had taught him all those terms when they were out walking once.

A young man in his early teens whom Seamus thought to be the next Lord Mayfair stepped through the front door and bellowed something. Seamus was too far away to hear the words, but he stopped and watched out of curiosity. Another, older man ran up the side steps and nodded toward the first man. After a few words were exchanged, the young man, who seemed to tower over the other because he was above him on the stairs, raised his arm and struck him with a riding crop. The second man dashed down the steps and around the corner, returning momentarily at a trot, leading a horse fitted with a saddle.

The young man with blonde hair descended the stairs slowly, fitting the fingers of his gloves and mounted the horse. He leaned down and spoke a few more words to the man holding the bridle before striking him again and galloping away.

Seamus could only assume that someone had taken too long to prepare the horse for the young Lord's afternoon ride. He felt sorry for the groom as the man sat down on the bottom step, rubbing his shoulders where the blows had landed. The situation nagged at his mind as he continued his journey home. He kept trying to push it aside and think about the more cheerful event that was taking place at home. He felt like he had been gone from home all day, though it was probably only a couple of hours.

He expected to hear something when he got home, some cheering, a baby's cry, but not dead silence. His folks had told him that his birth had been difficult but that it wasn't usually like that. As he approached the planked door, the Midwife came out, blocking his way.

"Why don't you sit here with me for a moment," she said, pointing at the bench against the sunny wall.

"But, can't I see the baby first?'

"Your Father is in there now." She paused and patted the bench, saying softly, "Sit, lad."

He bowed to her command and she sat down beside him, putting an arm around him.

"What is it then, Mrs. Fletcher," he asked, "a brother or a sister?"

She looked down at him; her face contorted as her eyes became like pools ready to spill over their banks. Her chin quivered as she said, "It would have been a girl."

"Would have been," Seamus repeated as he struggled to rise.

She held him back and brushed her hand over his hair. She pushed a stray hank from his forehead and searched his eyes. "There's naught you can do, lad. The good Lord has taken her back to him."

Seamus felt his own eyes pool, distorting his vision. "But she was only a wee small baby."

"I know, lad. But Heaven will choose where we may not." She brushed the same stray locks back again and gently took his chin in her hand. "He chose to take your mother too, lad." She pulled him into her ample bosom to comfort him as he realized what she was telling him.

"No! She can't be . . ." But he couldn't say the word.

She tightened her embrace as they both shook with tears.

He tore loose and stood before her and yelled in anger. "But you were here. Why did you let her die?"

"I didn't, lad," she explained. "It was all over before I arrived."

The door opened before he could say any more and Fahey stood in the opening, his eyes swollen and red. "Have some respect for your mother, lad," he said in little more than a whisper. "Now come and say good bye properly."

Seamus followed him on tiptoes to the bedside, as though his Mother were sleeping. She looked like she was sleeping, and so did the tiny little face next to her on the pillow. *This isn't right,* he thought, *death is supposed to be ugly. They must just be sleeping.* Then he remembered what Father O'Conner had told him, "for the Celts felt that death was an inviting thing," and he thought it must be true.

He leaned over and kissed his Mother's lifeless cheek and started to straighten. Instead he leaned across her and kissed the baby's forehead. He turned and silently left the room, his Father's eyes following him as he went. He willed himself to remain strong for his father's sake. He went out into the fields before he let his grief take over in great heaving sobs.

V

"She just seemed to be sleeping," he said to Father O'Conner again. "And her last words to me before I went to get Maggie were, 'I love you, Lad,' as if she knew she was going to die. Father," he said as he turned square on to the Priest, "could she have known?" His eyes again welled up with the memory.

They sat on the bench amidst the fragrance of the roses in the rectory garden. The Priest laid a reassuring hand on his shoulder. "It's impossible to know what another person knows. It's as I told you, lad. Death is not to be feared. It comes to each of us once in our lives. If we accept it when it takes someone we love, we won't be as frightened when it comes for us." He looked into Seamus' eyes. "Why do you think a wake is such a joyful occasion, Lad? We're sending the soul of the departed off to a better existence and securing an easier departure for ourselves."

He missed his mother awfully, but Seamus suddenly pitied his father. The wake for Lorna had been in the cottage, for she wished to be buried among her flowers rather than the kirkgarden. The plaster walls had known no joy those three days, but radiated the gloom that was on Fahey's face. He had loved Lorna so deeply that he could see only his own loss and not Lorna's gain. Seamus wondered if the cloud would ever lift from the O'Flarity roof. It had now been a month since his mother's death and Fahey showed no sign of ever smiling again.

Several of Fahey's friends from the pub had stopped by to see how he was coming about, but Seamus had sent them away rather than have them see his Father sitting at the table, staring at the cold hearth.

"What can I do about him?" he asked the priest.

"Give him time. He'll come around soon, lad."

"But Father, he's not eating. He's getting awfully thin."

"Aye, that worries me too, lad. But he'll get hungry soon and that'll be a sign that he's finally come to terms with your mother's ghost. I'll stop and have a word with him."

"Thank you, Father. I think it might help."

Several more days had passed with young Seamus working like a man in the fields. He didn't know how much longer he could do this kind of work alone, but he felt he had to keep the farm going. He walked into the cottage at the end of a grueling day of hoeing weeds to find his father sitting in the same place. But he had a hunk of cheese in his hand and a wad in his cheek. There was a pitcher of goat's milk in front of him, already half gone. He swallowed the cheese and gulped down more of the milk then smiled up at Seamus and said, "Eat lad, we have rocks to clear from the corner of the lower field yet today."

"Land ho," the look-out bellowed, announcing their arrival in New York. Seamus rejoined the present and peered westward for his first look at his new home.

Chapter 6

A lump had formed within his throat,
For there stood destiny off the bow.
Their port of call lay just ahead.
He humbly made a mental bow.

So that's New York? What an exciting town it is, just like you said it would be," Seamus said to Kyle as he stared in wonder at the skyline along the harbor. He couldn't believe all those four and five story buildings he saw. The wharf along the East River was lined with ships of every shape and size loading or unloading cargo. They stood at the bow, ready to heave the hawser to the man on the dock standing next to the bollard. "New York is awfully noisy, too," he added.

"You haven't seen or heard anything, yet," Kyle said. "I was here for two weeks on my last trip and the things I saw will amaze you."

Just then Captain Fowler gave the order and they heaved the heavy rope to the man below on the dock, who caught it deftly and ran it around the bollard one time. He proceeded to pull on the rope with the aid of another man who had come up and the bow tucked into the dock smoothly. They made the hawser taught and, without fanfare, returned to their previous task.

Seamus had watched the entire process in awe of their ability. "They made that look simple," he said to Kyle.

"They do it all the time," Kyle said matter-of-factly. "It should be simple for them."

They joined the rest of the crew loading the barrels laden with Irish whiskey into the nets laid out on the deck. Seamus watched as the hook was attached to the four corners of the net and the load was hoisted aloft before swinging over the side to be lowered to the dock below. He traced the line up to the jib and back down the boom to the stationary pivoting base of the crane that contained the twin treadwheels.

"Fascinating," he said to Kyle.

"What's fascinating?"

"The way they use that . . .," he didn't know the word for the machine, so he simply pointed.

"That . . . is called a crane," Kyle said. "And it's used to lift loads on and off ships."

"I can see that," Seamus replied. "It's certainly a lot easier than lugging each barrel like we did at the beginning of this voyage."

"This is a modern seaport," Kyle said. He raised his arm and pointed at the row of five story buildings across from them that ran up Fulton Street and added, "And those are the counting houses and warehouses that are making this place so busy. It's sort of like a world trading center, if you know what I mean. Come on, let's get our gear and go ashore."

Seamus stopped by Captain Fowler on his way to the hatch. He held out his hand and said, "It was a pleasure sailing under you, Captain."

"You're welcome to stay on, young man," Captain Fowler said.

"No thank you, Captain," Seamus said as he nodded at the building across the street. "My future lies there."

"Who really knows where their future lies?" the captain asked. "I know where I want to be, but that's not the same as knowing where I will be." He still held Seamus' hand and at this point he gripped it firmer yet. "I have great hopes for you, lad, and I wish you the best of luck wherever you fetch up."

"Thank you, Captain," Seamus said. "And I wish the best to you as well." He reclaimed his hand, stepped over the hatch surround, set his insoles on either side of the ladder, and slid to the deck below. He bounced lightly on the balls of his feet as though he had been doing it all his life.

Kyle looked up and asked, "Where were you?"

"I was saying good bye to Captain Fowler, since I'll never see him again."

Kyle stopped what he was doing and looked over his shoulder at Seamus. "How can you know that?"

"I don't. But I doubt that I'll ever sail from here again," he said as he looked back at his friend. "This will be my home, now."

He wondered where that decision had come from since he had not consciously made it before that moment. He sat down next to his half-packed belongings and looked at his friend, repeating the words with a glazed look in his eyes.

Kyle stood up straight and turned to face Seamus. "Does that mean that we'll not be taking any more voyages together?"

"I don't know, Kyle," he said. "But I'll not be going back to Ireland, I don't think."

"Pity," Kyle said. "I rather like your company. And you're a good teacher. I can read now and that makes me feel powerful, my friend. I would like to share that power with you."

Seamus wasn't sure how to respond to that so he simply stood and returned to his packing. He climbed the ladder with one hand and slung his pack onto the deck with the other. He knelt on the deck and reached down for Kyle's pack to make the climb easier for his friend. Kyle came up through the hatch and they turned toward the gangplank together for the last time on this voyage. They were in the New World. Seamus felt exhilarated and Kyle showed all the signs of excitement a young man can at another adventure.

They crossed the busy wharf which also served as South Street, and went into number two Fulton Street, the first in the line of buildings known as Schermerhorn Row. The clerk sitting at a desk just inside the door looked up as they entered. "Can I help you?"

Kyle squinted at the young man and said, "You're new since I was here last year."

"I am that," the man said. "A man's gotta work somewhere."

"True," Kyle said. "We just came in on that ship . . ."

"The snow?"

"You know your ships," Kyle said. "Anyway, my friend thinks he wants to stay here and he's looking for work."

"Work we always have," the man said. He held out his hand to Seamus. "I'm Heinrik. Peter Schermerhorn is a distant cousin. He gave me work when I finished school. I hire men who can give me a full day of hard work without complaining."

Seamus took his hand in his strong grip and said, "I can give you that."

"Then you're hired. Do you need a place to stay?"

"Aye. I don't know my way around yet. Where are there lodgings?"

"I can put you up on the sixth floor."

"I only saw five floors from the ship."

"There's the attic. We plan on putting in some dormers someday. But for now, it's a place to stay. You'll have to feed yourself though." He looked at Kyle. "Are you looking for work, too?"

"Only while we're docked," he said, glancing at Seamus. "I'm sailing back and forth as long as the captain will have me."

"Or until you get washed overboard," Seamus said with a snort of fun at his friend's expense.

"Yes, there is that," Kyle said with a smile.

"Done," Heinrik said. "Follow me."

They seemed to climb forever. On the fifth floor Heinrik stopped and took a lantern down from the hook next to a door. He lit it, opened the door, and led the way up yet another set of steep stairs. At the top was another hook like the one below where he deposited the lantern.

"You can sleep here," he said, indicating the four cots, two on either side of the room.

"Is anyone else living here," Seamus asked.

"Not at the moment," Heinrik answered as he glared at the graffiti on the walls. "Take a couple of days to get settled in and see the sights. Tomorrow is Sunday so we don't work. Monday, we start with the sunrise. I'll see you downstairs then." He turned and made his way down the stairs.

As his head disappeared below the floor level, Seamus turned to Kyle and they smiled at each other.

"I didn't hope to find work so easily," Seamus said. "Thank you for stopping in here and getting that started."

"I knew there was work here, even if it was temporary." He reached over Seamus' shoulder and turned him gently toward the stairs. "Let us go and find some food. I'm starving."

"Wait a moment," Seamus said as he peered at the same graffiti that had apparently bothered Heinrik. "Bring the lantern closer, Kyle."

Kyle took the lantern down from the hook and held it close. What they saw was a pretty good likeness of the ship they had just disembarked from drawn on the wall with the words *Irish Lassie* below, along with the name Mickey O'Roarke and the year 1829.

"That's our ship," Kyle said. "And wasn't Mick the lad who was resting on the bilge pump lever while his friend, Norris, removed the rat that was plugging the pipe?"

"Aye, he was. I wonder if he was the same Mick who made this artwork," Seamus said as he indicated the drawing on the wall. It was suddenly artwork rather than graffiti since they knew both the subject and the artist.

They made their way down the stairs and along Fulton Street. They finally came to Broadway, turned right and found a place for a meal a little way along. After they were satisfied, they made their way westward until they came out on West Street and the waterfront along the Hudson River. Seamus' mouth formed into an 'o' as he looked up and down the riverfront at the forest of tall ship's masts.

Kyle saw the look on his friend's face and laughed. "I told you that you would be amazed."

Seamus looked back at Kyle and said, "I thought we had docked on a busy wharf, but this is loaded with ships. I didn't know there were this many ships in the entire world. Where do they come from?"

"All over the world," Kyle said with a wave that included the entire world. "If you name any place on this Earth, there is probably a ship from that port at these docks."

Seamus squinted up and down the river again, shading his eyes with his hand against the lowering sun reflecting off the watery expanse. He shook his head and said, "Amazing."

"We've got a couple more hours of daylight at best. Come on and I'll show you some more sights that will amaze you."

They turned and wended their way back among the tall buildings that made up that part of New York City. Seamus had never seen so many four, five, and six story buildings in one place before. They came out of the shadows of the buildings into a grassy area with trees off to one side. There was a group of young men running back and forth across the grass as they approached. They held some kind of poles with little baskets on the end; now and then one would swing his pole and a white object would fly out. Another man would catch the object in his basket and start running in a different direction.

"What are they doing?" Seamus asked as they watched.

"It's a game. They told me last time I was here that the Indians have played it for a long time."

"It looks dangerous. Look how that fellow hit the other one with his stick."

"From what I've learned, that was mild. The Indians call the game 'little brother of war.'"

"I don't doubt that at all."

"Apparently, the Indians often had goals that were miles apart and the games could go on for days."

"What is the point of this game?"

Kyle pointed at the opposite ends of the grassy area and asked, "Do you see those two fellows?" When Seamus nodded, he continued, "They have to keep the ball from going into their net. If it does go in, it's a point for the other team. The team that scores the most points is the winner of the game."

"And you say this goes on for days," Seamus asked.

Kyle laughed. "Not any more. One of the fellows who knew a lot about the game told me that it did in the old days before the white man took up the game. Now they have a man with a watch keeping the time for the length of the game."

"What is this game called?"

"The Indians call it baggataway or Tewaaraton, depending on what language they speak. The French call it LaCrosse because the stick looks like a bishop's crozier or shepherd's crook. No matter what the name, it is a fast-moving game."

"I'll say it is," Seamus said as the teams raced by very close to them. Seamus was forced to duck as a crozier inadvertently came close to his head, but not before he got a good look at the stick. "I see what you mean about the stick looking like a shepherds crook, er, bishops crozier." He studied the webbing of the basket as the player continued away from him and down the field. "It looks like it would be fun to play."

"They're pretty tight with their membership," Kyle said. "I doubt that you could get on a team."

They watched for a while before they turned around to head south to Number Two Fulton Street. The light was fading in the western sky as they reached the corner but not before turning the clouds the most beautiful mixture of reds interlaced with orange and yellow. Lavender streaked the sky above all the other colors. Seamus stopped at the door and returned to the corner for a full view of the western sky. He stood as if mesmerized and gaped at the sky fire that welcomed him to this new land. He was sure now, that he would never leave these shores again. "This is home," he whispered. A single tear brought on by all the conflicting emotions within him moistened his eye.

II

Sunday morning broke over the horizon and the noisy day began below in the street. While the company was closed, it seems that the wharves were open for business as usual. There came a loud toot from a little distance away, rousing Seamus and Kyle to full wakefulness.

"Do you want to explore some more while we have a chance," Kyle asked in the nearly dark room when he heard Seamus rustle.

"Sure," Seamus replied. "Though I can't believe there is that much more to see."

Kyle had stumbled to the lantern and raised the wick to brighten the room. He turned to his friend and said, "Don't kid yourself. We've barely scraped the surface."

They got themselves ready and descended to the street below in time to hear a tooting from up the East River. They looked to the left to see great volumes of black smoke, erupting from some sort of a smokestack sticking up among the ship's masts along the harbor.

"What is that, then?" Seamus asked, deferring to his friend who had been here before.

"I don't know. Shall we go down there and see?"

They hurried along the wharf to find a sign by a pier that informed them that this was the Staten Island Ferry. Moored in the slip was a boat with rounded humps on each side and no sails. The acrid smoke belching from the top of the twin stacks made them momentarily gag before a breeze blew it away.

"What in God's creation is that?" Seamus asked.

"I don't think that is one of God's creations, my friend," Kyle said. "I had heard about those on my last voyage, but have never seen one." He snorted through his nose in disdain before adding, "That's one of Robert Fulton's creations. It's called a steamboat. They are supposed to replace real ships from what I hear. Personally, I don't want anything to do with Fulton's Folly. I understand that's what they were called in the beginning."

"There are no sails. How do they move it?"

"That's my point."

Just then, the crew untied her from the bollards and she belched more smoke, blew her whistle with a shrieking screech and began churning the water on both sides of her hull. She glided backwards out of the slip, turning her bow outward as she went, then stopped churning water. The passengers were lined up along the starboard side waving to those on shore. Suddenly the water erupted anew amid ship and she began moving forward and turning more to port than before. They watched as she presented her stern. She grew smaller as she crossed the East River bound for Staten Island across the river. The steady cloud of smoke continued to move upstream as she grew smaller.

Seamus looked at his friend in time to see a sour expression begin to fade. Kyle spat into the river and said, "That left a bad taste in my mouth."

"I take it you have no love for steamboats, then?"

"Well, no. But it was the smoke in my mouth that gave me the bad taste."

"You have to admit that it looked a lot more maneuverable than a ship with sails."

"I don't care. I don't want any part of them."

"So that fleet you talked about will be strictly under sail?"

"That is absolutely right, my friend. These are dirty, smelly boats and I don't think they'll last long."

The two spent the day seeing the sights of the city and ended up in a dockside pub for a pint as the sun was again disappearing over the western horizon.

They spent the next week working for the counting house on the docks doing manual labor. Seamus was no stranger to the rigors of hard work, but by Friday night they were both exhausted.

"I can't do this much longer," Kyle said. "I'm going along to see Captain Fowler tomorrow and see how soon he's leaving. The work isn't as hard. Are you coming?"

"I don't think so," Seamus replied. "Sure it's hard, but it won't last forever and you can begin to buy those ships you want."

"Just the same, I think I can make better money on the high seas than this job pays," Kyle said as he rubbed his aching lower back. "And I won't die from the effort."

Seamus accompanied him anyway later in the day to see Captain Fowler. Kyle expressed his desire to rejoin the crew.

"I don't see any reason why you shouldn't, lad," the captain said. He turned to look deep into Seamus' eyes and asked, "And you?"

Seamus shook his head and said, "No, but thank you. I've made my decision to stay here and I'll stick to it."

Captain Fowler shrugged and said, "Pity. You're a good man and I would like to have you aboard." He turned back to Kyle. "We're nearly full laden. We shove off in two days' time. Come aboard tomorrow morning and you can help with the final preparations to get under weigh."

"Aye, Captain," Kyle said.

They left the ship and made their way back to the place they had watched the lacrosse match the previous Saturday. Seamus wanted to find out if he could work his way into one of the clubs and learn the game. They found an empty bench slightly removed from the edge of the playing field and took possession of it, leaving room at the end for another person to sit and watch.

As they waited for the teams to appear and begin the action, a young lady, complete with spinning parasol, sat on the unoccupied end of the bench. They glanced at her then back at the empty field. Kyle gave her a second look, then a third that stretched into a stare. Seamus said something to him that he did not hear. The young lady glanced at Seamus when he spoke then looked Kyle full in the face.

"You're staring at me," she said coyly. "It's impolite to stare, you know."

Kyle shook his head. "I'm sorry, I didn't mean anything disrespectful. You're so pretty, though."

She blushed. He stuttered. Seamus nervously moved a little farther down the bench.

Kyle held out his hand to her. "I'm Kyle Owens," he said, "and this is my friend Seamus O'Flarity."

She cautiously took his hand and said, "I'm Marta Fairbanks. I'm pleased to meet you."

Kyle looked into her blue eyes then up at her golden hair. He still held her hand which she was trying to extract from his grasp. He finally noticed and let go as he blushed.

"I'm sorry," he said, "I don't know what came over me."

"It's alright," she said. "I have another."

"You have another what," he asked, still staring at her.

"Hand," she replied.

"Good, good," he said distractedly, not hearing that she had made a joke.

Seamus burst out laughing and broke the spell.

Kyle turned to him and asked, "What's so funny? Did I miss a play?"

"Oh yes, my friend, you certainly did," Seamus said. "You go on with your game, because there isn't room on your field for three. It seems they don't play Lacrosse on Sundays. I'll see you back at the rooms."

"Fine," Kyle said, still in a fog and having no idea what Seamus was on about.

Seamus rose from the bench as the two disappeared into each other's worlds.

III

Monday morning arrived and Seamus was alone in the nearly darkened room. He stumbled to the lantern and raised the wick. Kyle's bed had not been disturbed. The man was missing. He got himself shaved and off to the work at hand. It was the kind of day that is so busy it seemed to be over when it began. He was returning along the wharf to his room when he was hailed from above. He looked up to see Captain Fowler waving down to him.

"Ahoy, Captain," Seamus said as he waved back, "Did Kyle sleep aboard ship last night?"

"Nay, lad. Nor has he shown up today. I was about to ask if you had seen him."

"I'm afraid not. His things are still in the room but he hasn't been there."

"We shove off tomorrow, with or without him. Would you consider taking his place if he doesn't show?"

"I'm afraid not, Captain. I'll try to find him tonight if I can."

"I thank you, lad. I can't ask any more than that," he said as he started to turn away. He turned back and said, "And, lad . . ."

"Aye?"

"Keep writing."

"I will, Captain."

Seamus changed course and beat a hasty path for the place they played lacrosse only to find it deserted. There were obviously no matches on week days. There was also no sign of Kyle or the girl. What was it she called herself? Oh, yes, Marta Fairbanks. She was very pretty and Seamus could see how Kyle would be overcome with her beauty. He hoped that wasn't the reason for his disappearance though. How would he tell Captain that his worthy crewman had jilted him for a member of the fairer sex? He sat down on the same bench and wondered what he should do. Maybe if he waited for a while, Kyle would reappear. It was a mild evening, after all, and he had not sat and just absorbed nature as it was meant to be absorbed in some time.

He must have dozed because he awoke to the sound of feathers swooshing nearby. He looked over in the waning light to see an owl perched on the opposite end of the bench. It turned its head at the same time as he and must have been startled by Seamus' movement, because it took off and flew silently up into the nearby trees.

Seamus looked around and stood up in some alarm. He wondered how late it was getting and where his friend was. "Maybe," he thought, 'he's already back at the room."

He would just go back and hope his friend appeared. He didn't know where to find Kyle so going on a one-man manhunt made no sense. He didn't know where the girl Marta lived either, so that quest was out of the question.

The next morning found him as alone as Monday had. He was becoming concerned about his friend. When he reached the street, he saw that the *Irish Lassie* was indeed in her final preparations for departure. He dashed across South Street and up the gangplank and asked the first man he saw where the Captain was.

"Captain, he still hasn't returned. I went looking for him like I said I would and couldn't find him."

"Thank you, lad. I appreciate the effort. I'll have to sail without him if he doesn't show soon, though."

"I understand. I'll keep an eye out, but I have to work, too."

"It's alright, lad. Thank you."

Seamus descended the gangplank for the last time, sad that he couldn't help the Captain.

His work for the day kept him pretty well on the dock so he was a witness to the snow's departure. He gave a final wave and was surprised to see someone on board acknowledge and wave back at him. "Maybe Kyle had made the sailing time after all," he thought. He felt a little better and went about his duties for the rest of the day.

At the end of the day, he looked up to see someone tearing around the corner and heading toward the snow's empty birth. The figure stopped and stared at the void, raised his arms from his sides and let them drop. He slowly turned and walked in Seamus' direction. As he got closer Seamus saw that it was Kyle. His friend had not been the one on board waving back at him.

"Where have you been," Seamus asked in concern as Kyle drew near.

"Ach, you wouldn't believe me if I told you," Kyle said.

"I might," Seamus said. As he pointed at the empty slip, he added, "And by the by, you missed your sailing."

"I can see that," Kyle said as he blew air out his nostrils.

"So where were you?"

"Marta made me completely forget what day it was, Lad."

"Women can have that effect on a man, can't they?"

"Oh, aye. I thought it was still Sunday. We were playing and she was cooking for me and she has her own flat and . . ."

"Slow down, slow down," Seamus said, laying a hand on Kyle's shoulder. "You don't have to get all the words out at once. There isn't room in your mouth for that." He looked his friend full in the face and asked, "What do you mean she has her own flat?"

"Oh my," Kyle said. "It's bad, isn't it?"

"I'm afraid so, my friend. But it's a good kind of illness you have. I know because I've had it myself. It gets better with time. You've fallen in love."

"But why did it make me forget about the sailing?"

Seamus looked at his friend and thought over his answer before saying, "How many times have you seen a pair of robins fly straight at you during mating season, and not because they're attacking you but because they are so distracted with each other that they just didn't see you?"

Kyle looked at him in disbelief for a second then said, "It is like that, isn't it?"

"Aye, it is every bit like that." He patted Kyle on the back and said, "You're in love, my friend. Enjoy it." He reworded his previous question. "Girls her age don't usually have their own flats back home. Why does she have her own place?"

"Her Da' lives out in the country; somewhere up in Connecticut, I think she said. She works in the city so she stays here because it's easier."

Kyle looked at their surroundings then back at Seamus. "I guess I'm stuck here now, since the ship has sailed. Oh well, I don't suppose it will be that bad with Marta to see from time to time."

"That's the spirit, lad," Seamus said. "You'll be alright, and take my word for it—the hard work will make you stronger."

IV

The summer passed and cooler weather was moving in on New York. With it came the smoke from many thousands of fire places and wood stoves. The soot in the air was becoming so thick that the dock workers teased about every other man having to spend the day parting the air so his partner could see to work. It was a standing joke that wasn't so funny when the persistent coughing began.

Through a raspy throat Seamus said to Kyle, "I've heard about the farms out in a place called Pennsylvania. The air has to be easier to breath than this. Do you want to come along and try your hand at tilling the soil?"

"Can't you just see me as a farmer," Kyle rasped back. "Besides, I don't want to get too far from Marta. She is a little vixen but she is my vixen."

"Suit yourself, then. I can't take this any longer. I'm going to take my savings and move along."

"I'll miss you," Kyle said as he looked at his friend with sad eyes.

"I'll miss you, too," Seamus said. "Who knows, we may meet up again someday." He leaned back against the wall by his bunk and pulled a knee up to his chest. The external pressure seemed to ease the internal pressure on his ribs from the constant coughing. His eyes watered as the pain abated.

"Are you crying?" Kyle asked.

"No. I just hurt too much from this coughing to hide it anymore." He shifted to ease the pressure a little more. "I think I'll leave in the morning."

Chapter 7

Elsewhere

Yet in the wild and untamed places
There were such men who knew no bounds,
Who would forsake the gentle graces
For forested hill and rougher grounds.

The north woods were filled with the torturous screams of a man fighting the very precipice of death.

Stands-Near-The-Spirits poured more cold water on the hot stones in the low steam hut and chanted incantations to the great ones above about the glories of this man with white skin. He poured cold water on the parallel wounds of his unusual patient, bringing on more of the delirium-driven screams.

Stands-Near-The-Spirits stopped chanting and prepared a salve from the fat of the bear that had caused the wounds, adding herbs he had personally selected. He spoke the new name for the white man, a name he had chosen for the white man, for as speaker to the spirits, he had the right to choose and give names.

"Grandfather, who dwells in the forest with the bear; Grandfather of the bear, hear me speak to you about this man I call Bear Claw. Hear me speak of his honor and his valor. Grandfather, hear the tale of how this man of powerful strength fought with the bear; and Grandfather, hear how he killed the bear with only a knife."

He stopped chanting while he rubbed the concoction into the wounds on the man's chest and arms. With a grunt he rolled the big man over onto his side and, reaching over him, began rubbing the smelly ointment into the gashes on his back.

With a howl the hairy arm flew out, catching Stands-Near-The-Spirits across the side of his graying head, sending him toppling against the hot rocks. A shower of sparks crackled from the pieces of dried twigs falling from the low roof where his blackened, deer-hide-clad feet had scraped them loose as he tumbled.

"Grandfather, he has much strength, even near death," he chanted comically as he righted himself.

He crawled back to the prone figure and watched him cautiously for a moment. He would never know what the man had looked like before the bear disfigured him with slashing claws and gnashing teeth. The end of his nose was a bloody pulp. His left eye was in the middle of a set of vertical claw marks, deep and oozing, that reached the end of his hairy chin.

Stands-Near-The-Spirits wondered why the white man did not pluck his face hairs the way his other people did. But it was only a passing thought as he rubbed ointment into the wounds and chanted.

The tribe dwelt so far from the usual paths the trappers traveled that few were ever seen by his people, and then only from a distance. Therefore, when Bear Claw was found lying across the carcass of the dead bear with the first snow beginning to blanket them, he was quite a novelty. Curiosity was so high that Stands-Near-The-Spirits had a difficult time convincing the members of the tribe to leave them alone so that he could minister his medicine to him.

He had given the task of preparing the remains of the bear to his brother's woman. Several days had passed since the white man and the bear had been brought back to the encampment. Waving Grass had skinned the bear and stretched the hide in her lodge to dry, and carved the meat and distributed it to the tribe, saving a portion for Bear Claw, if he survived.

Her voice, in an unfamiliar babble, came through the haze to the semi-conscious white man, a soft voice that appealed pleasantly to his sore mind. Then a coarser voice spoke in the same tongue. He tried to move and the pain seared through his body. He stifled a howl and opened his right eye, realizing that the left would not follow.

He wondered what was happening to him. Was he the victim of these people's tortures? He had heard strange tales about the people of the North Country when he was a boy back in Kentucky. Then he remembered the bear and recalled the struggle vividly. His old brown Bess had misfired and the bear kept coming. He had disturbed it as it was about to enter its den to hibernate. He knew better than to tangle with a bear close in, but as he turned to run, he tripped over something hidden by the falling snow.

The bear was all over him before he could get up. He was committed to battle. The strong musk of the bear rankled his nostrils as his head and shoulders were crushed into the bear's chest by powerful forelegs. Hot, searing pain shot across his back from the long, bony claws.

He remembered the knife in his belt and managed to force an arm downward to grasp the hickory handle. He turned the point to the bear's midsection as the powerful paws again crushed him. With a howl, the bear released him, allowing him room to slash the knife upwards. In retaliation, the bear had slashed downward across his face and chest. The mauling stroke sent the knife flying into the snow, leaving him disarmed and in fear for his life. The blood running into his eyes prevented him from seeing well enough to run.

The bear lunged at him, entrails flying from its open belly, knocking him to the ground. His knuckles crashed against something hard. He rolled his hand over and grasped the chunk of rock and began bashing at the bear's skull just as the heavy creature's jaws closed across his nose. He continued to hammer on the thick bony skull as the two rolled down the hillside, locked in mortal combat until all went black.

Now he realized that, contrary to his childhood tales, these people had probably saved his life. He again tried to sit up, wincing from the effort, and contented himself with propping his right arm under himself.

"You there," he called to the figure squatted in the doorway.

The figure looked around and spoke in his tongue to the woman beyond the door. He heard muffled footsteps rush away as the man crawled across the dirt floor of the low sweat lodge to where he lay. The words were still unfamiliar as he spoke to Bear Claw. As best he could for his condition, Bear Claw tried to say in sign language that he didn't understand. To his surprise, the man answered in sign language, although it was a bit different. Bear Claw was thankful to his Chickasaw acquaintance back in Missouri country for teaching the basics of it to him. The acquaintance was not a friend for Bear Claw had no friends. He pretended well until he got what he wanted, then moved on. He trusted no one and that distrust engendered the same in return.

"I am Stands-Near-The-Spirits," his host signed.

After several attempts and because of the variations, Bear Claw finally understood and repeated the name, then spoke it in English. The Indian looked at him curiously and Bear Claw signed and spoke at the same time, "Stands-Near-The-Spirits."

The man of medicine repeated it several times, smiling at the rhythm.

Then Bear Claw began to sign his own name but was stumped, for there were no signs for the Anglo name Alfred Simpson.

Stands-Near-The-Spirits interrupted and signed, "You are Bear Claw."

Once again, it took several attempts before he understood. Bear Claw smiled and the smile broke into a laugh. He understood the significance of being named and, more importantly, named into the tribe. He was being accepted by these people and honored in their fashion. Because of the old tales, he had feared that he would be killed as he entered the land of the geysers and the yellow soil, for the Blackfoot were said to hate the white man. But they had great esteem for the man who could kill a bear with only a knife and a rock, and survive, pitiful though he must look.

He spoke and signed his new name. Stands-Near-The-Spirits spoke the English words *Bear Claw* several times the way he had done with his own name.

Both men laughed, Bear Claw for the simple pleasure of being alive and the man of medicine for seeing that joy on his patient's face. The moment passed as a new figure blocked the light of the entrance and spoke to Stands-Near-The Spirits. He was invited to enter, along with the woman who accompanied him. They sat near Bear Claw as the introductions were made in their language and in sign language. It was a slow and tedious process as

Bear Claw figured out the nuances of this version of signing. Bear Claw's name was spoken in English to accompany the signs. As the other man's name was signed, Bear Claw translated it to English for their benefit. 'Deer Stalker,' the newcomer repeated several times, then nodded his own graying head in approval.

Stands-Near-The-Spirits went on to explain that not only was Deer Stalker his brother but the head of the tribe, and that the woman was the one who had skinned the bear, dried the hide and prepared the meat, and that she was Deer Stalker's woman, Waving Grass.

Bear Claw looked at her for a long moment, absorbing the soft, doe eyes and gentle curve of her cheek before he spoke her name like a prayer. Deer Stalker shifted uneasily and Bear Claw caught the movement. He feigned soreness from his wounds to cover the way he had spoken her name and lay back with his eyes closed. He listened to their conversation, not understanding a word, then raised himself back up with a wince and a groan.

Stands-Near-The-Spirits again signed that Waving Grass was Deer Stalker's woman for his clarification. Bear Claw signed that he understood and said in English that he wished that it weren't so. They all smiled at his acceptance of the reply.

Then Waving Grass drew her hand from behind her back with the symbol of honor, which she had made for Bear Claw. She lowered it over his head as Stands-Near-The-Spirits explained that these were the claws of the bear he had killed and the symbol of its power, which now became his power.

As the cold, bony claws touched the naked skin of his neck and shoulders, a chill came over him. He wondered what supernatural powers these people possessed that could pass the power of the animal onto him. But he couldn't deny that they had done so, for he could feel himself strengthening already. He leaned on his elbow and looked at each face, seeing confidence in the fact.

Deer Stalker rocked forward onto his knees, his head just clearing the sweat lodge roof and spoke to Stands-Near-The-Spirits. He then gave Bear Claw a look of guarded acceptance and made the signs, which wished him a quick recovery. He then crawled to the door, motioning Waving Grass to follow.

She stayed for but a moment, staring at Bear Claws brawny, wounded chest, with streaks of hair missing, then peered into his hazel eyes with a look of sincere sympathy. He mistook the sympathy for desire. He watched her leave with a longing that he hadn't felt for some time. He turned to the man of medicine whose eyes were closed. He wished he knew what Deer Stalker had said to cause this sudden change of atmosphere, for there were heated words between the two men before Deer Stalker had left.

II

As time passed in the quiet forest, the muscles healed and the scabs began to slough away. Bear Claw spent a good deal of the time learning the Blackfoot language and teaching his own form of English in return. He had learned his English in the usual way, at home with 'pass the salt' and 'do your chores'. The backwoods of Kentucky didn't require a great deal of education other than what was needed for survival, but he felt qualified to trade what he knew for what the Blackfoot knew just the same.

His dreams of the fight with the bear had begun to bother him less and he was back to sleeping through the night and waking early and refreshed. One such morning, he crawled out into the dawning light and sniffed the moist air. He felt an urgency to explore his surroundings. Following his nose, he came upon a shallow valley where the rising sun glistened golden through the misty vapors that filled the spaces between the ground and the tops of the low-lying bushes.

A thrush perched on the topmost limb of a scrub oak, just above the fog, and sang to a male on a similar bush across the meadow about this being his territory. An unusual sense of tranquility possessed him as he slowly parted the waist high fog and made his way down the slope. The damp grasses licked his ankles until his step sank into water. He stopped and listened. A quiet, repetitive smacking sound came back to him. He backed up a couple of paces and sat down in the mist and moist grass to wait for the sun to dissipate the fog and turn the half-light into full-fledged day.

As the haze burned away, he discovered that he was at the edge of a marsh where a pair of teal ducks paddled and groped in the water for their breakfast. They were undisturbed by his silent presence as they upended so that their tails pointed skyward, then dropped level, their bills smacking and clapping the marsh grasses back into their gullets.

He was thankful for the warming trend during his recovery. The snows had melted and this pair of southbound ducks was lured to a pause in their journey. He felt at peace with himself for the first time in many years. Maybe near-death experiences did that to a man. He felt at peace with nature as well and wished it could go on forever. He was not accustomed to this feeling and he almost liked it and hoped it would continue.

Then Waving Grass' soft voice broke the silence from close behind him. He snapped his head around and looked into her doe brown eyes. He understood enough of the words to get by and as she sat down beside him, he replied, "I'm enjoying nature and the quiet of the morning."

She looked at him curiously and sympathetically touched the scars on his cheek. His eye still had vision but through lids that knitted sideways when they healed. She followed the path of the scars down to his chin and onto his chest. Her touch aroused a sensation that he could not ignore. His shirt was open and she traced each scar with the tip of her finger. He could no longer control the urge he had felt the first time he had seen Waving Grass, when he was crawling back from the brink of death.

He lay back in the damp grass, pulling her down with him. She struggled at first; then, against her better nature, relaxed and let the moment take control of her. She laid her head on his shoulder and caressed his chest guardedly with her open hand. He stroked her hair and then her shoulder. Her face came up to his and their lips parted together as sweet oblivion carried them away.

The grasses warmed and dried beneath them as they lay silently in each other's arms, their breathing calmed now. The ducks had long since left for quieter ponds, but Bear Claw and Waving Grass had been unaware of their departure.

Then a shadow came over them as Deer Stalker looked down at their naked bodies. Waving Grass shied away as Bear Claw leapt to his feet.

"I warned them not to trust you," Deer Stalker said in his own tongue as he set his jaw for the attack. They grappled in the morning grass and splashed out into the marsh. An obsidian knife glinted wet as it flashed through the air, plunging downward. But the strength of the bear grabbed the wrist and held it fast. They fell backwards into the water and disappeared beneath the surface. The water boiled as the two twisted and writhed like prehistoric beasts in combat. The birds ceased their song to listen to the deadly duel. The surface stilled, then erupted in a spray as they rose in unison before plunging below the surface of secrets again. A redness spread outward on the rippling surface before a lone head again broke it. The figure rose in the waist deep water and strode, dripping from the marsh to the naked woman cowering in the grass. He stretched out beside her and she lay her head against his scarred chest. She knew her husband of many years would not be rising from the pool and her life would forevermore be linked to this man.

III

The walk back to the lodge of Stands-Near-The-Spirits was a solemn one, with neither touching nor looking at the other. Both were wrapped in their private thoughts.

They sat silently before the fire pit as the man of medicine raised his head for the first time since they entered his lodge. They had not spoken, nor would they until he spoke first. He opened his eyes and stared trance-like between them for a moment, then slowly shifted his gaze to Waving Grass, and then to Bear Claw, before again searching the void between them. A single tear worked its way down his cheek.

"The Grandfathers have shown me," he said. "I have seen Deer Stalker among the Grandfathers."

Waving Grass shifted uneasily in preparation to speaking, but Stands-Near-The-Spirits raised his hand to halt her words.

"I should kill both of you, but the Grandfathers told me long ago that my brother's woman would be untrue in the presence of a man of white skin. They told me that my brother would die at the bottom of a reed-filled marsh. These things cannot change, for the Man Above has willed them. Because I have foreseen this, I am not as angered as I would like to be, for he was my brother. But I am truly saddened, for I had hoped that I was wrong. My brother was not angered, for he knew of my vision. He asked if you were the one who would kill him and I could not answer him. I knew. But I could not say, for it would change what Man Above desired, so I bowed my head." He looked at Waving Grass in dismay.

"You have two choices, woman of my brother," he said. "You may leave the village, never to return, with this man before the truth is known; or you may remain and take your punishment. Because you were my brother's woman, I will allow you three days if you go now, as you are," he paused before adding, "with nothing."

He looked into her eyes and saw the pain. "You knew this would happen if you were untrue. You were raised on the tribal laws and you knew how strict the laws were concerning a woman lying with a man who was not her husband. I cannot change the laws, and by them you must be tortured until you die. I think you should go."

"Then it will be," she said softly, bowing her head obediently.

"Can't we just act like nothing happened," Bear Claw blurted out. "I'll leave and she can stay here with her people."

"No!" Stands-Near-The-Spirits leaned forward and stared into Bear Claw's eyes, the good and the bad one. "Our sense of dignity is a strong thing. She knows that she has done wrong and must be punished. I offer her life because these things were willed by stronger powers than mine." He looked hard at Bear Claw before whispering, "She must go or die."

Waving Grass spoke quietly, "I will go. But before I do, can you tell me what you have seen for me?"

"Do you wish to know more sadness, woman?"

She shuddered and looked at Bear Claw before saying, "No, I will wait for the passing of time to tell me."

Chapter 8

I've given up my berth in trade
For muddy earth and rusty spade.
'Tis dig all day and die each night
Too tired to eat or drink or fight

Seamus flapped his blanket straight over his frame and rope bunk and lay the flimsy tick pillow across the top. He dropped to one knee and dragged out his tin cup, plate and fork just as the breakfast bell rang through the heavy morning air. He joined the hundred odd men rushing from their tents to form a hungry line.

"Mush again," complained a young fellow near the front of the line.

"Wouldn't be so bad," added another, "if they didn't flavor it with grease."

"Hell, back in Tennessee we fed this slop to the huntin' dogs," a third said.

The thick air was heating up fast from the boredom of the same breakfast as the crackling July sun rose above the canal bed. The men digging the canal in Ohio were a varied lot from different parts of the country, with a few immigrants thrown in for good measure. That made for some bitter battles. But no feelings were as hostile as those caused by the burly foreman, Tom Hodgekins. In fact, many potential battles were overlooked as the men formed a ragged front against Tom, he was that hated. It was not so much that they were going up against him as they weren't giving him anything more to use against them.

He purposely strode along the waiting chow line with steak and eggs on his tin plate, waving it as he went for all to smell. He stopped by the huge Tennessean, held the tray under his nose and asked in mock generosity, "Want some of mine, boy?"

The big man, a little slow of mind, thought he was serious and reached for the plate with a grin, only to have his knuckles cracked by the short club that Tom was never without. The Tennessean dropped his empty plate in the dust and rubbed his sore hand, glaring through soiled locks at the foreman.

"Ain't enough for all of you, boy," Tom said with a wave across the line, "and if I give some to you, I gotta give some to them."

When the man from Tennessee bent to pick up his plate, Tom kicked him in the backside, sending him sprawling between the legs of the man in front of him. Tom laughed as he sauntered away, flaunting his steaming tray as he went. The entire breakfast line glared at him as the man from Tennessee was helped to his feet.

"First day here?" asked the man who had helped him.

"Yup. Weren't a very genteel welcome, I don't reckon."

"Watch yerself 'round that one," another man said. "And make sure he don't catch ya' sluffin' off."

"Hell, he ain't as bad as the foreman we had back on the Erie Canal in New York," an older man said. "He used a whip on us if we breathed the wrong way."

"Yeah, but Kicker's got a mean streak as wide as this canal," said the previous man.

Seamus turned to the Irishman he had befriended and asked, "Who's Kicker?"

"That one," his friend said, pointing at Tom's back with his fork. "You saw what he just did, Lad. He likes to kick."

"Oh!" He paused for thought. "I'll remember that."

As he ate his thin, tasteless mush, he recalled a thin, young fellow with whom he had worked on the docks back in New York called Kicker. He was a pleasant lad, though. The only thing he kicked was a ball. He never seemed to eat at meal breaks during the long day. Instead, he kicked a ball against the warehouse wall the full time. He was a quiet, hardworking lad and no one minded what he did to amuse himself.

This would be Seamus' first full day in the canal. He had arrived in the late afternoon the day before, was given a pick, and put right to work. When the sun went down, he was too tired to eat and had gone straight to his bunk. Now he was rested, fed, and ready for a full day as he approached the tool shed. A familiar face showed above the arms of the man who had slung a shovel over his shoulder as he turned from the tool shed door.

"Kyle," Seamus called out, moving from his second line of the day and rushing to greet his one-time shipmate. They embraced in the Irish fashion of brotherhood, ignoring the curious looks of the men in line.

"Good to see you, Seamus."

Tom Hodgekins bellowed, "If'n you lovers is done huggin', you can git yer arses to the head of the canal now." He grimaced as he flung a pick at Seamus' feet. "Now git goin'."

"Step lightly around him," Kyle whispered as they hurried away.

"So I've heard," Seamus said as they walked. "I thought you were planning a fleet."

"I was. And I nearly had my first ship."

Seamus waited but Kyle walked silently on. Finally, he could stand it no longer. Grabbing Kyle's sleeve, he stopped him and asked, "And?"

He could tell by Kyle's expression that he was almost too embarrassed to talk about it. Then, with a sigh of resignation, he said, "A good friend of mine, whose name I shall not mention but whose initials are Seamus O'Flarity, went to a lot of trouble to teach me to read when we were shipmates."

Seamus nodded agreement.

"Like a fool, I thought I could read and understand anything that came along." He paused for a moment, his left brow forming a gable over the brown window of his eye, and asked, "Do you remember Marta, the lass I was seeing in New York while we were working the docks?"

"Aye, and such a pretty sweet thing she was," Seamus began.

Kyle waved him silent. "Sweet, my aching heart," he said, "She was bait. She and her papa were a real pair in cahoots. Beware of girls with looks like that who say their papas are rich and are willing to back you." Kyle snorted in disgust as he stomped his shovel into the canal head. He looked over his shoulder and caught sight of Kicker watching them.

"Look busy while I tell you the rest."

Seamus sunk his pick to its haft in the yellow clay of the canal head and pried loose a clump as Kyle continued.

"I was really in a turmoil over her and thought I wanted to marry her. I was seeing her every evening and spending weekends at her flat. She knew of my dreams of a ship. Finally, she told me that her daddy was interested in helping me get started. Well, do you remember how much money I had saved before you left for Pennsylvania?"

Seamus grunted agreement as he sank his pick into the canal face again.

Kyle went on, "I had doubled that. I had lived like scum to do it, too." His anger rose and dissipated with each plunge of the shovel. "Her papa, the good and honest Alexander Fairbanks," he said through clenched teeth, "said I would have to invest it all in the ship, which I expected, and he would make up the difference." He sank his shovel deeper into the earth as he grew more hostile with the memory. He went on, "He had an agreement drawn up, a contract he called it, that I had to sign. I read it over as best I could then put my name on the bottom line and handed him almost all my money. I kept a little to feed myself, but that's long gone now."

"Then what," Seamus grunted as he swung his pick.

"Then, a few days later, I asked the good and honest Mr. Fairbanks how soon I would have my ship. He asked, 'What ship?' I said, 'The ship we're buying,' and he acted ignorant. He said, 'I don't know anything about a ship.' I said, 'What about my money and the agreement I signed?' and he said, 'Oh, that,' like it was some trifling matter. To him, with all his money, it probably was trifling."

Kyle had dug deeper into the soil with each angry shovel full. "He brought out the contract and showed it to me. He said, 'Maybe you should read it over again, son.' But the big words were no more clear to me than the first time I read it. I said, 'What does all this mean?' He grinned like a cat with a mouse in the corner and said, 'In essence, what it says is that you were to locate and purchase a ship within three days or have no claim to any moneys invested or promised.' All my hard work and savings were gone and because I signed that paper, there wasn't a thing I could do."

The height of his anger sent him into such a digging frenzy that a cloud of dust formed around them. He stopped digging and as the dust began to settle, he said, "I took it out of his hide before I left New York and came out here. That was three months ago."

"It seems that you didn't get rid of all your anger," Seamus replied.

The loose dirt and gravel crunched behind him and he whirled to find Tom Hodgekins approaching. "What in the hell is going on over here? Are you digging a canal or a well?"

Kyle looked down at the three-foot-deep hole he stood in and sighed. He looked up at Kicker in dismay.

"I'm docking your pay for the time you wasted digging that and the time it'll take to fill it and tamp it down. You're lucky you're so far down or you'd have my boot up your backside for wasting the whole morning," he growled, and stomped away in search of prey he could reach.

Kyle leaned against the edge of the hole, pulled a kerchief from his pocket, and mopped his muddy brow. He looked up at Seamus with a grin and a grimace all mixed up on his face, as though he was fighting back tears, and said, "Fairbanks is still costing me money."

Seamus felt sorry for him but there was little he could do for his friend. Words of consolation would do little good at this point. He looked over at Tom Hodgekins and said to Kyle, "He's watching. You'd best start filling in your well."

II

The tankard of warm beer tasted good and helped to wash down the slop they called stew. It was nothing like good Irish stew. As a matter of fact, it was nothing like anything Seamus had ever tasted. He learned quickly that the meals never varied. They were served mush in the morning, stew at noon and, for a change of pace, stew with a tankard of stale beer for supper. Most of the men were in the habit of gulping down the stew in a hurry to get past the taste of rancid meat, then washing it down with huge swigs of the beer to clear away the aftertaste. The remainder of the beer was carried away to the various activities devised by the men, and savored for as long as there was a drop to drink. No one was ever allowed enough beer to get drunk. Seamus and Kyle generally joined in song with the Irish contingent, accompanied by a fiddle and a concertina. The tunes carried them back to the green pastures of home, which few would ever again see, but they would all cherish in memory forever.

Seamus' memories were a bit different. He saw the green of the willow and would forever mourn the sadness it brought. He had written to his father after his arrival in New York and received a reply after what seemed an eternity. When he read it, he was stunned, shocked, frustrated, and angry with himself in that order, for the letter carried news he would never have expected. The words had leapt from the page as he read.

*"Before you left, my Son, you had told me that with Patricia dead
you had nothing to lose by killing Lord Mayfair. I know how you felt
and I cried for you and your broken heart after you left.*

"Then Athlone was in turmoil, for when the servants at Mayfield Manor broke through the study door, they found Patricia standing over the Monster's body with a smoking pistol in her hand. They said she seemed to be in some sort of trance and could not explain why she had shot Lord Mayfair."

Seamus had felt a new ray of hope. Patricia was still alive. Maybe he could go back and find love after all that had happened. He sat still and stared out over the masts in New York harbor, dreaming of how it would be when he returned. Remembering the letter, he eagerly lifted it and read on.

"She was jailed for several weeks. Finally, they hanged her for killing an English Lord. As the hatch was released, the Priest who was her confessor heard her say, 'Be safe.'"

Seamus felt the hatch give way under his own hopes and watched his salty tears fall and mix with the salty waves along the wharf. What had he done? He could find no words to express this new grief. Through new tears, he read on half-heartedly.

"Son, you can come home to the Dad who needs you. There is no one to suspect you anymore. I'm getting too old to work the farm alone and there's no one but you to leave it to when I die. Please come back, my Son.

You're loving Father,

Fahey."

Seamus had read the letter several times, hoping that he had misunderstood the words. It was hard to believe that Patricia had been alive. But remembering what Mayfair was like, he realized that the beast could lie as easily as he could ride down a priest. He had said Patricia was dead to make him give up. Mayfair hadn't known how deeply Seamus had loved her. He was probably incapable of the emotion himself.

To find out that she had picked up the pistol and inadvertently taken the blame for his crime gnawed at his conscience sorely. That she had died in his stead had given him a new ghost, one that he could not wish away as he had done the others. But she was not an angry ghost, for, since that letter, she always came to him under the willow with a smile of acceptance and whispering, "Be safe." The tears had poured from his eyes when he thought of what she had done for him. He felt unworthy, but knew that he must go on or her death would be a waste.

He had finally, after a lot of thought, written back to Fahey. The words of resignation read,

> ". . . for, knowing that my beloved died for me, I cannot face the land where we should have lived our lives in happiness, nor could I look any of the Darcy's in the eye without wondering if they somehow know the truth. I cannot come back, ever.
>
> "I beg of you to see that my friend Robin Clancy has work. Take him in my stead as your heir. He will work hard and see to your needs as I would. Make him your son for me and treat him as you would myself.

*"Please understand, my father, that though I love you as a good
son should, I cannot return. I am destined to stay in this land for as
long as I live.*

Your loving Son,

Seamus."

He had sealed his fate with that letter and Fahey had accepted it with his
reply, stating that his friend Robin, having nowhere else to turn now that his
grandfather was dead, was thankful for the living.

"Though I wish it were not so," Fahey had concluded, *"I will accept your feelings
about coming home."*

Quite often, during a bout with his memories, Seamus would wander
the half-mile or so along the canal bed to where the last lock was being built,
in search of solitude. He would sit in the moonlight for a while and stare at
the quarried stones dumped haphazardly on the ground or at the mortared
walls made of the same material. The walls often curved back toward the
banks but the mortar joints remained the same, large and coarsely struck by
unskilled hands learning the trade. But, even though the mortar joints were
wide enough for a man to fit his hands into past the wrist, the lines were
even and the face of the stone was plumb.

He found a small amount of satisfaction in the shape of the stones and
was often fascinated by the images of plants and animals that seemed to
appear when the moonlight played across their surfaces. He never saw the
locks by daylight because the digging was too far away, but he promised
himself that he would visit them one Sunday when they were given free time.

III

The wizened old man working between Seamus and Kyle groaned and dropped his pick. He leaned his shoulder against the embankment and slid to his knees. Seamus dropped his shovel as the old man doubled up and fell sideways. Seamus bent to lend old Hank a hand as Kyle looked around to see if help was nearby.

"For the love of Christ," Kyle swore between clenched teeth, "here comes Kicker."

Seamus felt a shiver rise up his spine as he propped the gray head of the old man on his knee. The man's eyes opened and he looked around.

"It's my heart but I'll be alright," Hank said in a whisper, as he clenched the fabric on his chest in pain. "You'd best get back to work before Tom gets over here."

"You don't look so good, Hank," Seamus said. "Your face is kind of piqued."

"I'll be alright," the withered mouth insisted.

"Kyle, get some water, "Seamus said. As Kyle strode off toward the bucket, Seamus said to the old man, "You just relax for a moment. Don't worry about Tom or me right now."

"Now what are you playing at," Tom roared as he approached. "If you want to be a nurse, go somewhere else. If you want to dig canals, stay. But get back to work."

Seamus looked around at the gathering crowd, then back at Tom. "But Hank collapsed and . . ."

"Bull," bellowed Tom. "He's just faking it. I'll show you." Without warning, Tom planted the toe of his boot in the old man's ribs with bone crunching force.

Hank's eyes bulged as he sat bolt upright. Tom lashed out with the toe of his boot again, connecting with the same spot on the lower part of his ribs. Blood oozed from the corner of the old man's twisted lips just before he slumped, face first into the dust—dead.

The shock of the brutal moment wore off quickly. Like a breaking wave drags the next wave ashore, shock was followed by rage as Seamus roared, "No," and attacked Kicker with a vengeance he thought he had overcome. Uppercuts, roundhouses, and haymakers were all mixed up in a series of quick movements as the roaring crowd continued to swell. Seamus kept moving around Tom, who seemed too dazed to locate his attacker. In a final fist flying frenzy, Seamus laid waste to the owner of those specially made kicking boots.

Panting from the effort, Seamus sank to his knees and looked with revulsion at the writhing, moaning heap before him, rose, and walked away. He rubbed his aching, bloody knuckles as the crowd parted to let him through. He had been oblivious to their cheers as he pummeled and punished Kicker, and remained trance-like as he passed through the throng. He saw only the bulging eyes and bleeding mouth of the old man he hardly knew, a man in need of a little comfort in his advanced years, who had reaped only the wrath of a sadistic task master.

As he stumbled back to his tent, his fury spent, he began to feel shame for having again lost his temper. He heard a cheer from behind and hoped it meant that Kicker was on his feet. He turned and watched the milling circle of men, expecting to see Tom's head, perhaps being helped back to his own tent. He was glad that he had stopped before he killed Tom. His conscience was still raw from the ghost of a similar person back in Athlone, even though years had passed since that fateful day. As he watched, the cheer took on a lusty tone and the crowd parted.

A man on horseback galloped out of the crowd with a trail of dust rising behind him. Looking closer, Seamus recognized the familiar boots of Kicker at the leading edge of the dust cloud, tied to the rope that ran up to the rider's saddle.

Seamus lowered his head in dismay and continued on to his tent. He sat in silence, listening to the roaring cheers and ripples of laughter up and down the canal bed, especially near the lock construction. He tried to justify the beating he had given Tom by recalling the vision of the old man's bulging eyes. But instead, he kept remembering another fit of rage and its results. How could he justify anything in the events of mankind when he was but one of its members?

In disgust with himself and his fellow man's reaction, he threw his belongings into his bag. He tossed a book into the bag, then retrieved it and sat down glaring at the title. *The Praise of Folly* leapt off the spine at him and its title took on a new meaning for him. He could not recall the words Desiderius Erasmus had so carefully penned within that binding, only the act Seamus had committed, and the shouts and laughter of his co-workers as they dragged Tom along behind the horse. He thought of the face of his friend, Kyle, beaming with glee as he ran, bucket sloshing water, along with the crowd. Seamus didn't think much of Kicker, but he was appalled at the joy with which the crowd had undertaken his punishment once they had the upper hand, the advantage that he had so shamefully given to them. Such folly, he thought, and they were all praising themselves.

He pulled the cords tight on his bag and flung it over his shoulder. With the book in his free hand, he stepped from the tent and met Kyle who was about to enter. The two stared at each other for what seemed an eternity. Kyle's smile faded as he read the apparent disgust in Seamus' expression. He opened his mouth to speak as Seamus slammed the book into his chest and walked away with only his bag. After some distance, he looked back to see his friend on his knees in the dust, staring at the book's title.

When he passed the stone locks, he was not surprised to look up and see a pair of hands protruding from the newly laid masonry. He stopped for a moment to wipe the hot tears from his cheeks as a finger twitched on one of the dangling hands.

As the light began to fail, Seamus turned to the west. He walked toward the setting sun with one small, pink cloud floating just above the horizon, one small but significant piece of sky fire.

IV

Seamus walked slowly westward for several weeks, sleeping under the stars at night and avoiding the beaten paths by day. He wanted nothing to do with his own kind and their immorality, and so sought the solitude of the forest and the animals. He lived on the abundance of the autumn berries and drank from the unsoiled streams. There was a tranquility that he had not known existed, and he relished in the hope that it would go on forever.

He was in just such a mood as he followed the course of a river one day and the sky grew dark with clouds. The rain descended sharply. He spotted a willow and made a dash for its protection. Feeling secure and somewhat dry with the rain running down the outer limbs, he let his defenses drop, and at that moment Patricia came to him again.

He felt the hot waves of emotion welling behind his eyelids and heard the words "be safe," but there was more; the vision pointed past him and said, "love her as you have me and I will come no more."

His heart was torn asunder, for on the one hand he wished to be free of the heartache, but on the other, he cherished the memory and wished to hold onto his Patricia forever.

As the vision of her began to fade, he grasped for the vaporous form but caught only a handful of wet willow leaves. He slowly turned in the direction her ghost had pointed and saw the startled, wide brown eyes of a maiden who had also entered the willow's protection. He stared in disbelief and she in surprise.

Chapter 9

"I want this, thus it is mine,"
Spoke the man who had no soul.
"It is mine because I say,"
Spoke the man who was a fool.

A cross the southern wilderness of Canada, Bear Claw had provided meat for Waving Grass and himself with his brown Bess. A cousin of Waving Grass had retrieved it the day they carried Bear Claw's near lifeless hulk home to camp. While he had been healing, he had time to repair the damage that had caused it to jamb when he tried to fire at the bear.

Now, Bear Claw watched Waving Grass' belly grow thick as they trekked the forests of pine and spruce. They had lain each night under the stars and clouds or under a hastily built lean-to, which warded off little of the drenching rains. The mosquitoes buzzed by day and night, a constant hum, but he had learned not to scratch and make the painful stings burn worse.

As warmer nights began to wane, he decided that it was time to turn to the south and settle in before the snows began to fly. There was still plenty of time, he thought, to get to a warmer climate before autumn ended.

Waving Grass trudged along beside him as they passed through the trail-less forest of unspeakable green with tree trunks big enough to hide a man. When they saw the first signs of habitation in the form of paths, their journey became slow and cautious. The paths became more numerous and crossed each other with more frequency.

Dusk brought them to the edge of a vast body of water, where they were stunned by what they could see in the failing light. They stood close to each other as the wind whipped the surface into little waves. They decided to chance discovery, and camped at the water's edge and listened to the waves lapping at the rocky shore. Again they slept embraced after their urgent needs were fulfilled. They had been destined for this life since their first touch by the marsh.

By first light they were in awe of the magnitude of the sea, whose lapping tide had sung their lullaby through the night. There was no land in sight save to right and left, and that land was of stone walls as far as one could see. They were at a low point of the land, just above water level.

Bear Claw made a sharp stick and speared a lake trout the way Waving Grass' people had taught him. As the two halves of the fish smoked over a small fire, Waving Grass peeled off her doe skin dress; the soft hide made a gentle sound of protest as it slipped up and off her body. The dried quills that adorned her neck harmonized and scraped together. She lapped the garment over her arm and loosened the ties that held her leggings, letting them slide down her slender legs. In all her glory, with garments over each arm and tassels gently swaying, she turned and stepped into the chilly water to scrub herself and her clothing.

Bear Claw admired her from the shore as her long tresses fanned out around her on the surface of the water. They seemed to form a raft at the center of which rode the face he thought he had come to love, the face that spoke of all things gentle and kind, things he never knew before.

She looked up from her scrubbing to see him staring, and cocked her head as she smiled and said, "Why don't you come in?" She teased a bit as she rose waist deep in the water and, in mock bashfulness, laid the dress over her shoulder to cover her bare breasts.

He cupped his hands beneath his chest and replied, "I ain't got nothing to keep me afloat," and he caught the soggy dress when she playfully threw it at his flashing eyes.

As he hung it dripping over the bush near the fire, he heard a twig snap nearby and whirled to peer into the brush. With one hand he waved a warning to Waving Grass, who ducked beneath the surface and swam to the cover of an overhanging rock. A few moments in the cold water for a quick bath had been invigorating, but she had not planned on an indefinite stay. She began to shudder with chills as Bear Claw threaded his way through the growth in search of the intruder.

After a while, he stopped and squatted down to listen for telltale sounds but heard nothing. As he was about to turn back to camp, he spotted something in the dried leaves beneath the brush within arm's reach. He recognized it to be a toe—that of the right foot of a youth, by the looks of it. He made as if he had not noticed and was about to leave, but as he leaned to rise, he lashed out at where the ankle should be and snatched the foot from under its owner.

The young Indian crashed onto his back in the brush in surprise. Bear Claw leapt upon him, pulling the knife from the boy's hand. With his knee on the young man's chest, he examined the knife before shoving it into his own belt. He gestured, palms open, to the youth that he too was now unarmed and would do him no harm. Bear Claw slowly raised his knee and the young man backed away, into a sitting position.

Waving Grass had clambered out of the water, wrapped a blanket about herself, and sat shivering by the fire. She looked up as they approached but remained huddled under the blanket. She listened while Bear Claw told how he had made the capture. She asked in her own tongue where the youth came from, but he stared in complete lack of understanding.

Bear Claw tried hand signs, and was surprised to see him reply that they lived all around him. He asked how many; the youth answered that there were five.

"Small band," Bear Claw said in English. He signed, "Is that your whole band?"

The boy signed back, "No, only my Father's family, which is made up of my parents, an older sister and an infant brother."

"What are your people called?" Bear Claw signed.

"Anishinabe," spoke the youth with obvious pride.

Waving Grass said to Bear Claw, "I know that name. It means First Man. They think that all mankind came from their ancient Fathers. I think they speak the Chippewa tongue."

Bear Claw stared at the youth for a moment before grunting. He looked out across the vast waters and signed, "What are these waters called?"

"Kitchigama," the lad said. He seemed to think for a moment, then signed and spoke, "My people are also called Kitchigumiwininwug."

Bear Claw chuckled and said, "We'll stick with Anishinabe, it's easier to say."

The lad looked at him questioningly, so he repeated the jest in sign.

Bear Claw leaned forward, pulling his knife from its scabbard, and the lad leapt backward in defense. Bear Claw looked up, startled by the sudden move. He paused before pulling half the fish from the fire. He cut that in half and offered part of it to the lad as he sat down cautiously. With his free hand, he asked the lad what he was called.

He replied, "Miskwasi." He took a bite of the fish after his host, then signed, "What are you called?" He watched the mauled face as the answer came, and asked if that was what caused the marks.

Waving Grass interrupted and signed, "He is a very brave man. He killed a bear with only a knife."

Miskwasi looked from one to the other with a new expression. He no longer saw him as his captor, and knew that his father would approve if he invited them to his mother's lodge.

Waving Grass said to Bear Claw, "I will be glad for the warmth. I am so cold from the waters of Kitchigami."

As Bear Claw led Miskwasi down the bank a short distance to give Waving Grass some privacy, a muskrat waddled lazily across the clearing. The lad pointed at it and whispered, "Miskwasi."

Bear Claw looked from Miskwasi to miskwasi and chuckled. He patted the lad on the shoulder. "You are a muskrat, my young friend."

Miskwasi looked perplexed, for Bear Claw had spoken in English.

II

Bear Claw ducked his head and blinked as he entered the lodge, trying to adjust to the dim light filtering through the smoke hole. The smell of freshly cut cedar boughs caressed his nostrils as the matting cushioned his step.

The low walls of pine logs formed a square room twenty by twenty feet. The bark had been scraped from the inside face of the logs and saved for the winter fires. The roof poles were of birch trunks the size of a man's thigh where they rested on the walls. Pine saplings were tied crosswise on the birch poles, then covered over with the birch bark to repel rainwater and snow.

Along the walls, there were sleeping platforms, three feet above the floor to be above the drafts. The space below the platforms was used for storing the sleeping mats and other goods, allowing the platforms to be used during the waking hours for sitting and other tasks.

Miskwasi's father was seated on the platform, making snowshoes for the winter when they entered. His legs were dangling over the side with ankles crossed as he bored a hole in a willow limb with a flint auger. He looked up and nodded a greeting as he spoke to his son. Miskwasi answered while gesturing at them.

Setting aside his project, he rose and faced the two, saying, "I am Mittig Wagaukwut. I speak some English. Oondous—come, warm yourselves by the fire."

"Much obliged," Bear Claw said, indicating Waving Grass. "Her clothes are still a little wet and I'm sure she's cold." He looked around and added, "Cozy lodge you have here. Looks like it would be warm in the winter."

"It will be," came a woman's voice from the doorway. "My husband's name means 'tree axe,' for he is the best builder from our village."

"Mishewin Autig, nin go je," said Mittig to his woman. Then he said to Bear Claw, "I told her to go."

"Wait," said Waving Grass. "May I speak with her? I have not spoken with another woman for a long time."

Mittig stared at Waving Grass's belly for a moment before her reasons dawned on him. "Stay," he said to his woman. "I will walk with . . ."

"Bear Claw," said Bear Claw.

". . . Bear Claw in the forest for a while."

As they were leaving, Bear Claw heard Mishewin Autig say that her name meant apple tree, and the two women laughed at the irony of Tree Axe marrying Apple Tree.

Mittig's daughter, who was ready to become a wife soon, approached with an armload of firewood to be put away for the winter as the three men were leaving the clearing. Bear Claw found it hard to hide his interest in the ripe young maiden as she passed with a nod.

III

The following day found Waving Grass fevered and delirious from pneumonia. The extended bath in Kitchigami had begun to take its toll. Apple Tree set about the task of mixing herbal concoctions and trying to control the fever. She sent the men away when Waving Grass began showing unusual contractions. Therefore, only she and her daughter were present when Bear Claw's son was born without breath or heartbeat.

"It was too soon," Apple Tree explained later to Bear Claw. "The baby was not yet whole."

"What do you mean, not whole?"

"The fingers and toes were still like the frog," was her reply. "Not like this," she showed him her own baby's fingers.

"What about Waving Grass, will she be alright?" he asked.

"Your Siksika woman will be well in time. She still does not know day from dark, but I have made much of the herb medicine. See, I keep it in this mocuck," she said, touching the birchbark container normally used for large quantities of maple sugar. She raised a portion on a wooden spoon and said, "I give her this much four times each day. Already she is better."

Bear Claw grunted and left the lodge to wander in the woods. He discovered a creek hidden in a glen and sat by its edge to watch the bream swimming in the hollow, and think.

Plenty of fresh fish close by, a tight shelter for the winter, a lot of firewood stored away already, moose and deer meat dried for long keeping; what more could a man want? A woman, of course. Once she healed and got over the fever . . . fever . . . of course. But she wouldn't remember much that occurred during her illness, and there was time, just enough, before her illness ended. So Apple Tree had said of his Siksika, his little Blackfoot woman. She would not know what had caused her illness and fever, or how contagious it was, and that would be to his advantage. After all, there were almost enough supplies for two people to last the winter, especially if one of them was ill and not eating. But seven people would require a lot more hunting and gathering, a lot more work.

He smiled to himself and leaned back against the sun dappled birch tree, staring through the forest. There seemed to be an abundance of everything here, an abundance that he would be a fool to ignore.

He didn't want to work at hunting and gathering for the winter. He didn't want to share the work—or the benefits. He shared enough as a child, until it hurt—painfully. For he had refused to share. His parents had fourteen children and he had had his fill of sleeping at the foot of the bed and eating cold potatoes.

He had been caught stealing food and hoarding it for himself. His father had beaten him severely with his bare fists and allowed him only a crust of bread while he watched the others eat his portion. After a week of that punishment, he had left home at the ripe age of fourteen to make his own way.

Determined to be his own man, he had hunted and fished his way north and west, occasionally selling pelts, but never staying in one place for very long.

Now he had found a place to settle down for a while and would not share it with anyone, except Waving Grass to keep him warm. He was relieved that the baby had not lived, for that would be one more to share with, one more mouth to feed.

As far as Mittig's family was concerned, he would have to get them out of his way. He would simply await his opportunity and kill them one by one. That didn't bother him; he had already tasted blood, and once the bear tastes blood it is no longer content with berries.

He began to think of the possible ways to eliminate them, when a pair of blue jays wheeled through the glen, screeching back and forth at each other, interrupting his thoughts. He saw movement off in the near distance and rose to explore. He watched through a thicket as Waubi Nebec, Mittig's daughter, picked berries and put them into a basket. She was alone, providing him with his first opportunity, one he dared not pass up. He would just have a little fun with her before . . .

As they struggled for her virtue, they rolled over the basket, crushing the berry juice into Bear Claw's buckskin covered hip. Her face showed revulsion for his maniacal features, enhanced by the scars. She called out for help during the struggle, but the lodge was too far away. He feared that someone would be close enough to hear, so he slugged her into silence. She lay unconscious, on her back, moving only with his movements.

It had begun. He would have what he wanted. He must insure that and did so with the edge of his knife across her silken throat. She would not speak of this incident to anyone. He dragged her still form into the thicket and covered her over with the broken berry bushes. He made his way to the nearby creek to clean the blood from his hands.

IV

Inside the lodge, Bear Claw heard the moan of the still delirious Waving Grass. He entered and blinked to adjust his eyes to the fainter light.

Apple Tree was administering more of the medicine from the mocuck and wiping Waving Grass' forehead with a dampened piece of soft doeskin. She looked up and smiled as he approached.

"She is getting better," she said. "Soon she should goosh kooz in— awake."

"Good, good," he said. After a moment he asked, "Where are Mittig and Miskwasi?"

"They have gone to follow the moose. They will be back later when the sun rests."

Bear Claw rubbed his hairy jaw where White Water had scratched him in their struggle. He sat down on the platform and compared the unfinished snowshoe to the completed one and decided that he could finish the work. It would be a necessary item of winter wear.

"Did you see Waubi Nebec in the forest?" asked Apple Tree.

Keeping his eyes lowered to hide the lie, he answered, "No," and said no more. He wanted to rest before he confronted her, knowing from her own lips that the time was growing short, but wanting to prove his manhood again before he killed her.

"She was gathering berries," she said.

"I know. You already said so." He was getting agitated with her talk.

"And you did not see her?"

"No."

"What is this," she asked, touching the stain on his hip. He had not noticed it before, and had no planned answer.

She saw his agitation and backed away. He charged at her before she could reach the door, and flung her sideways against the cradleboard with her infant strapped in. He heard the startled baby begin to screech, and then silence as it was crushed by its mother's weight. Ignoring her own safety, Apple Tree snatched up the baby, but saw that it was too late.

Still holding the baby in her left arm, she screamed in anguish and hurled herself at him, flailing with her right fist. He drew his knife and sheathed it in her charging body. She clawed at his chest as she slid to the cedar boughs on the floor, struggling no more.

He moved her body and that of the baby out of sight, built up the fire so all would look normal on the return of the hunters. They would now become the hunted. He laid out a bow and a few flint-tipped arrows on the platform and sat down beside them, leaning his back against the wall and pulling his knees up under his chin.

V

He had been dozing with his forehead on his knees when he heard the pack dogs barking in the distance. He jumped off the platform and stoked the fire to give himself light and make all look right from outside. He took his place by the bow and waited, listening.

He heard Mittig say something to his son, then the quick padding of feet running toward the door. Bear Claw notched an arrow, drew back the string and waited.

Miskwasi dashed in, jabbering in Ojibwa, and saw Bear Claw just as the arrow pierced his heart. His eyes stared in disbelief as he stood suspended, before crashing to the floor.

Bear Claw raced over and peeked around the hide covering. Seeing Mittig busy with the carcass of a moose, he judged that he had time to move Miskwasi aside to better surprise Mittig. He looked out the door afterward in time to see Mittig turn and call again for his son.

His dead son did not answer.

"Michelin Autig," Mittig said to the silent door.

His dead wife did not answer, either.

"Waubi Nebec," he called in a concerned voice.

Bear Claw took up his position again as Mittig came through the door. The arrow thunked into the hide as it was thrown back. Mittig looked around it as Bear Claw notched another arrow. Mittig took a quick look at his son's body and charged at Bear Claw with the fury of a wounded moose.

The bow cracked under their weight and the arrow flipped end over end, landing fletches first in the boughs on the floor. The two men, equal in size and strength, rolled and grappled, fell off the platform with a crash, and separated. Mittig lunged again and Bear Claw lashed out with his feet, kicking Mittig over backwards onto the floor.

Bear Claw leapt to his feet and started to pounce on Mittig when he saw the shock in Mittig's eyes and the glistening point of flint protruding from his belly, red with blood. Bear Claw stood over him and heard him ask in a raspy voice, "Why?"

"I don't like to share," Bear Claw said with a shrug.

Mittig's eyes closed forever.

After the sun rose, he set about the tasks of burying the bodies, including the one in the berry thicket. He fabricated a story for anyone asking about them. He would simply tell them about the fever that had struck the encampment and show them the graves as proof. He then settled down to the job of nursing Waving Grass back to health. After all, a man needed someone to cook for him and keep him warm in the winter.

He had what he wanted for now, a well provisioned home for the winter, water nearby, and a woman, when she was well again. He would become wealthy with a few beaver traps along the creeks and lake shore through the winter months. He laid his plan for the fur trade as the first snow covered the graves.

Chapter 10

Seek her love, my lonely lad.
Be her love 'til the end of day.
I shall come no more to thee
Nor haunt thy dreams in any way.

The atmosphere was strained. Neither Seamus nor the girl spoke or moved from where they were when they first ducked into the shelter of the willow, waiting for the downpour to end.

He admired the way her long tresses were braided with strips of doeskin and laid over her shoulders, rising and falling with each breath. Her shoulders were clad in doeskin, and the front of her dress was decorated with colorful beadwork artistically done in the shape of the leaves of the trees and the flowers of the fields. The strands of the skin were tied in small knots along each seam of her shoulders and sleeves, leaving little tassels as a fringe. Her moccasins were made of the same material, except that the beadwork on the toe of each slipper was sewn with yellow and white to look like a moon.

The softness of her eyes captivated him each time she raised her head to glance at him. He dared not look directly at her for fear that she might run away.

Finally, the rain slackened and she disappeared when he glanced away for a brief moment.

"Wait," he called, ducking out the way he thought she had gone. But she was nowhere to be seen. He retrieved his bag and began searching the forest for that single pair of doe eyes.

He ignored the fact that there might be hostile Indians in the area, suppressing the thought that it may be to them that she belonged. He had heard gory tales about the people of this wilderness, but cared only for the owner of that alluring pair of mysterious brown eyes.

The day wore on as he walked in ever widening circles around the willow. He stopped with a jerk at the sight of a single feminine footprint in the mud, in the middle of the trail. He looked down the trail cautiously, turned, and followed the direction the toe pointed. When he looked to his left, he saw the dolomite cliffs for the first time. They were so pretty that they momentarily distracted him from his search. He changed course to get a closer look at the rock face. It wasn't a solid wall, but broken now and again by small caves and crevices.

As he strolled along, occasionally ducking limbs and dodging bushes, he admired the contours and wondered how these formations came to be in the middle of a forest. He was thus engrossed in thought when he came upon a gap in the rock big enough to fit a very large house. He followed the gap to his left and now found the wall to be on his right, with the ground sloping gently upward on his left. A creek ran along the wall and out the gap. There was a thin grove of older trees. Within the grove was something else he didn't recognize.

He jumped the creek and, staying near the rock, began moving forward. It looked like some kind of dwelling. As he moved closer, he began to see more of them. People were moving around from one to another of the dwellings. He could hear their voices but couldn't make out what they were saying. He was sure now that it was a village of some sort.

Now came the time of decision. If he entered the village, he might be killed as an intruder. If he remained where he was, he might be discovered and killed as an—intruder? If he turned back, he might be found by other members of the village who were returning and what—killed as an intruder?

"Seamus, lad, get a hold of your imagination. Intruder indeed," he said to himself. This may be the village where the maiden came from. To see those magic eyes again was worth any risk and, of course, the pride of folly. He decided that boldness would perhaps be his best line of defense. Thus it was that he rose and strode into the Potawatomi village.

He stopped in the middle of the square as though in a trance, for there she sat, among a group of women shelling corn. Her nimble movements stopped when a murmur went around the circle; she looked up and stared at him, mesmerized. A bond had formed between his eyes and hers. In that brief moment, they became one, aloft, out of the reach of ordinary mortal touch.

The trance was broken by the phrase, "Queue faire vows manqué," close by his shoulder. He whirled to face an older man with graying hair and wrinkles just beginning to form on his face.

"Je venire dams paid," he stammered in half remembered French. He rephrased it in English. "I come in peace."

"You speak English?" the chief asked.

"More readily than French, if you don't mind," Seamus replied.

"I speak both," the man answered proudly. "What do you want here?"

Seamus found himself in a quandary. How could he say outright that he was looking for the lass with the big brown eyes? But what other reason had he for coming here? He had never felt so muddle headed before. Finally he said, "I am but a traveler who has lost his way."

"You may stay and rest. Come," the man said as he led the way back to his lodge. Before leaving the square, he spoke in his own tongue to the women.

At the lodge, the older man sat on the raised platform outside the door, and offered space to his guest to do the same. Seamus dutifully sat and crossed his legs in front of himself. He felt the strain of not knowing what to say to this man who he thought would be hostile, but proved to be able to speak three languages.

The girl with the dark eyes approached timidly with a rush basket and placed it between the two men. Up close, she was smaller than she had appeared at a distance under the willow. She stepped through the door and came back out with a wooden bowl of water and a gourd ladle, which she set next to the basket. She dipped the ladle into the water and offered it to Seamus with both hands. For a moment, their fingers touched and a tingle ran along his spine. He presumed that she felt the same by the gentle smile that spread quietly upward into her eyes.

The older man spoke and the girl's eyes darted to him then back to Seamus. She pivoted and returned to her duties at the shelling basket.

"My daughter's eyes have fastened upon you," he said.

Seamus realized that he had not taken his eyes off her, and that he still held the full ladle as he had received it. He took a long draught and settled the gourd back into the bowl.

"And your eyes are upon her, I see," the chief added.

Seamus blushed and looked sideways at the neatly combed black and gray head, with three eagle feathers attached to the locks by thongs.

"You say so little, White Man."

"I don't know what to say, or how much I may say without offending. I don't know your customs."

"But you speak honestly." The man paused thoughtfully before he continued. "Hear now, what I say. I am called Sinago, Gray Squirrel in your language. I am chief of this tribe. Bright Moon is my oldest daughter." He indicated the girl who had just walked away. "My kiwi, that was my woman, has gone on to join the grandfathers long ago and Bright Moon has taken care of me since." He paused and offered Seamus pone from the basket. Seamus was delighted from the first bite, for the little corn cakes had been flavored with bits of black walnut and maple sugar. Sinago watched him with interest, then continued, "Several young men of the village want Bright Moon to be their kiwi. Soon she will have to choose and the rest will have to accept her choice, unless . . ." he looked squarely at Seamus now, ". . . her choice is from outside our village." He paused for effect. "If her choice is from outside, he must prove himself, his strength, his value, and his love of her and for her people. He must do this because she is the daughter of the chief, and one day he will be chief himself."

Seamus felt a shiver of destiny but kept it hidden, for Sinago was watching him closely.

Sinago continued, "As chief, he will have many enemies outside the tribe as well as within. He will have to be strong enough to withstand many

163

attacks so that his son may one day be chief. He must know these things before he takes Bright Moon to be his kiwi."

Seamus realized that Sinago had seen the looks that he and Bright Moon had exchanged. He knew that this man had deep feelings for his tribe and his daughter and would protect them at the cost of his own life. He also understood that Sinago loved his daughter and would go to any length to see her happy, as long as it was within the moral laws and beliefs of his people. These things were obvious even to Seamus.

Sinago swallowed a morsel of pone and looked at Seamus for a long moment before going on. "But, if her man is not of our people at all, if he is white, he may never become chief, for the people of the tribe will not want this."

Seamus felt the fragile crystals of his hope plunge and shatter. He had been so suddenly taken by the maiden with the brown eyes, that he had given no thought to such things.

"What are you called?" Sinago asked abruptly.

"What?" Seamus asked, for he had been going over the implications of Sinago's monologue. "Oh, I am Seamus O'Flarity." He thought for a moment about how he would phrase the next question, then asked, "Tell me, Sinago, are there no alternatives? I mean, suppose a white man did marry Bright Moon and did not want to become chief, what then?"

"If the council approved the marriage, my second daughter's man would be the next in line," was his reply.

One tiny little crystal remained hanging desperately yet delicately within his reach, if he had the courage to grasp it. One tiny crystal lit the entire canyon where they sat eating pone on a warm summer day.

II

Feeling dejected and frustrated, Seamus sat down on a boulder by the river to pity himself. He wondered if he would ever again belong anywhere among any people. Many weeks had passed since his arrival at the summer fishing camp near the O'Plaine River; weeks of learning the Potawatomi customs, methods of hunting and fishing and, in general, the life style. He had run a grueling course for the love of Bright Moon and was still not accepted. What more could he do?

The summer fishing encampment would close up and move with all its possessions and people in a few weeks. Most of the tribe would rejoin the larger village on the Du Page River where the winter hunting would be better. He would either leave or move with them, depending on Sinago, the council and Bright Moon, but mostly on the council.

He had picked up a branch as he thought and watched the current flow steadily and surely by. He trailed the end of the branch in the current. He felt the water tugging at the stick and saw the ripple start there and dance merrily off down the stream, laughing as it went. The river met the obstruction head on and if it could not move it, happily shrugged, divided and went on its way without stopping. He realized that he must do the same.

He strolled along the bank, trying to decide how best to face his obstruction. How could he move these people who stood in the way of his love for Bright Moon? If he couldn't move them, would he be able to shrug and walk away laughing like the stream? He casually tossed the stick into the river and watched it float away with the current.

The sun was setting in the cloudless west and he knew that the council would be meeting on other important matters soon, so he turned back toward the village.

The council fire had been lit by the time he arrived and the decision makers were gathering. Many other interested parties stood outside the circle to listen or occasionally whisper comments to those within. This reminded him of one of Father O'Conner's history lessons about the Roman Forum.

He approached Sinago and waited until the noise of gathering had subsided.

"May I speak to the council?" he politely asked the chief.

Sinago raised his arms to silence the protests of a few of the members who knew of Seamus' desires and wished to hear no more on the subject. In his own tongue, Sinago said, "I will hear what this man has to say." He looked back at Seamus with a look of sympathy and urging.

Seamus stepped within the circle and began to walk slowly around the fire. When he began his second revolution, he said, "The water in the river is pure." He looked from face to face as he strode around the flames. "It flows forever." During the translation he bent and picked up a stick that had not made it into the fire. "I threw a stick into the water, but the river did not return the stick to me." He waited for the translation as he walked. "The water accepted the stick and the stick became one with the water." A murmur went around the circle as the translation ended. "The stick floated with the water all the way to the sea." The faces reflected the fact that they were accustomed to parables and they awaited the finale with patience. "You are the river and I have been cast among you. Will you throw me upon the bank or let me float along with you?"

The Shaman spoke, "I have heard through the spirits that you left your brother when he most needed you. How can we trust you?"

Seamus answered in defense, "I have never had a brother. I am afraid your spirits have spoken falsely of me."

"If Bright Moon joins with you, she will one day leave and she shall never smile upon us again," the Shaman added.

Without answering, Seamus made one more circuit of the council fire and stopped in front of Sinago. "I will await your decision by the river," he said.

III

A coolness swept across the river as Seamus squatted by the bank, the cool of autumn approaching. The sweet, musty odor of the forest in fall danced gently on the breeze. He was aware of the soft tread of someone's presence but remained motionless, fearing a final and lasting rejection.

The tender touch on his shoulder was not among the greetings he had been expecting at that moment. He looked up into the face that had lured him into his present situation, the eyes that had captivated his soul in that instant under the willow and again over the shelling basket.

"They are still talking," Bright Moon said in a voice equally as gentle as her eyes. She spoke English as well as Sinago, who had taught her what an old trapper had taught him years before.

She sat down beside him and took his hand, saying, "I have come under your magic, but I must obey my father. He wishes that I be happy but that I do as the council says, for these are his people and mine. We must live among them all of our lives."

"But you don't," Seamus quietly interrupted. "You can go away with me if they object to our union. Say you will, my love," he pleaded.

Bright Moon stared into the night sky at her namesake for a while, then said in a carefully controlled voice, "I must be honorable to all of my fathers, the one living and those who are not. They watch. They see us here now, sitting by the water. They hear you speak of running away and they hear me answer that I cannot, for the shame that I would bring to them."

Seamus' mind raced. He saw Father O'Conner's stern yet gentle face and thought of all the teachings of honor the old priest had given him. Honor or love—how to choose.

He saw the face of Patricia under a willow at Lough Ree and again, recently, urging him to love Bright Moon. Love or honor, why must there be a choice?

He saw his mother's face, serene and silent, in her final sleep. He saw his father's face, but that one living and unlike the others, seemed to be telling him to follow his heart. After all, had he not condoned what Seamus had done for love once before, or had he merely accepted the facts as they were—something already done and irreparable?

"We were born to each other," he said, "You know that, don't you?"

"I feel it too, but . . ."

"Then how can you accept their answer if the council says no? How can fate be changed by a group of men who can only see that the color of our skin is different? Come with me, Bright Moon."

She looked deeply into his eyes and said, "Fate is the one who will decide the vote."

Chapter 11

The winter snows had come and gone
Skipping northward acre by acre,
Leaving a trail of flowers in her wake,
Showing the bounty of man's maker.

A tang of frost still teased the air until the morning sun chased it away and warmed the day. Birds sang about spring's journey, telling in their own tongue about the adventures and conquests of the season. A fox squirrel looked on with interest as two of its mates played tag up a tree and across a limb, among the infant leaves.

Bear Claw straightened as the hide door closed behind him, stretched as far as his fingertips would reach, and yawned in the cool morning air. He smiled secretly as he walked to one of the shed-like structures he had built over the graves of Mittig's family. No one intruded on a grave. In fact, it was safer than one of those eastern bank vaults. Gifts and food were often left for the departed, and it showed Mittig's neighbors that Bear Claw 'honored' them for taking care of Waving Grass and him while she recuperated. It was convenient that they believed his story about Mittig's family losing their lives to the same fever that almost killed Waving Grass.

He looked around to ensure his solitude, and lifted the planks from the end of one of the sheds. He slid the first of two large bales of beaver pelts out into the sunlight, followed by the other. He then replaced the planks and used a limb to brush away the drag marks.

He shivered as he passed the little grave at the end of the row of five. It was the one that Mittig had built when his and Waving Grass' own child was born lifeless. It was the one where he had so carelessly dumped Apple Tree's baby, the place where two souls resided. He always skirted that one with an uneasiness he could not explain. Here lay what little conscience he retained.

He loaded the bales onto Mittig's sled and hitched the dogs into the harness. Snow or not, they would be made to pull the load. When he was done, he called out to Waving Grass that he was leaving.

She stepped out on still shaky feet with a parfleche full of dried meat for his journey.

"You will come back," she asked in a strange tone.

He nodded without looking up from packing another parfleche with powder and shot as well as other things he might need.

"I will be stronger when you return," she said in a slightly seductive voice.

He looked at her now and a twinkle showed in his good eye. "So will I," he grinned. "I go now," he whispered as he casually embraced her.

He drove the dogs south, following trails described by Mittig's neighbors during the winter months. Sometimes there was snow and other times none. The trails would lead to the St. Croix River, where he would trade the sled and dogs for a canoe that would take him all the way to the Mississippi River and on to New Orleans. He knew there was a good market for furs there because he had been there in his earlier ramblings. With the currents all going that way, he wouldn't have to work hard.

When he traded with the Ojibwa for the canoe, they had warned him, "Take care as you pass the lands of the Sauk and the Fox, for Black Sparrow Hawk is making war on the Whites. The Whites call it Black Hawks War because he is the one stirring up the people to fight. Our brothers, the Potawatomi, have refused to fight and will help you if you are in danger."

With those warnings, he set off, traveling by night and concealing himself and the canoe by day until he thought he was past Black Hawk's territory. Unfortunately, he had miscalculated the distance he had traveled. The first morning that he chose to go on rather than hide, he received a shock when he looked upstream and saw, at some distance, two canoes gaining on him. They had the advantage of no fur bales and more paddlers.

He looked ahead and saw the mouth of another river spilling into the one he was on and, with the last of his strength, rounded the point and landed. He frantically pulled the canoe into the brush and covered himself and the craft in time to see the lead canoe come around the point. He was glad that spring had arrived earlier here than farther north.

The two canoes slowed as they went by and the occupants jabbered back and forth in another of those languages he would never understand. He waited and watched, keeping to the shelter of his thicket. Once they rounded the next bend, he dashed back to the shore to obliterate the marks his canoe had made upon landing that he had not seen before in his haste. He knew they would be back and was surprised they had not seen the marks the first time.

As the midmorning sun began to warm the thicket and bring out the perfume of the forest, he dozed in a semi-alert state. It was well after noon when his eyes flashed open at the touch of cold steel at his throat and a hand over his mouth.

"Don't move a muscle," the bearded face whispered into his ear, "they're all over the place and you were startin' to snore."

Bear Claw lay perfectly still as the knife and hand were removed. He asked many questions with his eyes but only received more questions in return. He quietly sized up the man with the hazel eyes who had taken refuge with him. His gray hair stuck out of his knit cap at angles to his head and the matching beard was half way down his chest.

They could hear the motion all around, the nearly silent motion of men searching for men. As the sounds retreated, Bear Claw began twisting his head back and forth to ease the tension of the awkward position he had maintained for so long. He sat up slowly as the stranger put a finger to his lips in caution.

The man pointed through the undergrowth and Bear Claw followed with his eyes to see the back of a young brave left behind to watch and listen. There would be several sentries left to alert the main party of any movement. The two White men would have to be as patient as Black Hawk's men were and then some if they hoped to survive. It was a long wait full of many unasked questions, whose answers would have to be postponed until the braves returned to their camp after dark.

Finally, Bear Claw blew out his breath and was about to thank the stranger when he said, "Save it. We ain't safe yet. Let's git the hell out a' here whilst we got the chance."

They slid the canoe into the water and paddled as quietly as they could, until they were well away from the confluence of the two rivers. They continued up the river and as the sky began to lighten, the questions began to flow.

"How'd you know I was in that thicket?"

"I seen ya' land with them hot on yer birchbark backside," said the stranger. "I knowed ya'd be in trouble if'n I didn't help ya' out, so I worked my way over to ya' before they come back with a search party." He gave a knowing little laugh and added,

"Jest in time too, by the sounds of yer snoring."

"I sure do thank you, stranger." They paddled on for a ways and Bear Claw said, "By the way, I'm Alfred Simpson. But friends call me Bear Claw."

"That how ya' got all chawed up?"

"Yup. Tangled with a bear out in Blackfoot country and won. They nursed me back to life and renamed me. What's your name? I can't keep calling you stranger, not after you saved my life back there."

"Elliot Pratt, simple as that," he said. After a silence filled with the swishing of paddles and waves lapping at the canoe, he continued, "Used to be a surveyor's helper. I worked with Pascal Enos back in '29. We laid out the town of Calhoun. Harrumph! Ain't the same no more. Now they calls it Springfield and they got the state capitol set up there."

"Capitol of what state?" Bear Claw asked.

"Illinois, of course." Elliot stopped rowing and stared at the back of Bear Claw's head. "Where you been that you don't know where you are? I mean, you been out with them Injuns a long time?"

"Yup! Been learning how to trap and track real proper."

"That where you got all them bales of furs?"

"Yup! Should draw a pretty penny down in New Orleans, I ever git back to the Mississippi."

"Hell, you don't want to go back there lest you don't never want to collect for your efforts. 'Sides that, you'll draw more money for 'em by goin' to James Kinzie up on the Chicago River. He's got a cabin set up for traden' over by Fort Dearborn. There ain't no guvermint factors there no more, jest private traders."

"Better pull ashore and take cover," Bear Claw warned. "Sun's coming up."

"Don't fret none, we're in Potawatomi country now." After a moment he added,

"Don't 'spose it'd hurt to rest a spell though."

They built up a small fire. Elliot surprised Bear Claw by pulling all the makings for coffee out of his pack.

"I ain't had coffee in a long time. You always carry it with you?"

"Yep, wouldn't be without it," he said as he set to work. He laughed to himself as he worked, and then spoke his thoughts, "Funny thing is, they call that little village by Fort Dearborn the same as the river. Must really make the Injuns laugh, 'cause checaugo means smelly waters or oniony waters or some such name in their language." He looked sideways at Bear Claw as the water started to boil. "Can you 'magine namin' your town Smelly Waters?"

Bear Claw shook his head and shooed away the gnats.

Elliot went on, "I got me a gut feeling that Chicago is going to be a big town someday, though. Why, there's already Easterners comin' in there and buyin' up land. Spec-u-lators, they's called." He handed a steaming cup to Bear Claw. The two leaned back and speculated on the rest of the trip.

II

Bear Claw found the going tedious and much to his dislike, for it meant constant work paddling upstream. He wondered to himself why he had decided to become a trapper of all things. It certainly wasn't a lazy man's work. But in a short time, he'd have enough money to be as lazy as he liked. For that he'd do it. They paddled up the Illinois River to the Des Plaines River, also called the O'Plaine by some folk, then upstream some more, day after grueling day.

"Jest 'round that there bend and we'll stop for the day," Elliot said as the sun was setting behind them. "There's some folks I want to see there."

They pulled to shore and beached the canoe next to a creek. After hiking a short distance up the creek through a gap in the bluff, they came to a village.

The amount of fish carcasses drying between the lodges made it obvious that it was a fishing village.

Elliot pointed at the group waiting in the square and said, "That's the chief, the tall one. His name is Sinago. The Chaskyd, or Shaman, is the one next to him on the right. He's the one who talks to the spirits. Sinago's oldest daughter is on his other side. Last time I seen her, she was only waist high. But there's no mistaking that beautiful face and those big, beautiful dark brown eyes. Hello," he said under his breath, "looks like there's a white man in camp."

"Greetings, my friend Sinago," said Elliot.

"And to you, Elliot Pratt simple as that, and to your friend."

All the eyes of the welcoming party were fastened on the clipped nose and nearly closed, scar-covered eye, as the Shaman leaned close to Sinago and whispered into his ear. Sinago waved him off as a distraction.

"You come now, we'll talk," Sinago said to Elliot and Bear Claw. The resident white man fell into stride with them, hoping to partake of a little white man talk. Bright Moon followed along to see to the needs of the guests, her father, and her husband, Seamus O'Flarity.

Each time he was sure no one was looking, Bear Claw peeked back at Bright Moon, assessing the possibilities. He thought a little diversion with this maiden would be nice.

"There was much snow two winters ago, friend Elliot," Sinago said as they seated themselves. "Many of my people were cold and hungry."

"Did you lose many?" Elliot asked with sincere concern in his voice.

"No. My people are strong."

"What of the white folks up in Naper Settlement," Elliot asked. "How did they do?"

"Trapped like beavers in a snare for two moons, but they lived. New experience for them," he laughed.

Elliot turned to Bear Claw. "Why don't you persuade this here young feller to tag along with you to Kinzie's and Fort Dearborn?" He patted Seamus on the shoulder.

"I don't know," Seamus said guardedly.

"What's your name?" Bear Claw asked.

"Seamus O'Flarity. But I couldn't leave Bright Moon now, not just yet."

"Bring her along for company," Bear Claw said. The scars hid the twinkle in his eye.

Seamus turned to Bright Moon and asked, "Would you like to go?"

"I will follow wherever you go, Husband," she said with obvious love in her voice.

"Then it's settled," Bear Claw said, slapping his hands together with glee.

Sinago turned back to Elliot as Bear Claw, suddenly full of charm, began describing his journey to Bright Moon and Seamus. But Seamus was more interested in what Sinago was saying to Elliot.

"There are more white settlers coming, Friend Elliot. They are close to our winter hunting camp. And they are up the Du Page River a day's walk, in a new settlement called Barber's Corner. They are friends of Captain Naper."

" . . .don't you think, Seamus," Bear Claw was asking.

"I'm sorry, I was listening to Sinago. What did you ask?"

"I asked if we could paddle all the way to the fort."

"Only in the early spring when Mud Lake floods. But it's too early and the waters are still down, so we'll have to portage five or six miles to get to the Chicago River."

Seamus' attention was again drawn to the other conversation. Elliot was speaking. "I warn the settlers as I go but I'll bet they won't go to the fort. Sinago, my good friend, if Black Sparrow Hawk does come this far, will your people help the settlers?"

"Shabbona thinks we should," Sinago said. "I think we should, too. I am tired of wars, and Black Hawk's war on the White man is useless. If he continues, we will all be forced to leave these lands. We have proven that we can live in peace with each other. French traders have married our women for years. My own daughter has a white husband. What more can we do to prove that we accept the river's current and will flow with it?" He glanced at Seamus and nodded thanks for the use of his phrase. "Yes, we will help the settlers against Black Hawk. I will speak with Aptikisic about this also."

Seamus admired the eloquence of his father-in-law, the man of a race the Whites called savage, and who commanded two White man tongues as well as several Indian dialects. Seamus knew that every day spent among Bright Moon's people was embarrassing for Sinago, because of those who opposed the union of the red and white skin and the difference of beliefs. He made up his mind in that moment and turned back to Bear Claw.

"We'll go with you," he said firmly.

He relaxed now that the decision was made, and Bright Moon gently laid her hand on his arm and gave him her eye smile. She knew it was the best for all concerned and gave her approval with that small gesture. Seamus leaned back to listen to Elliot. He was telling about a fight that he had observed.

"It was down in New Salem, a fairly new settlement on the Sangamon River. Well, first off, there was this bunch of rowdies that called themselves the Clary's Grove Boys and one of them was this big, burly feller called Jack Armstrong. I swear he was the strongest feller I ever did lay eyes on. Then there was this storekeeper, Denton Offutt his name was. He spouts off about how his clerk could lick any man around. His clerk was an outsider to boot who come from Kentucky. I thought it was kind of funny cause I'd seen this feller Abe Lincoln several times and he always seemed quiet to me. Well anyway, they finally had a wrestling match that lasted and lasted. Why, they'd still be trying to throw each other around if this Abe feller hadn't said, 'Jack, let's quit. I can't throw you and you can't throw me.' I'll tell you, he ain't no outsider no more. That kind of man ain't no outsider nowhere. Got what you'd call a quiet strength to him. I like a feller what's strong and still sensible."

He eyed Seamus and said, "You kinda' strike me as being that sort yourself, young feller. That's what put me in mind of the story. Why, you ain't said two words since we got here."

Seamus fidgeted a little as they all looked at him. "I haven't had much to say. I don't know all these people you're talking about, so I figure it's best to just keep shut about them."

"That's true enough," Elliot said. "Never smear a name you don't know." He tossed a twig into the fire. "You folks better git some shut eye or you won't git very far after Mud Lake tomorry."

III

Seamus pulled his foot out of the sucking mud of the prairie swamp and took another step. He looked at Bright Moon with an expression of apology and said, "Elliot was right about needing a good rest before coming to this. We ought to go back and wait for the spring floods." He added a laugh to show Bear Claw that it was only a jest.

"Yup," Bear Claw said, "'cept we'd miss another whole winter's pelts."

They slogged on a ways before Bear Claw added, "You *are* going to go north and run trap lines with me, ain't you?"

In her own tongue, Bright Moon repeated the words of the Shaman. "Beware the man with the scarred face, for he is evil."

"The shaman also thought I had a brother," Seamus reminded her in Potawatomi. In English, he said to Bear Claw, "I hadn't given it any thought.

I suppose we could. Sure and why not. But, we need to find an easier way to get to market next year."

"We'll leave at the right time for the floods. That's easy to figure."

"Hey! There it is," Seamus said with excitement. In the near distance lay the sparkling ribbon of the Chicago River, beckoning them to be free of the prison of mud.

"Over there," Bear Claw nodded with his shaggy head. "That looks like the shortest way."

Their feet sucked in and out of the mud with renewed energy. At Seamus' bidding, Bright moon was the first to sit in the canoe and clean the mud from her legs in the fresh water while the men held the canoe steady. Seamus took his turn while Bear Claw braced the bow. When he was done, Bear Claw tumbled into the canoe, not caring if he wallowed in the filth for the rest of the trip.

They arrived at Kinzie's as the sun was sneaking off to sleep, but James Kinzie, owner and proprietor, was still open for business. A few of the local Potawatomi and Ottawa still lingered, half drunk, sipping at what their government annuities would buy, not willing to sober up and wait for the next payment.

Seamus opened the door and heard the conversation as he entered.

"I tell you, Elijah, if they can pull this off in congress, and we get this canal to the Illinois River, we're all going to be rich men. Why, just think how big this town will be. Instead of a hundred and fifty people, we'll be thousands, and they'll name streets after those of us who were here first. Think of it, man. Hubbard Street for you and Kinzie Street for my pa and me." Turning to the new arrivals, he said, "Howdy strangers. What can I do for you?"

Bear Claw hiked up his muddy breaches and said, "Got a mess of beaver pelts to sell. You interested?"

"Yup. There's still a fair market for them."

"Good. We'll bring them in." Bear Claw led the way back to the canoe. As they re-entered the store, Kinzie was saying, "But we'll need a harbor for lake shipping. The storms get too treacherous for anchorage while the bateau shuttle back and forth. Let's see what you've got," he said, turning back to the trio.

He untied the bundles and went through the pelts, uttering uh huh from time to time. Finally, at the end of the second bail, he said, "That's what I like, an honest trapper. One who doesn't try to slip in a few rabbit and squirrel pelts to make up the difference. I don't always go through them this thoroughly, but since you're new to these parts, I have to find out what you're made of. You keep packing them like this and we'll both prosper for as long as there's a market."

Bear Claw winked his good eye at Seamus, who missed the gesture among the confused features of his face.

James Kinzie went on, "These are pretty nice pelts. Where'd you trap them?"

"North," Bear Claw said, "up near the west end of the lake the Chippewa call Kitchigami. By the way, with Black Hawk on the rampage we daren't go back to the Mississippi. You know of any other rivers between here and there?"

"Well," Kinzie thought a minute as he waved good bye to Elijah Hubbard. "I've got an old surveyors map. Don't know how much good it'll be since it's kind of old, but it's better than nothing."

He reached up to the back of the top shelf and retrieved a roll of paper three feet long. Spreading it open on the plank counter and weighting the corners, he said, "It's forty or fifty years old now, drawn by French Voyagers as they called themselves. Let's see," he pointed to the legend in the bottom corner, "here it is—1788. Can't make out the name. Now, you're looking for the western end of Lake Superior," he looked up, "that's the same as Kitchigami."

He traced the shoreline with a finger and stopped at the western end, which was about as far as the map was drawn. "That look about right?"

Bear Claw bent over the map and compared the streams to those he remembered during the winter of trapping as best his lack of education would allow. "Yeah, I 'spose so. Where are we now?"

Kinzie tapped the map with a rounded fingernail at the site of Chicago, and the two began tracing rivers and streams with their eyes. Seamus and Bright Moon looked on with interest.

Finally, Kinzie pointed at a river and said, "Looks like this'll be the least amount of portages, but you're going to have to do some paddling."

"Would you be willing to sell me this map?" Bear Claw asked.

"Can't do that. You see, it's the only one I have. Tell you what you can do though," he said, bending to reach under the counter, "here's some brown wrapping paper and some charcoal. If you care to take the time, I'll let you copy what you need from it."

"I'll do it," Seamus interrupted. "I've got one question though; how do we get from here to St. Martin Island? That's a long stretch of lake shore to follow in a canoe with heavy water all around."

"Heavy water," Kinzie said, sizing Seamus up. "Sounds like you've done a little sailing."

"Aye, I have," he said as he bent to the task of sketching the rivers, "I worked my way over from Ireland a few years ago aboard a snow."

"You may be in better luck than you thought. A friend of mine owns and captains a barkentine that he runs from here to Detroit. Several of his crew are down with the ague right now, so the *Western Lady* is sitting at anchor. Captain Fernell said last night that if he had one more well man, he could set sail."

Seamus' eyes lit up. He had enjoyed his short-lived career as a sailor.

"You come back in here tomorrow morning and I'll introduce you. He comes in here about ten o'clock to chew the fat when he's in town."

They agreed and were about to leave when Kinzie added, "By the way, the *Western Lady* usually calls in at St Martin Island, right where you want to disembark."

IV

Robert Fernell stood at the railing with his arms folded across his broad chest. The brown in his high collared sweater would have blended with the deep tan of his face if the graying whiskers on his square jaw had not separated them. The gray stopped just above his ears, as though the top of his head belonged to a much younger man than the bottom. He held a reserved smile as he welcomed them aboard, glad to be able to get under weigh. But the furrows on his forehead spoke his concern for the unknown seamanship abilities of this young Irishman with the Indian wife.

"Swing the davits out for the canoe," he ordered in a deep voice. As two crewmen leapt to obey, Seamus dropped his bundle and descended to secure the lines to the bow and stern of the birchbark craft.

"You can stow your gear over there," the captain said to Bear Claw and Bright Moon, pointing at a space between some crates near the mizzenmast.

"'Preciate yer giving us passage, Cap'n," Bear Claw said as Seamus reappeared on deck.

"Thank him, not me," he said, nodding toward Seamus. "Hope you can do all you say, young feller. The farther north we go this time of year, the rougher it'll get."

"All I can do is my best, Captain. I hope it's good enough. Who does the schooner belong to?" he asked nodding toward a nearby ship.

"Captain Naper and his brother John owned her. I sailed with them a few years ago out of Ohio. Now they've brought their families here and sold the *Telegraph* to someone local. She hasn't moved since."

He looked doubtfully at Bright Moon, who was staring at the ship and her trappings in wonder. "Well anyway, some of the sick should be well before we get to the rough waters." He cupped his hands to his mouth and bellowed, "Lay out the sails, lads, weigh anchor and let's get under weigh." He turned to see shock on Bright Moon's face. Perhaps she had never heard anyone bellow before. He looked at Seamus and said, "Well, don't just stand there. You're part of the crew now."

Bright Moon's head swiveled from man to man across the deck and up into the rigging. She had never seen so many men move at once at one man's beckoning. She could feel the deck begin to move, and was amazed that this house in the water could pick up speed like a well-paddled canoe.

V

As the Captain had predicted, his men were able to return to their duties one by one. Seamus was glad of that, for the captain's other prediction had also come true. The going was getting rougher. He realized that the Captain's years of experience on these Great Lakes had become invaluable. It was obvious that he sailed nowhere else. He had become completely attuned to the seasons of these waters, like a carpenter is accustomed to his tools. He knew how to use every wave and every gust to his advantage.

Later, as they shared the wheel, Captain Fernell shouted above the wind snapping canvas, "If my guess is right, I'll be wanting to grab the wind as soon as we reach St. Martin and head east through the Mackinaw Straits ahead of the gale-force winds."

Seamus looked at him blankly before the Captain clarified for him, "It means something different for both of us. For my ship and me, it means survival. A gale could dash us on the rocks in the straits, and in order to stay ahead of it, I may not have time to call at St. Martins."

"But . . ." Seamus was knocked sideways by an unexpected gust from port. As he regained his footing, Captain Fernell reached out and grabbed his elbow, steadying him back at the wheel.

"See what I mean? Already the winds are shifting around. I'll lower you within sight of the island though, and you should have plenty of time to make land before it hits."

They fought the shifting wind as though on a tacking course for a while. Finally, Captain Fernell yelled above the wind, "You've been a great help and proved yourself well. I wouldn't mind keeping you on permanently."

Seamus smiled his gratitude and strained his arms the harder.

VI

Bear Claw clung to the bottom rung of the rope ladder with one foot holding the canoe in close as it bobbed by the dwarfing hull of the *Western Lady*. Seamus hung over the rail to steady Bright Moon as she began her descent to the canoe. He noticed that Bear Claw still looked a little green around the edges from his first voyage. But at least he was smiling as he looked up, watching Bright Moon's progress. It was the first time he had seen anything but anguish on Bear Claw's face since they had weighed anchor at Fort Dearborn. The man was positively grinning. *Perhaps it's the prospect of setting foot on solid ground,* thought Seamus.

Once Bright Moon was safely seated, Seamus scurried down the ladder like the seasoned seaman he was. They cast off the lines and yelled a farewell as the wind hauled the *Western Lady* away, dragging them a little ways in her wake.

Seamus took one last look at her before settling to the task of paddling ashore. The instant he lowered his gaze to search for the paddle, he realized that there was a familiar face at the rail, a face he had not seen during the short voyage, a face that must belong to the last of the ague plagued crew. He snapped his head up for another look. Standing at the rail, arm stretched above his head, was his friend, Kyle.

Seamus was almost timid as he raised his own arm to wave, but turned it into a hearty fare thee well as the face blended into the departing canvas.

"Who is that, Husband," Bright Moon asked, "your Brother?"

"No, no. I have no Brother, remember? Just a very dear friend." He replied. "I had no idea he was aboard ship or I would have had many words with him."

He became quiet for a while. She seemed to read his thoughts as she said, "You know what my people say, Husband. If a man touches another man's heart, then they are truly Brothers. I see the strong feelings you have for him. I sense that you would trust him with your life. Therefore, you are Brothers."

The shaman's words came tumbling back to him accompanied by a tingle to his spine. 'You left your Brother when he needed you,' echoed through his conscience. He had thought the shaman an old fool for making that statement and had sworn that he had no Brother. It was only a difference of word usage. To him, a brother was a man with the same parents. To Bright Moon's people it was a kinship of spirits. Truly, he had left the canals and Kyle after hurting him with his pride and folly remarks. He should have stayed with him or convinced him to leave but he was in too much pain at that moment to consider anyone else's feelings. "We are rather like Brothers should be," he thought.

What about the prediction that she would never return to her village? What had he done to her? Perhaps they should turn back now. But he had given his word to this scarred man and his word was valuable. He wondered what the shaman meant when he said that she would never smile on them again. Was there another turn of phrase or obscure meaning to those particular words? He would have to take special care to protect her now.

Another chill rose rapidly up his spine as he recalled the words she had translated that the shaman had said about Bear Claw. What lay in store for them now, he wondered? But Bear Claw had shown no sign of being dishonest, just vulgar and dirty.

"You going to help me paddle, or not?" Bear Claw growled.

"Sorry," was all Seamus said as he dipped his blade into the water. He glanced one more time at the *Western Lady*, as she became part of the low, scudding clouds.

He let his mind dwell on Kyle, their last meeting and their entire relationship. Kyle wasn't a bad sort; he had just been swept up in the tide of the moment. He felt bad for his friend. But he felt worse for missing the opportunity to mend their relationship. Then again, he reasoned, he hadn't known that Kyle was on board the *Western Lady*.

"The waters are angry," Bright Moon said as she gripped the sides of the canoe with white knuckles.

"We'll soon be on the island," Seamus reassured her. "We'll wait there for it to calm before going on to the river."

They bounced and bobbed like a twig. He had never seen the Mackinaw Straits, but from what Captain Fernell had told him, he began to fear for the safety of the ship, and her crew, even more now that he knew his friend was among them.

They beached the canoe and dragged it as far from the water as the rocks would allow. Seamus turned and stared at the swells being whipped up by the wind. Bright Moon laid her head against his shoulder and asked, "Will they be alright, Husband?"

"I pray to God, they will."

"If we don't take shelter soon, we won't be," Bear Claw interrupted." There's a place up there." He pointed to the top of the rise.

They climbed the small rise to the tavern at the top. The bottom half was quite what they expected for the area, having been built from logs that were square hewn and stacked, the chinks filled with earth. The top half took them by surprise. It was covered with overlapping siding and double hung windows that slid up and down, like the ones Seamus had seen back in New York.

There was a name painted on the bottom panel of siding, just above the door. Seamus read *Michigan Road Inn* as they passed through the entrance. He wondered about the road on so small an island. Then it occurred to him that he had heard the term before in reference to certain water routes.

Bear Claw called for a room and paid for it from his beaver pelt earnings. They carried their belongings up the narrow stairs to the room. Seamus thought back to the last time that he had slept in a real bed. It was in New York when he was working the docks.

Bright Moon stood in the open doorway with a look of wonder as she glanced around the room. "These things are strange to me, Husband," she said in a hushed tone, as though she was afraid of waking some evil spirit.

"That's right," he said in the voice of one with a new discovery. "You have never been in a White man's house. You've never seen stairs or a bed before. You'll like sleeping in that," he said, gently drawing her into the room by the hands and trying to reassure her.

The brass bed, and those in the other half dozen rooms, had been brought in on the *Western Lady* according to the innkeeper. It had a real tick mattress over springs. He led her over to it and sat on the edge, drawing her down in the same motion. The springs groaned a little under their weight and she sprang to her feet in horror of this bed that spoke.

"It's alright," he said. "It will not hurt you. Sit."

She cautiously obeyed and felt the give and push of the springs. She gave a little bounce, sensing the results. She giggled and bounced harder. Seamus enjoyed the sound of her happiness, rather like a child with a new toy.

She looked at him with a pleading smile that he had only recently begun to understand. He rose and took Bear Claw's elbow, leading him toward the door, turning his head briefly with a wink for Bright Moon.

"May I buy you a pint," he asked Bear Claw. "I have a few coins left."

"Sounds good to me," he replied, not one to turn down an offered drink.

As they descended the stairs, Seamus secretly hoped that Bear Claw was the type who would keep on drinking once he had begun, allowing him and Bright Moon time to explore the bed with some privacy.

As it turned out, Seamus had three pints at Bear Claws urging, but left him with two more in front of him as he ascended the stairs. He found Bright Moon rolled up in the blanket, asleep on the floor beside the bed. He sat down in the single chair and watched her sleep for a bit with sympathy in his heart. Finally, he knelt and gently kissed her cheek. He did not intend to wake her, for the trip from the *Western Lady* to the Island had been grueling for her. For that matter, the entire day had been exhausting.

She woke anyway and he saw her brown eyes focus on him first with alarm, then with the happiness he had come to know was deep in her soul. She raised up on one elbow and said, "It moves too much."

He looked at her in confusion before it dawned on him that she was referring to the bed.

"Come, we'll try it together."

She rolled over once, freeing the edge of the blanket and said, "Please, no, let us sleep here." She held the blanket open for him, exposing all her beauty to persuade him.

She grinned as his strange combination of canal digging pants, Indian moccasins, and shirt and Irish underclothing flew haphazardly in all directions in his haste to oblige. He doused the hurricane lamp beside the bed and dove under the blanket as she giggled over his cold feet. Soon the air was alive with the perfume of their love and they were sated.

An hour later, Bear Claw clomped into the room to find them fast asleep in the same embrace that sleep had found them earlier. He grumbled and stumbled in the dark after closing out the light from the hall, but still they did not awaken. He crashed down on the bed and fell asleep fully clothed and highly intoxicated. The dirty toes of his boots hung over the foot of the bed.

VII

Seamus and Bright Moon sat at a table, eating breakfast. This was another new experience for her. They were waiting for Bear Claw to put in an appearance. The day had begun calm and bright, just as Seamus had hoped it would.

"You see," he explained around a bite of freshly baked bread, "Some white men find it necessary to go on a drinking binge from time to time until they're 'blind,' especially if it is to be their last drink for a while." He knew he was partly to blame, and heaved a sigh of contrition. "I'll go up and see what's keeping him. You wait here."

Bear Claw lay on his left side with the scarred side of his face buried deep in the pillow. He looked like an overgrown baby with a hairy face and Seamus was reluctant to wake him, but he wasn't sure how long the weather would hold and knew that they must be on their way.

Bear Claw grumbled as Seamus shook his shoulder, but his eyes opened anyway.

"We've got to go."

"Yeah, yeah, I'm comin'."

He swung his feet over the side of the bed and steadied himself. "You sleep on the floor all night?" When Seamus nodded, he asked, "You prefer that to a real bed?"

"No, but Bright Moon said it moved too much and she couldn't sleep in it," he said, pointing at the bed that he'd never gotten to stretch out upon. He changed the subject before the soft mattress attracted him too strongly. "I'll get my drawing of the rivers so we can plan our course."

"Ah, don't mess with that," Bear Claw said. "Toss me that bedroll."

Seamus obliged and was surprised when he pulled the original map from the middle of the roll. "Where did you get that," he squawked, "He said he couldn't sell it."

"He didn't sell it. I helped myself to it. Besides, what good is it to James Kinzie? He don't have to tramp these woods, but we do."

Seamus resigned himself to the fact that his new partner was a little on the larcenous side, and bent over the map as it unrolled. They figured out about where they would have to leave the island in order to land at the mouth of the Ford River. They descended the stairs so that Bear Claw could have breakfast before they left.

While he ate, they asked the innkeeper about the landscape around the mouth of the river so they would recognize it. Fortunately, he had been there a few times, and was able to give them a detailed description. For their benefit, he added, "Then you take the Ford River to Michigamme Lake to the west, and up the deep river as far as it goes. Portage twenty miles over to the East branch of the Ontonagon River, then downstream to Superior. Follow the shoreline around the point with all its islands and keep going west to the end. Watch out for the waves. It can get rough this time of year."

They thanked their host for the lodging, food, and directions, and took their belongings back down the hill to the canoe. The winds had blown the canoe upright and it was partially filled with rainwater. They dumped the water, stowed the gear, and paddled to the shadowed side of the island to set their course for the river.

Chapter 12

Thus in you I shall put my trust,
Yet, being vigilant from day to day,
As we travel here and yon
Of folks we meet along the way

The trio was near exhaustion when they reached the western shore of Kitchigami. Bear Claw grabbed his bundle and headed up a path without looking back. Seamus and Bright Moon dragged the canoe out of the reach of the lapping waves and hurried to catch up so they wouldn't get lost. As they reached the edge of the encampment, Bear Claw was cupping his hands around his mouth and began to call out Waving Grass' name to the four winds. They waited for a few minutes before Bear Claw looked at them, shrugged his shoulders and said, "I guess she's gone," as though the fact were unimportant. He turned and went into the lodge with his traveling gear.

Seamus felt a twinge of worry over this man. Between the minor theft of the map and his flippant attitude over the absence of Waving Grass, he wondered if joining him was the best choice.

"Well, aren't you going after her?" Seamus asked as the hide covering dropped over the door.

"In time," came the muted answer. "Right now, I'm tired."

Seamus looked into the worried eyes of his bride and whispered, "What kind of man is he? Doesn't he care?"

"Do not forget the Shaman's words," she said. "He is not to be trusted." As their eyes met again, she added, "He is right, though. It was a hard trip and when one is weary, one does foolish things. Indian women often go into the forest alone to gather roots and berries or sticks for the fire."

"That may be so, but I think I may worry for as long as we are with this man. We know so little about him. What if he attacked you?"

"I am with you, husband. As long as you are near, I will be safe."

"That's very reassuring but I don't know how safe it will keep us from him. If the shaman said not to trust him, we should keep an eye on him. Perhaps we should return to your village straight away."

"Let us wait a while," she said.

He reluctantly picked up their belongings and they entered the lodge. Bear Claw was laying on the raised platform, arranging a hide robe over himself to ward off the nip in the air.

"I'll be more up to searching for her after I've slept awhile. You should rest, too," he said matter-of-factly.

When he put it that way, it sounded logical to Seamus, and he wondered why he was having these nagging doubts about Bear Claw's character.

He looked around the one room lodge and sensed that nothing was amiss. Everything seemed to be tidy enough, except that the cedar boughs on the floor were dried out and brittle. They should have been replaced with fresh ones long ago. "Perhaps," he thought, "Waving Grass was not familiar with this custom. Hadn't Bear Claw said she was Blackfoot? Maybe they didn't use cedar boughs to keep out the bugs and soften the step."

Seamus looked up from his musing over floor coverings to find Bright Moon examining the cooking utensils. Her eyes darted along a raised shelf where she found some pemmican. She took down the skin bag and scooped some of the contents into a clay pot. He watched as she added water until it was the right consistency.

Bear Claw, with one side of his nose nearly sealed shut from the scar, snored wheezily on the platform. It reminded Seamus of the metallic zing-chaw of a crosscut saw. He looked over at his new partner and marveled at how a person could fall asleep so quickly. What was it that Father O'Conner used to say, 'Innocent as a . . .'

Bright Moon interrupted his thought as she asked, "Do you want it cold or heated up?"

"I think warm," he said. "I'll get some faggots for the fire."

He stepped out into the sunlight and picked up an armload of the twigs that he had seen stacked beside the door. As he raised up, he saw a woman coming out of the forest dragging a sled loaded with more of the same.

"Bright Moon," he said through the door, "come here. I think Bear Claw's missing woman has just reappeared."

She stepped out and followed his line of sight. Together they waited until the woman entered the clearing. When she saw them, she stopped and stared.

"It's alright," Bright Moon said in Chippewa. To add reassurance, she indicated the hide door and said, "Bear Claw is here, too."

"Bear Claw," she said almost inaudibly.

Seamus indicated the lodge door with a nod of his head.

"Bear Claw, he came back," She said louder as she dropped the rope, ran past them, and disappeared into the lodge.

Seamus put his arm around his wife's shoulder and squeezed her to him. "I don't think she expected him to return, but I think she missed him."

"He has been gone long."

"About four months, by his reckoning. I wouldn't care to be away from you for that long," he said.

She smiled at him as they entered the lodge. Waving Grass sat on the platform, stroking Bear Claw's shaggy, sleeping head. He had shifted so that the snoring had stopped but he had not awakened at her touch.

Waving Grass smiled at them and said, "I was afraid that he would not come back."

Bright Moon approached her and said, "He has."

The two women began to chatter quietly in Chippewa. Seamus bent over the fire pit. He knelt beside the dry kindling and began turning a stick with a strung bow like his wife's people had taught him. Soon there was a curl of smoke where he had bored into a split log.

II

They began to settle into a routine as the colder weather approached. Seamus learned the trapper's ways quickly, as he and Bear Claw began setting out the traps for winter. They worked together until Seamus knew how to build a snare that would hold for the three or four days it took to make the rounds, checking them. Then they went in opposite directions, thinking they could trap twice as many animals before spring. They would have many more pelts and become wealthy men. That was a foreign thought for Seamus, as he had never known much more than poverty, though to him it was not poverty but normal.

Each time they met back at the main encampment, the men noticed that their wives were growing. They would both be fathers about the same time in the spring. Seamus' excitement grew each time he came back from his rounds. He could not understand why, instead, Bear Claw was becoming morose. He should be pleased and proud.

The women worked well together, each bringing new methods to the partnership. Even though she had been here for nearly a year, Waving Grass marveled at the wildlife and plants that she had not known in the western country. Bright Moon taught her how to find the roots she did not know existed. The best part was being able to talk woman to woman, for there were things that were not to be discussed with men.

The winter passed quickly and pleasantly for the foursome, and the stash of pelts grew to such proportions that they chose to stop trapping. Otherwise, they would not be able to transport them. Instead, they set to building another canoe like the one they had beached on the banks of Kitchigami. They would need the space. Seamus had suggested a coracle to tow along behind, full of pelts, but after he had described it to Bear Claw, they determined that it wouldn't hold the weight but would probably sink, taking a full winter's work to the bottom of Kitchigami.

The women contributed suggestions on the construction according to the customs of their people; and in the end, they had a serviceable canoe which would hold the weight of half the pelts and two people.

As the spring thaw arrived, so did the babies. Within a week of each other they came, squalling into the world. Waving Grass had told Bright Moon of her ordeal the last time, caused by the frigid waters, but neither woman thought there would be a problem. But within two weeks Waving Grass was suffering from chills as she had before. Soon she slipped into a deep coma from which she did not recover.

Bear Claw was in the forest when Waving Grass died. He wasn't expected back for a few days, so Seamus and Bright Moon saw to her sad, lonely burial. Bright Moon took over the feeding and care of Bear Claw's son. When Bear Claw returned, he barely acknowledged Waving Grass' departure and he began to act as though the child never existed. Seamus became quite alarmed at his cavalier attitude. He wondered how a man could not want to hold his own son and watch him grow. Bear Claw would stay out in the forests for many days at a stretch under the guise of scouting for the next winter's trapping locations.

One day in April, Seamus came back from a short hunting expedition to hear Bright Moon screaming. He dropped his kill and ran to the lodge to find Bear Claw trying to force himself on her. He grabbed Bear Claw by the shoulder, spun him around, driving his fist into the side of the man's face as he was spinning. Bear Claw stumbled and fell across the edge of the platform, knocking himself unconscious. Seamus embraced his bride protectively.

"I told you I would be safe with you near," she said with a sob as she looked into his eyes with adoration.

"What if I had not come back in time?"

"I knew you would. The shaman told me about this, too."

"Is there nothing the shaman hasn't foreseen," Seamus said in frustration.

"Not much," she said with a little hiccup. "He told me that now he will go," she added, nodding toward the unconscious figure on the floor, "He will take his share of the furs and leave."

Bear Claw chose that moment to return to awareness.

"Yeah, I'll take my share and leave right now." He staggered to his feet, picked up his few belongings and stumbled out of the lodge, not taking the time to apologize for his behavior.

They watched him from the lodge as he loaded his things into one of the canoes, and their eyes followed him back and forth as he took half the pelts to the shore, loaded up, and shoved off.

"What about your son," yelled Seamus as the canoe slid away from the bank.

"You can have him," he replied, and added, "never wanted the little whelp anyway."

They stood on the shore, arm in arm in stunned silence, and watched him paddle away.

"Father O'Conner would say that he was a particularly ugly man, inside and out," Seamus said as they turned back toward the lodge.

"It is as though my shaman and your Father O'Conner were the same person," Bright Moon said. She put her arm around her husband's waist as they walked.

"Maybe they were," he mused.

They entered the lodge as the boys were stirring awake.

"Poor Waving Grass," she said.

"Yes, to have died before she knew her son."

"That, too. But, to be betrayed by her husband. It was his duty out of love for her to take care of their son, and she couldn't trust him to do that." She thought for a moment, then added, "She didn't get the chance to name him."

"We will name him something that will honor her memory."

"You're a good man, Husband," she said with her eye smile.

She had lifted the lad who was making the most noise and begun nursing him. Of course, it was Bear Claw's son who was the most demanding. She would have to stop thinking of him as Bear Claw's son and instead consider him always as Waving Grass' boy. She wondered how Waving Grass could ever have gotten mixed up with that reprobate. She certainly was never like that herself. But every time she had brought up the subject, Waving Grass had found a way to change it without being insulting. She would never know what to tell the boy about his parents. Perhaps, if they raised him as a twin to their own son, the question would never come up, and the past could stay hidden. It would be too much of a burden for the boy to grow up knowing that his father didn't want him.

As he fell asleep, her own son roused completely and demanded feeding. As she switched babies, she told her thoughts to Seamus to get his opinion. He pondered for a while, then asked, "You don't think it will be too much of a burden?" He nodded at her swollen breasts, where his red headed son was busily taking in life.

"I can do this if you are willing to help me."

"Of course I'll be helping you. My name isn't Bear Claw."

She smiled at the jab at his recently departed partner.

"Speaking of whom, I think we will give him a day's head start before we begin the trip back to Fort Dearborn. We'll leave early tomorrow morning."

"As you wish, Husband. The boys won't remember their first canoe trip, but it would be good to be away from these bad memories."

III

Seamus awoke with the robins before the sun had put in an appearance. He dressed quietly and slipped out to load the bales of furs into the canoe. When he opened the shed where they were stored, he discovered that most of the remaining bales had been removed. "Bear Claw," he thought. He must have come back during the night and taken as many as he could put into his canoe without it floundering.

He stormed back to the lodge and found Bright Moon making him a meal. "He took most of the pelts," he said.

"It will be alright, husband. He is gone and we will make do as best we can."

"Aye, that's the truth of it, my love." Whatever made Seamus think he could become a wealthy man? Of course someone would have to come along and smack him back down where he belonged. Wealth seemed to be the privilege of the stingy or mean-spirited people of this world anyway. And Bright Moon wouldn't understand the use of money, so what was the point? He loved her so much that it almost hurt sometimes. That would be his reward in life.

Bright Moon gently stroked their son's red locks as she cooed to him, and he realized that no one could take this from him, and that he was the luckiest Irishman in the world. He went out to collect the rabbit he had dropped the day before when Bright Moon had screamed, and found that it, too, was gone. "Why wouldn't it be," he mused, "it was a free meal left lying around." He went to the shed, collected the remaining pelts, and put them into the canoe. At least they had something to show for a hard winter's work, meager though it was.

When he got back to the lodge, he saw that Bright Moon had packed everything she thought they could use into a couple of parfleches she had found under the platform. After he ate, she cradled the boys, one in each arm, and nodded for him to take the parfleches. They set off for the shore and settled into the canoe with her and the babies in the front to give them the smoother ride, and Seamus and the load back of center.

It promised to be a more arduous trip with Seamus doing all the paddling, but they were in no hurry, and if he tired, they could rest on the shore. The memories of this place would forever be bittersweet but they would have to become part of the past. They had the boys and the future to think about and little else mattered.

As he paddled east along the southern coast of Kitchigama, Seamus realized how different everything looked in the spring than on their trip here in the fall. He spoke his thoughts to Bright Moon.

"It will be alright, Husband. We will find our way." She paused in thought. "Or another way."

"You are so philosophical," he said.

She thought about that for a moment, then asked, "What does this phil-o-soph-i-cal mean, Husband?"

He laid the paddle across the canoe and rested his arms over it as he thought about the best way to phrase his answer. "In your case, love of my life, it would mean acceptance of the things you cannot change. Instead of becoming upset, you simply nod and move on."

"I like that word. Philosophical. Yes, that is a good word."

"The people in New York called the natives of this land savages. I have to say that nothing that I have seen makes me think that is even close to the right description. In fact, some of the rowdies of New York were far more savage than your people."

"Thank you, Husband. But you should know that there are certain of my people who can be very savage. This Blackhawk is one of those people."

"I heard about him when we were still at your village. What's his problem?"

"He is not very philosophical, husband. He cannot accept that the White man is coming here to stay. He is a very selfish man and doesn't think we should share the land with your people. It is not his land. It has been lent to us by the man above, no more."

"See, that is what I mean when I say that you are very philosophical," he said. He thought for another moment, then admitted, "I knew a man back in Ireland who was so much the opposite of that, that it cost him his life."

They coasted nearly to a stop as they mused over the mysteries of life—and death.

"How did that happen, Husband?"

"I took it," he said and looked down at his hands as though they were the culprits. She waited and he finally looked up to see concern on her face over the tear in the corner of his eye. "It's a sad story," he began. He told the tale of his Priest, his first love, the death of Mayfair, and his departure from the only home he had ever known. During the telling he had begun to casually paddle again, and when the tale was over and he returned his awareness to their surroundings, he realized that he had turned into the correct river back toward Fort Dearborn.

"You are a marvel, my love," he said to Bright Moon.

"Why do you say that, Husband?"

"You said, 'we will find our way, or another,' and then distracted me long enough for us to do just that. This is the river we want."

She looked around at their surroundings and smiled. "It does seem right, doesn't it?"

"Aye, and you are still a marvel. Have I told you recently that I love you?"

"With your eyes and your smile, often."

At that moment, the boys awoke, and the spell was broken by reality. They would need feeding and he would need to concentrate more energy paddling against the current.

IV

Seamus had discovered the real difficulty of the trip when they reached their first portage. With the boys' need for constant attention, Bright Moon was unable to be of much help. That meant unloading the canoe, hauling it to the next waterway, making the return trip for their belongings and his family, and then returning to the canoe. The longer the portage, the more grueling that portion of the trip. After one such trek, they chose to make camp and resume the next day.

"How much farther do you think it is, Husband?"

"By the direction of the flow of this river, I would say we are about halfway. I don't think I'll have to battle the current anymore. That will be a relief. My arms were ready to give out, between the paddling and the portaging."

"The boys are asleep. I will make you something to eat."

"Wait, my love. We need some fresh meat for a change. Let me find some game instead."

"If that is what you want. We will wait here."

Seamus rested for a short while then slipped quietly into the woods with his old musket. He had bought the musket, the lead press, and powder horn, from an old man after leaving the Ohio canal. The man lived in a small town and had no further use for it, but he did need the money for whiskey. It seemed ancient. The man said he had received it from a veteran of the revolution and this was already the eighteen-thirties. Seamus had used it several times, and it was about as accurate as he could want.

He saw movement out of the corner of his eye, and slowly raised the gun as he turned. He stopped short when he saw the doe with a fawn. He could not shoot either of them. That would be criminal. He lowered the muzzle and watched as they grazed peacefully, unaware of his presence. After they slipped behind some brush, he turned away in search of other prey.

"You were so long, Husband."

"I saw a doe and her fawn, my love," he said as he handed her the gutted rabbit. "I couldn't shoot either of them. Besides, what would we have done with that much meat?"

"You did the right thing. Families should not be broken apart. This will be a good meal," she said as she began removing the pelt. "I can make good shoes for the boys for their first winter from the skin." She looked around him and asked, "Where is the rest?"

"The rest, what? How many rabbits do you want?"

"No, Husband. Where is the rest of this rabbit—the insides?"

"Why would you want the innards?" he asked with a puzzled look on his face.

"Oh, Husband, you have so much to learn about my people's ways. We use everything."

"I didn't know. I tossed the innards into the tree limbs for the ravens."

"What are ravens, Husband?"

"Those big, black, noisy birds."

"Those are crows and it is best not to feed them."

"I thought they looked smaller than the ravens we had back in Ireland. Why shouldn't I feed them?"

"They are pranksters and will follow you and play tricks on you for being kind to them."

"You have some funny ideas, my love. But I will remember that in the future."

"Look, here they come already. They followed your scent. Don't leave anything laying loose when we go to sleep or it will be gone in the morning."

"You're serious about them playing pranks, aren't you?"

She nodded as she put the rabbit laden spit over the fire. "They would take this meat from the fire if we walked away. They are thieves."

"I could throw rocks at them or shoot them if you wish."

"You mustn't harm them, Husband. They also bring good luck, and if they are harmed, it will turn to bad luck."

"There is a bit of irony for you. Don't feed them or they will harass you, but don't harm them or you're really in trouble. And I thought my people had some crazy notions." He looked up at the growing congregation in the trees and winced at the noise they were making. "I'm sorry I brought this upon us, my love."

"No matter. If we ignore them, most will lose interest and leave. A few will stay to spread the word if anything looks worthwhile."

"All the same, I am sorry," he said as he turned the spit. "This is beginning to smell wonderful. What did you do?"

"I have learned a few things from Waving Grass. She used some things on meat that my people didn't think of. This was my first chance to try it out. I hope it tastes as good as it smells."

After they had thoroughly enjoyed their meal, Bright Moon said, "Husband, I have been thinking, would you like some help with the paddling and portages? You have been working so hard to get us there."

"What do you propose we do with the boys?"

"We could take the time to make two cradle boards, and it would give you time to rest."

He thought for a moment, then said, "I've never made a cradle board, but I've seen them. You could show me what to do, couldn't you?"

They set about collecting willow limbs while the boys slept, and while under the tree, they relived their first meeting under another willow. The passion was greater because there were not the inhibitions of that first meeting. Afterward, they smiled contentedly as they finished collecting the limbs they needed. She showed him how to curve the larger limbs for the frame, then lace the smaller ones in to make it firm.

"It is easy to do and we'll work together. Could we use some of the furs?"

"I don't see why not. It's not like we're going to make a fortune on them anyway."

As they worked, she said, "We still have not named the boys."

"I was thinking of Light from the Moon for our son," He said, with a smile at his own cleverness.

"Too long. How about Fahey for your father, or Robin for your friend?"

"I like Robin. Shall we call him that?"

"It is a good name. Yes."

They wrapped the framework with the beaver pelts doubled over to provide both warmth and softness for the boys to rest against.

"Are you sure you are not of my people?" she asked. "That is as good a cradle board as I have ever seen before."

"Yours is pretty good, too," he said. He looked around and said, "We could stay here for a few days, if you'd like."

She lolled back on her elbows and looked around, too. "It is nice here. Would you mind not hurrying?"

"Not at all, my love. Now I'll show you a trick I know." He began chopping and hacking with the hatchet he had found in the shed during the winter; and when he was through, they had a fairly decent lean-to shelter for their stay.

"It is nice, Husband. May I make a cover from more of the pelts?"

"Yes, and while you are doing that, I have another project to work on."

"Pro-ject, Husband? What is that?"

"A project is like a task or a job. I will show you when I am through."

They set to their separate tasks, she cooing to the boys, who were now sleeping in the lean-to, and he whistling an old Irish ballad as he whittled away at some of the shavings left from hewing out parts for the lean-to.

"I like the sound you make with your mouth," she said. "How do you do that?"

"Do your people not whistle?"

"Whis-tle? Is that what it is called?"

"Yes, whistling is done by blowing air through puckered lips, like this," and he proceeded to demonstrate with a lot of trills and grace notes.

"It is so beautiful," she said, "like a bird. No, like several birds."

"You try," he said.

She puckered up and blew, but made no whistling sound.

"Try moving your tongue around as you blow."

She did as he instructed and jumped when the sound came out. "I like that, but it tickles," she said, and went on to do it a few more times.

"Now try moving your tongue and tightening and loosening your lips."

She found that with a little effort, she could warble like the thrush in the brush.

"I will be able to whistle to the boys when they get restless. Will you teach me to make the songs that you were making?"

"I will, my love."

"What have you been making?"

He held up one of the fishhooks he had carved and she stared at it, then she looked the question at him.

"They are for catching fish," he told her.

She took it from him and acted out scooping a fish out of the water with it. "I don't think you will get close enough to the fish for this to work."

"No, no. Not like that. You tie it to the end of a piece of twine."

"Twine? What is that?"

He thought for a moment, then picked a piece of thread from his raveled sleeve and held it up for her to see. "This is thread. Twine is several strands of thread twisted together to make it stronger."

She went over to where she had cut several strips from the pelts to lash the hides over the lean-to and returned, handing them to him.

"They are too wide, my love, but you've got the idea."

She proceeded to slit them into thinner strips and hand them to him. He tied the ends together as she handed them over. He then took a medium size willow branch from those left over and tied the loose end of the line to the thin end of the branch. She watched as he turned over a stone, collected a grub, and stuck it on the hook. He crawled out onto a low branch that hung over the water and lowered the hook and grub into the water. The wooden hook floated on its side on the surface.

"Of course it floats," he chided himself, "it's wood. I shall have to weight it." He crawled back along the limb. He tied another length of hide to the hook and found a suitable rock to secure to the end. This time the hook sank below the surface as it was intended.

As they waited and watched the fish circling the bait, Bright Moon said, "My people would spear them as they swam by."

"I doubt that I am that good with the spear, my love."

"It will be faster."

"Where is that philosophical notion of waiting?"

Just then there was a tug on the line. Seamus was able to set the hook and land a good-sized walleye. He set the pole aside and removed the hook from the fish's mouth. As he handed the catch to Bright Moon, he said, "This is how I learned to fish in Ireland and it works well for me."

"It's very clever, husband."

While they chatted about differences from his world to hers, she scaled and gutted the fish, poked a stick through it lengthwise, and leaned it over the fire that Seamus had started. They had become a team, observing what the other was doing and making the necessary moves to balance the action. He smiled at the thought that two people from such different backgrounds could become so well suited to each other.

Once again, she used some of the herbs Waving Grass had taught her about, and they enjoyed a tasty meal. When they were through, she heaved the remains of guts, scales, and bones into the fire.

"What, you don't have a use for those," he teased.

"They would go into the soil to make the corn better if we were at my village. But we will not carry them home with us. They will stink soon. Also," she said pointing at the trees, "we don't want the crows to stay."

"Aye, that is true enough." He fell silent for a moment as he looked around them. Finally, he looked directly at her and said, "What if this were home? There are fish in the river. There is game in the forest all around us. There are berries and herbs. Why do we have to move on or go back?"

She looked at him in amazed silence for a moment. Then, she too, looked around and really took in their surroundings. She finally broke the silence as she stood. "I like it here. We can make this our home if you like it, too."

"Oh, love of my life, I like it very much. With you by my side, what more could I ask?"

They rested until the boys began to stir. While Bright Moon attended to their needs, Seamus pulled the canoe farther from the rivers rippling current and unloaded the rest of their gear. He upended the canoe to keep rain from filling it on the off chance they would need it in the future. With that task finished, he leaned back on his elbows and watched her gentle way with the boys and whistled her favorite tune.

"I think I'll build the lodge under the willow tree, love."

"No Husband, you must not."

"Why?"

"Fire from the smoke hole is not good under a tree."

"That makes sense. I didn't think of that."

"The willow is close when we want it," she said with a wink. She had learned that wink from him and he thought it charming coming from her.

"You have a way with them," he said, nodding at the boys who were looking around in curiosity. "They seldom cry or make a fuss."

"It is not safe for them to cry. It would bring the wolves and coyotes, or worse, the cougar."

"In Ireland, it seems the bairns are always squalling about something."

"What do the women do with them?"

"They put them in their cradles while they do their chores. They're close enough to hear them if they cry."

"We keep them with us and know when they are about to cry, so they don't need to."

"That also sounds more civilized. I've learned so much from you already."

"But you taught me to whistle," she said, and she proceeded with a tune which enthralled the boys.

Chapter 13

This home I make for you, my love
To raise our bairn and make a life
Away from all the crowded towns,
Away from all the daily strife.

Seamus spent a great deal of time felling spruce and pine trees to build a cabin in the method he had seen in these parts. It was so time consuming since the only tool he had to work with was a hatchet. He would have to go to Fort Dearborn after he got his young family settled and buy some decent tools. He collected boulders from the river and built a solid fireplace with a chimney on the downwind side to keep sparks off the roof. He chinked the stones with river mud since no mortar was available. He used dry dirt to thicken the mud to a mortar like paste.

He had found an open meadow full of tall grass that he was able to turn into the type of thatched roof he had learned to make so recently in Ireland. He knew it would hold the warmth. When it was done, he moved his family in with as much ceremony as he could muster, for this was their palace.

Bright Moon made a great show of being impressed, but as soon as he was out hunting, she began making little changes so that it would be more utile and comfortable. She had found a stand of cedars and covered the dirt floor with their boughs. Most importantly, she thought about all the things that Seamus would have to add to make it complete. Men just didn't think of things like the high ledge to keep animals out of the food supplies, or sleeping platforms to keep them off the cold ground in the winter. He would have more work to do when he returned, and she hoped he wouldn't mind.

"Of course I don't mind," he said. "I will do whatever will make you happy, my love. You just tell me what and where and consider it done."

After taking care of those chores, and making the cabin a home for her, and bringing in enough game and fish to keep her supplied, he set off for Fort Dearborn.

"I'm going to trade in the rest of the furs for some much-needed supplies," he explained as he loaded up the canoe. "Are you sure you'll be alright while I'm gone?"

"Of course, Husband. This is a good lodge and I know my way around the forest. Go now, and don't worry."

His trip was much faster without the extra weight and the need for frequent stops. He set up an account with James Kinzie from the remaining furs, and thought about the necessities for living far from civilization. Primary items included fresh powder and lead for the musket, a good crosscut saw, a rip saw, a file to sharpen them with, a double bit axe and stone to sharpen it, a good drawknife, and many other essentials. He debated over the price of a plow and horse but decided to delay that plan. To top off his purchases, he bought a harmonica to impress Bright Moon even more than he had done with his whistling. He thought he could remember how to play, even though it had been a few years. When James told him that he had a fair amount still on account, he asked him to bank it for future needs.

He was amazed at the number of small lakes he came across on the return trip. He told Bright Moon about them when he arrived. "They're only a short paddle away to the south," he said. "I'd like to show them to you some time."

He showed her the tools he had bought and how they worked. Soon he was ripping trees into planks and making a door and shutters to hang on the hinges he had bought.

While he worked, she explained to him that she had finally decided on a name that would be fitting for the son of Waving Grass. "We will call him Tall Grass."

"That would be fitting," he said with a smile, "because he will be tall like his father. And to call him Tall Grass after his mother would be good. I like it."

He showed her how the door latch worked and the shutters opened and closed and said, "These will keep the animals out of the food better than the high shelf."

"These are good things, Husband."

As she sat with a baby on each knee and admired his work, he pulled out the harmonica and started in on an Irish ballad that she had heard him whistle. She snapped her head around and stared at the source of the unusual sound.

"What is that, Husband?" she asked when he stopped.

"This," he said, holding it out for her to take, "is called a harmonica. I learned to play it as a lad in Ireland."

She reached around Tall Grass to take it while supporting the baby with her forearm. After a thoughtful pause, she said, "I would like to see this Ireland someday. You have so many wonderful things there."

"There are some wonderful things and there are some not-so-wonderful things. I'm afraid the people of my country would find you hard to accept. That is one of the not-so-wonderful things."

"Why, Husband?"

"To begin with, your skin is not as pale white as they would like. Then, there are your eyes, nothing like Irish eyes. And you have quite an accent."

"What is an accent?"

"Do you hear the difference between the way I speak your language and the way your people do?"

"Yes."

"That is a difference in accents."

"My people accepted the difference in your accent," she said matter-of-factly.

"Most of them do, but they are more tolerant than mine."

"I think I would still like to see your Ireland and the place you were a boy."

"Perhaps someday we can manage that. We'll wait and see." He took the harmonica back from her and put it to his lips, concentrating on one of his favorite ditties so he wouldn't have to think about all the reasons that trip would never happen. Afterwards, he slipped into his favorite lullaby and watched the boy's eyes as they went from playful to sleepy. Soon, they had nodded off and Bright Moon was able to rest for a while.

"I'm thinking that I'll spend a little time making a better trap for the coming winter," he said. "I've been thinking about a design I want to try," and he described it to her. "Will you and the boys be alright while I go off into the woods to find what I need?"

"Yes, Husband," she nodded sleepily in the warm summer air. The lullaby had had its effect on her as well.

He quietly set the harmonica aside, collected the tools he would need, and slipped away, leaving the three of them dozing in the shade of the cabin.

II

It was nearly pitch dark by the time Seamus gathered up his tools and the trap he had created and made his way back to the clearing. He didn't see the dark form on the path as he came out of the woods and stumbled, dropping everything in his attempt to stop his fall. He crawled back to see what had caught his foot, feeling as he went. His hand touched fur and he froze. His thoughts raced through the possibilities as he groped the fur to find a head. He suddenly realized what it was when he felt the ears. Why was a wolf lying in the path, and why was it not moving? Where were Bright Moon and the boys? Why was there such a chill going up his spine?

He cried out in a panic, "Bright Moon, where are you?"

There was a groan to his right. His eyes finally made out her shadowy shape huddled against the cabin wall next to the door. He raced to her side to find her body wrapped around the boys to protect them and her shoulder ripped open by the jaws of the wolf.

"What happened?"

"We were napping and I heard a sound. I woke up when the wolf was about to take Tall Grass. I pulled my knife out and jumped on his back. He rolled out from under me and bit down on my shoulder." She flinched at the memory of the wolf's teeth sinking into her flesh. "I stuck my knife into him and he tore at me with his teeth. I cut him with my knife as he pulled away.

He let go and ran over there. He sat down and stared at me and all I could do was protect the boys."

"He's dead now," Seamus said as he eased the knife from her iron grasp. "You killed him."

"I am sorry, but he should not try to take the babies."

"Let me help you inside so I can fix your shoulder."

She winced as she scooped up one of the babies with her good arm and he took the other. They made their way into the cabin, where he lit one of the candles he had brought back from Fort Dearborn and fixed it to the platform.

"Let's get this off," he said indicating the deer hide top she wore. He helped her get it past the wounds on her shoulder. "That's a nasty tear, my love. There's a piece of loose skin hanging. I don't know if it will grow back together right."

"Do what you think best, Husband."

Seamus proceeded to quickly cut away the torn skin with his own sharp knife. He then cleaned the wound as best he could with the limited supplies and knowledge he had.

"I brought some medicine that Waving Grass had left," Bright Moon managed to say. "She said they used it on her when she was sick the first time," she said through gritted teeth. The wound stung from the cleaning. "It did not help her the last time. But maybe it will help me."

"Where is it then, love?"

She pointed to the parfleche stowed under the platform and he pulled it out from under her feet.

"Let's hope this works."

The concoction had grown thicker as the water evaporated. It was no longer a liquid, but more of a gooey mess in the satchel. He spread a gob of the pasty stuff on her shoulder and her eyes rolled back in pain. She moaned, then sucked in air through gritted teeth.

"Should I take it off?" he asked.

"No, it will be alright," she whispered as she bit down on her lower lip, drawing yet more blood.

"Perhaps now is the time to go back to your people and let them treat this," Seamus said in concern.

"No, Husband. It is not that bad. Just let me rest for a while."

"As you wish, my love."

She slumped over sideways, rolling away from him, and he gently lifted her feet onto the platform and covered her with a blanket. She lay with her back to the room, so he did not know when she dozed off.

III

Seamus tried to gently waken Bright Moon after little Robin showed no signs of going back to sleep. She did not respond, and he began to worry about the effects of the tear in her shoulder. He held Robin and rocked him to comfort him as he thought back through what knowledge of bites he had, until he came across the memory of that fearful word rabies. "God help us," he thought, and prayed to his Maker that it not be that. He wouldn't know how to deal with rabies.

After two more unsuccessful attempts to rouse her, he bared her breast himself and laid Robin down to suckle. He hoped it was the right thing to do. The child needed sustenance and she was not awake to do it herself. He watched as his son went from sucking greedily to occasionally remembering in his sleep what he was supposed to be doing. Then he removed him from his mother's bed so she could sleep peacefully. What was he to do if this state she was in went on for long? She would have to have sustenance herself in order to produce milk for two growing boys.

He dozed off with that thought, and woke later to the sound of Tall Grass stirring for his turn at feeding. He was grateful when he opened his eyes to see Bright Moon picking the baby up to feed him.

"How do you feel, my love?" he asked quietly so as not to startle her.

"My shoulder is sore," she whispered, "but I will be alright."

"You had me worried when I couldn't wake you earlier."

She looked over at him in the dim light and asked, "Why did you try to wake me?"

"Robin was hungry."

She looked over at the sleeping form of their son with worry on her own brow. "What did you do, Husband?"

"I took care of the problem myself."

Her glance shifted to his chest as she asked, "How?"

"Well, certainly not like that," he said when he saw where her gaze fell. "I put him on your breast myself until he was done. Then I put him back where he is now."

She thought about that for a moment and smiled. "Thank you for letting me sleep," she said.

Tall Grass snuffled and let go, so he too was put back to finish his nap.

"I was so afraid for you, my love."

"Why?"

"I was afraid that the wolf might have been rabid, and that you might get it too."

"What is rabid?"

"It's a disease that some animals get, that makes them act odd and slaver and attack people they usually would run from."

"Oh, Husband. It would not have been that bad this soon. Besides, he did not attack me. He wanted the babies." She shook her head and added, "This is not rabid."

"Rabies."

"You said rabid before."

"Rabid is how an animal with rabies acts."

"Oh," she said. After a thoughtful pause, she added, "Sometimes your language is confusing."

"I keep forgetting to explain as I go. Sorry, love."

"It is alright. I will get it someday."

"The point is that I was worried that you would get rabies and I wouldn't know how to take care of you and the boys." He smiled forlornly at her before adding, "Please don't get sick."

His sincerity brought a tear to her eye and she thought again how lucky she was to have become his woman. She knew that he would always treat her well.

"You have not told me about your new trap, Husband," she said to get him off the subject.

"I completely forgot about it when I tripped over the wolf. I will get rid of the wolf and bring in the trap for you to see."

"Don't get rid of the wolf until morning. I want to see it again. I must tell it I am sorry for killing it."

He looked a question at her, but did not ask it. Instead, he said 'okay' and brought the newly designed trap into the cabin and explained how it would work. She looked it over with her practical mind as he explained, and she nodded her agreement. She pulled and tugged and saw how sturdy he had made the device. As she handed it back to him, she said, "It would be better if beaver did not have teeth, but if you leave them alive, will they not chew their way out? They do chew trees down for dams."

He sat down next to his invention, perplexed that he had not thought the project through to that one last little detail.

"Maybe I can use it to trap other animals that don't chew, like rabbits for our meals. Besides, that will cut down on the amount of powder and shot I need to feed us."

"That will be good, Husband. I am sorry about the beaver, but it would have been worse to find out later."

"It's okay. After all, that is what makes us good together."

She rotated her shoulder and winced. "I would like to rest some more while the boys are still asleep."

"You go ahead, my love. I'll listen for the little ones." He kissed her on the cheek and sat down by the dying fire to think about his trap. Maybe he could redesign it to keep the beaver from chewing. Perhaps he could devise some way of preventing the beaver from moving its head around to get a tooth into the wood. He would have to think about that.

Chapter 14

Not all the folks we come to know
Are fit to be a person's friend.
But there are those who come and go
Who have a very evil trend.

B ear Claw had cashed in on the beaver skins. He came away with a substantial amount of money, considering the number of pelts he had stolen from Seamus. He figured the extra was his due. After all, hadn't he taught the little Irishman how to trap, and shouldn't there be some kind of teacher's fee? He would have taken more, but the canoe was hard enough to handle as it was. Still, he had enough money to avoid hard work for a while. Maybe he'd head south to winter in the warmer climates. He could always come north and trap again if he ran out of money.

After collecting his money from Kinzie, he had gone on a bender that had made him unconscious during the time that Seamus was at Fort Dearborn, so the two did not see each other. Now he was sober again and he wasn't enjoying it much. Maybe he'd just go have a couple more beers before he started south.

II

"What do you mean, he was just here," Kyle asked.

"Just as I said," Kinzie replied. "He was here about a week ago and sold me that little bale of beaver pelts over there. He bought some tools, loaded them into his canoe down there on the river, and headed out again. I can't be much clearer than that, young feller. Why are you asking anyway?"

"Seamus is a friend of mine. We sailed over here from Ireland together. We worked the docks in New York and dug canals in Ohio together. I was sick when he sailed on the *Western Lady* so I didn't know he was aboard until he shoved off at the island."

"He and his squaw joined up with—"

"Wait! Did you say, 'he and his squaw'?" Kyle asked in confusion.

"Why, yes I did. Anyway, they joined up with that feller, Bear Claw, and went trappin' together. I thought it was kinda odd when Bear Claw waltzed in here loaded with pelts and then Seamus comes in last week with a few more. But that's none of my business, is it?" He described Bear Claw to Kyle.

"Do you know where he went?"

"Bear Claw's around here somewhere. I hear he got stinkin' drunk . . ."

"No," Kyle waved that answer away, "where did Seamus go?"

"Let's see. He said he was goin' up to the north woods. Let me get my surveyor's map and I'll try to show you. Last time I had this down was to show him and Bear Claw how to get to the west end of Lake Superior," he said as he rummaged around blindly on the top shelf. "Seamus sat right where you are and drew the route and the rivers out on a piece of paper I gave him. Now where has it gotten to? I don't feel it."

"It's alright. I wouldn't be able to find my way there anyway, and I've got to get back to the *Telegraph*. We sail in a couple of hours."

"I heard she was sold again. Who owns her now?"

"I do," Kyle said as he turned to leave.

Kyle was feeling low for missing Seamus by so little time. He worked his way back to one of the few taverns in Chicago. *And where did that name Chicago come from anyway*, he thought, as he sidled up to the bar next to a large man with a lot of hair on his face and head.

"I'll have a pint," he said.

The hairy man's head snapped around at the sound of his brogue. "You another one of them Irishmen?" he asked.

"Aye, that I am," Kyle said, staring at the odd scars on the man's face.

"Worked with an Irishman fer a while trappin' beavers. He was okay ta' work with but kinda funny about sharin' his Indian woman. Finally had ta' leave 'em behind and go my own way."

"What was his name?"

"He called hisself Seamus somethin'. Why you askin'?"

"He is a friend of mine. I've been looking for him."

"Last I seen him was on the western shores of Kitchigami."

"Where is that?"

"If ya' wanna folla' me back to my room, I can show ya' on this here surveyor's map I found."

Found, Kyle silently questioned in his mind. He wondered if this smelly creature was the one who liberated the surveyor's map that Mr. Kinzie was just searching for. Maybe he could do Mr. Kinzie a kindness and re-liberate it for him. "Let me buy some whiskey to take along."

"Yer' my kinda man, young feller."

Bear Claw showed him where he had last seen Seamus, then proceeded to guzzle the whiskey straight from the bottle. It was a good thing Kyle had bought two bottles of the cheap stuff. It might take every bit of it to put this one out. When Bear Claw fell into a stupor, Kyle took possession of the map and left.

III

"That's amazing," said John Kinzie when Kyle explained how he had come by the map. "I didn't really think your friend would take it. He just seemed too honest. After all, he is the one who offered to draw what they needed when I refused to sell it to Bear Claw. I don't much like that fellow, Bear Claw."

"I don't think there is very much there to like," said Kyle. "He is dirty, profane, dishonest, and a host of other things I can't think of right now. And that is from only knowing him for an hour. I can't imagine how Seamus stood him for an extended period of time."

"Your friend strikes me as being a decent young man. I expect I'll see him again in the spring. Can I give him a message for you?"

"Would you do that for me?"

He raised the map and said, "You were good enough to bring back my map. It's the least I can do in return."

"Would you let him know when the Telegraph is due back? I would like to see him again, if he can come."

"Certainly, my young friend. Consider it done."

IV

Dawn found Seamus sitting cross-legged outside the cabin in the north woods, staring at the carcass of the wolf. He was amazed at Bright Moon's courage, and yet worried over the safety of his small family. He knew that she was comfortable in the woods, for hadn't the forests been her whole life's existence? But what about the safety of her and the boys when he was out trapping or on a trip to Fort Dearborn? What if there were another attack and he was not here to find her in time? There were so many dangers in these north woods that he knew about. Wolves normally didn't attack people, but cougars did, and he had seen signs of them all over the area. How many other dangers were there that he was not familiar with?

The sun shone through the trees but it brought no answers. He thought he should make a stronger case for taking them home to her people.

"Why are you sitting alone out here, Husband?" Bright Moon asked as she came out of the cabin.

"I couldn't sleep," he said as he stood and gently embraced her, being careful of her wound.

"You are still worried about my shoulder?"

"I'm worried about you and the boys. What if I had not come back when I did?" he asked. "You would have lain there, injured and bleeding. The smell of fresh blood may have attracted other wild animals. If you were too weak to defend yourself and the boys, what would have happened?"

She sat down with a thump and stared at the wolf. She couldn't deny that he was a big one. She had been lucky with her knife. Seamus squatted down beside her and they looked at each other. She saw a single tear form in Seamus' eye.

"I couldn't bear to lose you, my love," he whispered.

She touched his cheek gently and her soft smile assured him that she really did understand.

"We really need to head south to your village."

She looked over her shoulder at the cabin. "What about this?"

"It's not important. You and the boys are what's important."

"Then, we must go soon." She looked earnestly at him and added, "If I look at this home you made for us too long, I may change my mind."

They began packing things into the canoe and by the time the boys were awake and fed, they were ready to start their journey south.

His relief at her agreeing to go home elated Seamus. In his new joy, he said, "We will take that new passage I told you about, the one with all the small lakes. The people in that area told me it is where the Fox River starts." He unrolled his tracing of the map and showed her where it was. "I understand that this river goes near the winter hunting grounds for your village, which should be about here," he said, pointing at a spot on the sketch.

She looked at him skeptically. "I don't know what all that means, but I will trust you."

"As you said the last time we were going south, 'we will know when we're there.'"

They reached the area with the lakes, and she truly did admire the beauty of it as he said she would. They rested for a day before going further. The remainder of the trip down river was uneventful except for the occasional hang up due to the shallowness of the Fox River. They arrived at the spot Seamus thought to be their final portage and spent the night on the banks of the Fox River for one last time.

V

In the morning Seamus cut saplings and built a travois like he had seen Bright Moon's people use, to move their goods when they changed camps each season. He took the cradleboard with Tall Grass and strapped him onto his back while Bright Moon took Robin's. He lifted the arms of the travois and they began the journey east, leaving only the canoe as proof of their landing.

On the third morning, as Seamus was lifting the arms of the travois, Bright Moon sidled up to him and whispered, "We are not alone. He is not of my people, but we are being watched from behind those trees."

Seamus slowly set the travois down and pulled his musket from the tethers. He loaded it and primed the pan just as he heard the distinctive zing of an arrow in flight. He dodged sideways, raised the musket, took aim at the small movement he saw and squeezed the trigger. A dark figure with a crested headdress fell out of the bush at the tree line. Seamus reloaded and waited. He looked back to let Bright Moon know that he thought the danger was past, only to find that the arrow had missed him and struck her in the chest.

"No!" he bellowed as he rushed to her side. He slipped Robin's cradleboard from her shoulders and helped her sit down.

"The wolf was tamer," she managed to whisper.

"Let me pull . . ." he started to say as he reached for the arrow.

"No, leave it," she said as she stayed his hand. "Let me look at you while there is time." She grimaced as she lifted her hand to touch his face again. "Take care of the boys." She smiled all the way to her eyes. "I loved you." With that, she slipped quietly away.

He held her and rocked back and forth, oblivious to the fact that both boys were crying from the sudden noise of the muzzle blast. "Why," he roared. "Why is the world so cruel?" It seemed that every time he found happiness, someone had to spoil it. He broke off the arrow and flipped it away from himself in a rage. He looked skyward from the depths of his watery eyes and asked, "God in Heaven, why are you doing this to me?" He remained on his knees with Bright Moon in his arms and wept as he had never done before, rocking her back and forth.

Finally, when he was spent, he laid her down and removed Tall Grass' cradleboard form his own back. He slowly rose to his feet. He had to see the killer up close. He memorized the look of the dead brave before going back to Bright Moon.

He chose to take her back to her people rather than bury her here. They would know the proper way to handle her remains. He gently lifted her onto the travois and secured her, followed by the boys, who had surprisingly gone back to sleep. He picked up the arms of the travois and trudged on in a state of numbness. As it was growing dark, he looked around to the west in time to once again see the sky afire. Even at a time like this, he was amazed at the blending of the colors of the leaves and the sunset. "Bright Moon would have loved to see this sight," he thought. "Oh, Bright Moon, I miss you already."

Chapter 15

I tried! O God above I tried
To keep her safe for thee and me.
'Twas not the wilderness that took her
But human beings such as we.

By a stroke of luck, Seamus found the hunting camp on his first try. He saw it across the DuPage River as the sun was setting, on the second day after Bright Moon was slain. Sinago was the first to spot him, and sent people across to help him carry the travois over the shallow waters of the river and into the camp.

"Where is Bright Moon?" Sinago asked.

Seamus wordlessly pointed at the travois and sank to his knees, hanging his head in shame. As the villagers began to gather around them, Sinago put his hand on Seamus' shoulder and asked what happened. He squatted down in front of his son-in-law so Seamus wouldn't have to look up. He told the story, beginning with the wolf and his concern for his family.

As he was telling the tale, Bright Moon's sisters picked up the crying boys and took them away for much needed feeding. The other women took Bright Moon's body from the travois and into one of the lodges.

"I was trying to make them safe," he said as he looked at Sinago with teary eyes.

"I know you were," he said quietly. After a pause he laid a hand on Seamus' shoulder and added just as quietly, "You made her happy, you know."

One of the men came over from the travois at that moment with the broken arrow. It had landed on the travois when Seamus pitched it away after breaking it off.

"One of Black Sparrow Hawk's people. Some of them are still angry about the treaty," Sinago said through pinched lips. "What of the brave who did this?" he asked Seamus.

"I shot him dead. He was alone. I think he was trying to kill me because I was white. I dodged and fired back. I waited but there were no more." Then it struck him, if he hadn't dodged, Bright Moon might still be alive. He had unwittingly sacrificed his beloved. How could he handle more guilt? Sinago watched his face as he worked through the implications of what he had said.

"You could not know what would happen. You were looking at the warrior and trying to protect your family," he motioned toward the lodges where Bright Moon's body and the boys had been taken.

"Fine job I made of that," Seamus said in disgust.

"Come," Sinago demanded as he rose and walked away.

Seamus rose and followed his father-in-law to his lodge, not knowing what to expect, but trusting him anyway.

The shaman sat near the fire pit when they entered. He looked up with sadness in his eyes as they approached. Sinago motioned for Seamus to sit. They were quiet for a while before the shaman began speaking. Seamus understood a little but asked Sinago to translate for him.

"He said that he foresaw her death. It is why he said she would never smile upon us again. But he also knew that she would send two boy-children back in her place. We will mourn her loss. But we will be thankful for what she has given us, for those boys will cause many things to happen when they are men."

Seamus looked sideways at the shaman with a curious expression and Sinago added, "Do not doubt what he sees. He has never been wrong."

"How can a person know what the future will hold?"

"He speaks to the Fathers and they tell him," Sinago said matter-of-factly.

"Bright Moon said he was always right."

"She was very wise for someone so young."

Seamus wept silently over his loss. Sinago and the shaman sat quietly, observing the depth of his sorrow. Finally, the shaman leaned over to Sinago and whispered to him at length before he rose and went out into the sunlight. Sinago remained by Seamus' side, quietly waiting for him to come to terms with his loss.

Seamus looked at him and said, "I don't know how I'll go on without her."

"You will do as you did before you met her."

"But what of the boys? How will I feed them?"

"They will stay with us for now. You may stay also, if you want to."

"Maybe for a few days, until I figure out what to do. Oh God above, I miss her."

Sinago reached over and laid a kindly hand on Seamus shoulder. When Seamus looked into his eyes, he said, "I missed her mother when she left. I know your heart. Remember that Bright Moon will always be with you," he said as he gently tapped Seamus' chest. "She also knows your heart."

"May I sleep here for a while?"

"My home is your home. Rest." He went out into the watery afternoon light and left Seamus to toss and turn as he relived the death of Bright Moon over and over again, trying to find a way in his mind that he could have saved her. He was sure he should have done something differently to protect her from that arrow.

II

Seamus came into the lodge with two freshly killed rabbits and laid them on the stones by the fire pit. As he dusted the snow from his shoulders and hair, he noticed someone new sitting by the fire.

"This is Aptikisic. He is known to the white people as Half Day." They nodded to each other as Sinago added, "He is a friend to Joseph Naper. He is the one who warned them to go to Fort Dearborn back when Black Hawk started raiding." He spoke to Half Day in their own tongue for a few moments with occasional glances at Seamus. He knew they were discussing the loss of Bright Moon. He turned back to Seamus and, nodding at the rabbits, said, "You're getting better with the bow."

"Your people are good teachers," he replied. "I have learned so much." He paused, hoping that this was the right time. "I've been thinking that it is time for me to move on, though."

"I felt that you would go soon," Sinago said.

"Now that you won't be moving camp anymore, I'll feel better about leaving Tall Grass and Robin for a while. It is a shame about the boundary line for the canal, but the white man just doesn't seem to trust anyone, not even themselves."

"The boundary line has been there for many years. Only now, with so many new settlements coming, has the white man started to worry about it. The people in Plainfield are not worried about us. The people in Lockport only want us out of their way so they can dig their ditch. Will you go work on the canal?"

"No! Definitely not that. I had my share of the canal life in Ohio. I Think I will go up to Naper Settlement and see if anyone needs farm help. That is what I grew up doing."

"You will always be welcome here. The boys will be looked after well."

"Thank you. Maybe when they are bigger, they can go with me and learn about the white man's world, not that it's better, but they should see what both are like."

"Remember that they will not look like the white man and may not be accepted."

"Robin's hair has strong red coloring. Maybe that will confuse them and they won't notice. We'll cross that bridge when we come to it."

"How soon will you leave?"

"Not before the snows melt. Even the white man knows that you can't plant seeds in the frozen ground."

"When the time comes, you will cross over the river and follow it to the north. The settlement is on the river bank so you will not have trouble finding it."

"I will keep that in mind. Thank you." He sat down next to the boys and gently played with their hands as they cooed at him.

Sinago said thoughtfully, "I don't understand how Bear Claw could walk away from his son."

"Neither could Bright Moon, nor I. The man isn't human."

III

Seamus found the going much harder than the crossing from the Fox River to his father-in-law's village had been. As he went north the prairie grasses became thicker and taller than he remembered them. He was constantly wading through boggy areas that abutted the river, but were prevented from draining into it because of natural berms along the banks. The berms were caused by the spring foods depositing silt as the water rose over the banks. The river moved slowly enough that the silt was not washed very far, therefore making the bank higher each year, trapping the flood waters on the other side until they evaporated or sank into the soil as summer approached. His toe would often get tangled in the horizontal, dead grasses that were washed flat during the spring floods, now hidden by the new growth that was already two feet high. By fall, it would be twice as tall.

He thought back to the name he and Bright Moon had given their adopted son and realized how appropriate Tall Grass would be for him. He had grown so much faster through the winter than Robin. His mind wandered over the past few months as he stumbled along.

Both boys were walking and even beginning to run. They would respond to their names and were able to form a few words in Bright Moon's tongue. He would always think in terms of Bright Moon, he thought. Of course, it was Sinago's tongue also, but he thought of her first in all things. He appreciated how fortunate he had been that Bright Moon's people were so willing to take on the responsibility for the boys while he re-established himself.

He was trudging through the early morning dew when he stopped dead in his tracks. He had noticed movement across the river out the corner of his eye. He slowly turned his head and saw a herd of ten white tail deer, some standing in the water drinking, and some on the opposite bank watching him. The big buck was on his side of the river, twenty feet away and staring at him. It chuffed and lowered his head menacingly. Seamus backed slowly away. It was a small rack of antlers the buck carried, but lethal all the same. He stopped after a few paces, thinking the buck would feel less threatened. He couldn't help watching such a beautiful sight as this small herd of deer. He backed a few more paces and they resumed foraging and drinking from the stream, all but the buck who kept a cautious eye on Seamus. After a while, the herd began to wander away into the small forest on the other side of the river. The buck, looking back over his shoulder, was the last to leave.

What a treat, Seamus thought as he resumed his trek north and east along the river's bank. He had seen deer before, such as the doe and her fawn that he couldn't shoot. But to see a herd that size and be allowed the privilege of watching them was not something he ever expected. He would love to share the experience with Bright Moon. But, of course, she already knew about it, didn't she? Maybe she sent them. Was that possible? "Get a hold of yourself, Seamus. Stop fantasizing and get on with your travels," he said to himself.

Once again, he saw movement up ahead between the trees along the river. He stopped and watched long enough to determine that it was human and wearing a hat, and therefore must be a white man. He called out and the head turned in his direction and stared as he approached. At the same time, he noticed that the river split, as though going around an island.

"Would this be the Naper Settlement?" he asked as he got closer.

"'Fraid not, friend. This is Fountaindale. Some folks call it the Scott Settlement. What can I do for you?"

"I'm looking for work. I can plow and plant or do whatever else needs doing."

"I'm Willard Scott," the young man said as he offered his hand. "My Pa and I own this property. He's Stephan Scott. I'll take you to him but I don't think he's looking for help right now."

"Thanks," he said as they released each other's hands. "I'm Seamus O'Flarity. I'd appreciate any work I can get."

They got to the ford and as Willard took off his boots, Seamus asked, "Do you live on the island?"

"It's not an island. This is where the forks of the east and west branches of the DuPage River come together."

Seamus began removing his own footwear and asked, "Where does that name come from, anyway?"

As Willard picked up his boots and turned toward the river, he said, "Story has it that there was a French trapper back in the 1700's that had a trading post right about there," he said, pointing to a spot across the confluence of the rivers. "His named was Du Pazhe, but like everything else, it changed over the years. Least ways that's the story as I got it from Half Day."

"I know Half Day. I met him this winter when I stayed with my father-in-law, Sinago."

"Half Day is a good friend," Willard said as he waded ahead of Seamus. "He saved our hides back in the early days when Black Hawk was making war."

"I was with Sinago when all that started," Seamus replied from behind as he stepped up onto the bank. "I remember him saying they would help the white man if it came to war."

By this time, they had crossed the river, put their boots on and were walking up the path between the two branches. Seamus marveled at how lovely the area was and how lush the vegetation grew. "This must be very good farm land."

"It is that. We grow corn, wheat, buckwheat, barley, and oats mostly. Ma has her garden for vegetables and herbs. Most anything will grow here."

"What about potatoes?"

"Never heard of anyone trying those. Why do you ask?"

"That's what my da' and I farmed in Ireland."

"I thought I detected an Irish accent. Here we are," he said pointing at the house on the rise that overlooked the west branch. The one-story log house was set high enough to avoid the spring floods. "Ma," he said to the figure bent over and planting seeds in the newly loosened soil on the south side of the house, "this is Seamus O'Flarity. He's looking for work. Is Pa around?"

"He had to go up to the blacksmith's." She straightened up, pressed her hands against the small of her back and sized Seamus up. "I'm sorry, but I don't think there's much for you here, young man. Stephen's somewhat funny about being self-sufficient. But you might check with Bailey Hobson.

He usually knows who needs help. Son, show him where the road is up to Bailey's."

They walked down the hill to another well-used ford and again removed their footwear. After the fording, they went a short distance and the private lane joined a well-traveled road that ran north and south.

"You won't have to ford any more rivers from here on. Hobson's is about three miles north from here. Give Bailey my regards."

"Thank you. I will," he said as he turned north along the wagon track. He realized that this area must be better settled than he thought to have so well used a roadway.

IV

"Sorry Son, I don't plow fields and I don't need anyone else to plow fields," said Bailey Hobson. "I run a grist mill. People bring in their grain and use their own teams to turn the millstone. I do hear things from time to time, though." He thought for a moment then said, "I'll tell you what. I am going to put up a tavern for the folks to stay in while they wait their turn for milling their grain. You ever built anything?"

"Yes sir, I have. I grew up on a farm in Ireland. My father taught me the use of tools." He had never built anything major but he did have a working knowledge of tools. The important thing was that it was work and he wasn't going to turn it down. He was raised on common sense and knew he could figure out how to do what was required.

"Come with me," Bailey said. "Harry, I'm going up to the Naper's saw mill with this young fellow." Harry Boardman waved acknowledgment as they left.

"Toss your stuff in the back," he said as he climbed onto the seat of the wagon. "What did you say your name was?" he asked as they started the two-mile ride north.

"Seamus O'Flarity."

"I can tell you're Irish, but where did you come from just now?" he asked, as he whipped the horses into motion.

"I spent the winter with Sinago's people at the Potawatomi village down the river."

"Did you, now? They're good people. It was Chief Half Day who warned us when Black Hawk started on his rampage. It gave us time to get the women and children to Fort Dearborn where they'd be safe." He shook his head and snorted in disgust before adding, "Then the army sent troops out to Fort Dearborn and made the women and children move out so they could be safe themselves. It made us all mad but it made Captain Naper furious. We went down to Ottawa and petitioned the government to let us have our own fort. Finally, General Atkinson sent Captain Payne and fifty men to help us out. We call it Fort Payne. That's it over there," he said, pointing to the right as they forded the river and turned left to follow the riverbank.

Seamus saw a stockade-type fence with raised blockhouses on two opposing corners. It was all built from peeled logs and the blockhouses had openings to shoot from without being exposed to fire coming the other way. It was almost as impressive as Fort Dearborn.

"It's almost as impressive as Fort Dearborn," he said.

"You've been there then?"

"Aye. My wife and I saw it when we were at Kinzie's."

Bailey looked around. "Where is your wife?"

Looking like a cloudy day, Seamus answered, "She died."

"Oh. I'm sorry. How?"

"One of Black Hawk's braves shot her."

"That was cowardly, shooting a White woman."

"He was shooting at me. She was Potawatomi."

"Oh. Still, that was a rotten way to lose your wife. I'm sorry for you."

"Thanks."

"Joseph," Bailey said as he braked the wagon and hopped to the ground. He extended his hand to the gray-haired man coming out the door. "This is Seamus O'Flarity. He's going to work for me building the tavern. Have you got much of the lumber cut yet?"

"Right over there," he said, pointing at stacks of lumber separated by boards and drying in the sun next to the mill. "That's about half of it. It's still drying, though. The rest will be cut in about a week."

"Of course, I didn't intend to start quite this soon, but this young fellow came along looking for work and I couldn't turn him away. Besides, he just lost his wife to Black Hawk and he needs work to keep his mind busy."

"Sorry to hear that, son." He turned back to Bailey. "Why don't you let him stay here and help me get your lumber ripped for you?"

"Now, there's a good idea. Then he can haul it back to my place when the time comes. You let me know when it's ready and he can come get the wagon." With that he took his leave after handing Seamus his bag from the back of the wagon.

"Are you ready to do some work, young man?" asked the tall, broad shouldered man.

"Aye."

"Where are you from?" he asked as they walked toward the door.

"Originally, from Ireland. But I've worked the docks in New York and dug some canals in Ohio. Most recently, I was trapping up north."

"I thought I detected a bit o' the brogue when you said 'aye'. My brother and I are from Ashtabula County in Ohio." It suddenly got too noisy to carry on a conversation. Captain Naper turned to Seamus and, putting his mouth close to Seamus' ear, said, "Watch and learn from my brother, John, over there."

Seamus nodded, put his bag down by the door and went closer to see what John was doing. He slowly turned a crank that moved a table holding a log across a large, spinning blade. Seamus followed the path of the blade shaft with his eyes to a pulley with a belt that went up to another pulley on a shaft that went through the wall. Suddenly, the high-pitched sound stopped and a plank fell from the side of the log onto the table.

"Mind the blade," the Captain said, "but help John stack the plank."

"Aye."

"John, this is Seamus. He'll be helping with Bailey's lumber order. Then he's going to build the tavern."

"Pleased to meet you, Seamus," he said, offering his hand.

Before moving the plank to the stack, John pulled a lever, releasing tension on the belt and the blade began to slow down. "There's less wear on the belt if it doesn't run all the time," he explained in answer to Seamus' quizzical look before adding, "We used to stop the horse that powered the whole rig before we changed to the wheel in the river."

As the day wore on, they worked at each end of the planks, shifting them to an existing stack as they came off the blade. Afterward, John showed him how to reset the blade to get the maximum use out of each plank.

"These are called spacers. They go between the blades," he said as he added another saw blade to the shaft. "They're four inches wide. When the two-inch-thick plank comes out the other end, it will be turned into several two by four boards."

"I made boards for doors and shutters with a rip saw when I was in the north woods, but it was a lot harder work since I had to cut each one by hand."

"So you're not a stranger to hard work, then," John stated. He nodded at the crank he had been operating all day and said "Crank that handle and move the table back to the other end."

Seamus cranked. He was glad for the work. It gave his mind something to dwell on besides his losses. John showed him how to place like-sized planks on the table against the tail stock and tight to the fence. He let Seamus crank the table forward and later marveled that he went at the right pace the first time, never binding the saw. The pile of planks shrank away as the pile of boards grew. People had come, chatted with John, and left all day long as Seamus worked at the milling.

"You're a natural," John said. "Now we'll stack them out in the sun to dry."

He taught Seamus how to place the boards with spacers between layers so that the wind could blow between the tiers, removing the moisture and keeping the boards from warping.

"There will be a new load of timber here tomorrow. We'll unload that first, then go back to cutting. Where are you staying?"

"I haven't had time to find a place."

"No matter. You can stay at the Preemption House and pay up later. I'll vouch for you for now. Anyone who can work as hard as you did today is worth his weight in gold."

"Thank you, sir. You have been very kind."

"Ain't just kindness. It's also good business. We need more people like you around here. I'll go over with you and introduce you."

They went out into the late afternoon sun and started up the wagon ruts they called a road. John pointed to their left and said, "That's my brother Joseph's cabin at the top of the hill. He was the second one to settle here. Bailey was the first to start a business with his grist mill, but everyone calls it Naper Settlement because Joseph seems to be the one always taking the lead when something needs to be done." He looked at Seamus as they walked and asked, "Did you know that he captained our ship on the lakes? We built her ourselves. She was called the *Telegraph*. After we brought our families, along with thirteen others over from Ohio, we sold her."

"I saw her at anchor off Fort Dearborn. She's a beauty."

They reached the ford that Bailey Hobson had brought him over earlier. A portion of the settlement was south, across the river, but they turned left, away from the river and proceeded up the hill a short ways. There stood the two-story Preemption House. This would be home for a while. It was only a few minutes' walk each day to the mill.

"Can a man get a meal here, too?"

"Sure can," John said as they entered the building by its single front door. "This is John Stevens," he said. "He's the proprietor of this fine establishment. John, this is Seamus O'Flarity. He will be working at the mill for a while. I'll vouch for him while he's getting started. Would you see to his room and board for us in the meantime?"

"Sure John. Your word is good enough for me. I will ask you to sign the book though, Seamus."

"Aye, I'll be glad to, thank you."

"I'll be seeing you bright and early tomorrow, then, Seamus," said John Naper. They shook hands and he added, "Welcome to you, lad. We're glad to have you."

After he was gone, John Stevens said, "You must have done something very right to gain that much respect from one of the Napers so quickly."

"All I did was cut logs into boards all afternoon. That's nothing special."

"You have to understand, young fellow, that Joseph and John are the oldest settlers here after Bailey Hobson. They came from Ohio where everyone was a farmer or a seaman and worked hard all day. Many young people today don't want to work hard. The Napers have had a few like that at their mill, and you must have been like a refreshing breeze to them."

"I worked hard on my father's farm in Ireland. I worked hard on the ship to get to New York. I did the same on the docks and in the canals of Ohio. It's second nature."

"You just keep doing that and you'll be alright. Come, I'll show you to your room. When you're ready, come back down and have your supper."

The few people in the room looked at him quizzically as he passed by, but no one spoke to him.

Seamus spent the next half-hour stripped to the waist and washing the sweat and sawdust off in the basin. Finally feeling refreshed, he looked out the window to see if the coast was clear before dumping the basin into the bushes beneath the window. The promise of a meal was calling to him, so he made his way down the stairs and into the dining room where several other boarders and locals were already seated and tucking into their meals. The air was rich with the aroma of roast beef and his mouth began to water.

"Come in and sit," said a woman's voice near his shoulder. "I will bring you a plate."

He sat and she returned with a heaping plate of roast beef, boiled potatoes, and an ear of boiled corn. He gaped at the amount of food set before him and wondered if he would be able to eat it all. He decided the best thing to do was to try. Thank goodness he had built up an appetite.

His fellow diners, most of whom were locals, glanced at him from time to time, some wondering who he was. He saw the curious glances as he ate. Finally, when he had eaten enough to fill the void, he stood, turned in a circle and announced without pride or rancor, "I am Seamus O'Flarity. I have come here to work and earn a living. I am helping cut lumber at the Naper's mill so that I can build a tavern by the Hobson's mill. I will learn all your names as time goes by. But for now, I thank you for your welcome."

There was a stunned silence as he sat down and resumed his meal, and then someone applauded, followed by the rest. Seamus raised his head after taking a bite and looked around in surprise. They were all smiling at him. Finally, the man at the adjacent table took pity on him and said, "Most people, when they're being stared at and gossiped about, would just put their heads down and keep eating in hopes that everyone would leave them alone. But you had the audacity to speak up."

"Did I do wrong?"

"Not at all. We are the ones who got it wrong by staring and gossiping. You're going to fit right in here, young Seamus. Welcome to Naper Settlement."

"Thank you, sir. And who are you?"

"I'm Harry Boardman, Bailey Hobson's partner. We almost met at the gristmill when Bailey took you off to the saw-mill."

"So I'll be working for you, also?"

"That is correct. Now if you will excuse me, I must get home. I only stopped for a cup of coffee after my errand. My wife will have supper ready and I have my own farm between the rivers to see to."

Seamus watched him leave, thinking as he resumed his meal how hard these people worked to carve out a life here. He realized how much of an appetite he had worked up today and was determined to do justice to this fine roast beef dinner. Voice levels resumed at a normal volume and he was glad to be in the company of people holding every-day conversations. He thought a stroll through the town after his meal would be a good idea.

People began to leave their tables and go out the door. Many of them slowed or stopped at his table and welcomed him to the village He smiled and thanked them and continued to eat in hopes of finishing while it was still warm.

John Stevens was in the main hall when he came out of the dining room. Seamus walked up to him and said, "There sure are a lot of friendly people in this town."

"They are that. But considering how hard the first years here were, they are especially nice to people who are not afraid to work. Your name made it around town before you left the mill. Most of them knew who you were, and they are all marveling at your work ethic. My advice is to enjoy the notoriety while you can. Once the novelty wears off, you'll be just another hard-working man like the rest of us."

"Thanks. And thanks for the meal. It was very tasty." He started to turn away then turned back to ask, "Do you lock the place up at any particular time? I'd like to take a stroll around the town."

"Enjoy your stroll. We don't lock the doors here. And, by the way, we start serving breakfast at five o'clock in the morning."

"Thanks again."

Chapter 16

What wonderful smells
These woods exude,
Each one is distinct
Like an attitude.

T his isn't oak," Seamus said after they unloaded the last log from the wagon.

"No, it's black walnut," John Naper said. "We're finished with the framing lumber. Now we'll start making the siding." Seamus must have had a question on his face, because John went on to explain, "Black walnut has a tighter grain than the oak so it will shed rainwater better. We use different wood and different dimensions for different purposes."

They set the blade for thinner cuts than the day before and began ripping a new log. Seamus wrinkled his nose and sniffed the air. He found it interesting that each type of wood had a distinctive odor. He liked this one. He'd have to make a point of learning about all the different kinds of wood that grew around here. Most of what he had cut in the north woods had been spruce.

"When we get through with the siding, we'll start making the plank for doors. Those will be out of pine. Have you ever done any mortise and tenon work?"

"I know what it means, but I've not done it."

"The framing lumber needs to dry a while longer, so I'll teach you how to do some of the fancy stuff that Bailey wants. It's like the trim he told me his folks had back in Orange County in Indiana. I'm familiar with it because we had the same thing in Ohio. It's called millwork."

"I meant to ask, has Bailey ordered the nails?"

"He's had Israel Blodgett making nails night and day for two weeks now. Israel is the blacksmith. You do know he has to hammer each one out separately, don't you?"

"I saw a blacksmith in New York doing that a few years ago. It's a wonder that no one has found a faster way to make them. I have an idea of a way to do it faster. Do you mind if I take some time and talk to Mr. Blodgett? Maybe he would be willing to give it a try."

"Stop by the smithy tomorrow on your way here. He always starts before sunup any way."

"I'll do that."

II

"It sounds like a good idea, but I'm not a potter, young fellow," said the brawny man named Israel Blodgett. "'Course, I gotta make the fire hotter than it is now to melt the iron enough to flow. But I think I can do that with the right kind of fuel."

Seamus scratched his head and asked, "Is there a potter in the settlement?"

"'Fraid not. I'll tell you what; you come up with something and we'll try it out. If it works, maybe I'll buy it from you. How does that sound?"

"I'll see what I can do, but in truth, I'm not a potter either," Seamus said in dismay. "You have to admit that it would be a time-saver, though."

"I'll give you that. See what you can come up with."

Seamus took himself back to the mill, deep in thought as to how he would make a mold out of clay to pour hot iron into to make nails without having to hammer each one. To begin with, where would he find the right kind of clay? For that matter, what was the right kind of clay? He knew the mold would have to be broken to get the nails out after they cooled, but could you reuse the clay? He would just have to ask John for enough free time to experiment.

John said, "There was a lot of blue clay down about ten feet when we were digging the well up on the hill. It got pretty hard after it dried out. I wonder if that will work."

"Where is this blue clay?"

"You know what, we're far enough ahead that this can wait. C'mon, I'll show you."

They walked up the hill, past the Captain's house a ways, to the newly dug well, where there was still a pile of raw earth. John kicked aside some of the top layer with the toe of his boot, uncovering the moist layers below. As he had hoped, there was some of the moist blue clay he had mentioned. Seamus reached down and pried a large chunk of the semi-soft clay loose from the pile with his fingers. He felt the texture and squeezed a fist full to see what happened.

"I'm no expert," he said, "but this might just work. I'll take this for now and see what happens."

He hefted the chunk that was about the size of his head onto his shoulder and they strode back down the hill. "I'll take this over to the smithy and work on it there, since I need some of the nails he's already made as a pattern."

"Good luck with it. I'll see you when you get done."

Seamus plopped the clay down on a clean spot on the floor of the smithy. "I think this may work," he said as Israel came over to see what he had brought. "I think I have to moisten the clay more, though. It seems pretty dry."

Israel handed him a large pail. Seamus broke a good portion away from the rest, put it in the pail, and covered it with water.

"I need to build a frame. I'm going back to the mill for some lumber. May I use some of your tools when I get back?"

"Use what you need."

After explaining his newest thought to John, he gathered up some of the scraps of lumber that were lying around and raced back to the smithy. He built a four-sided frame that would sit flat on a broad board. He laid out a row of the nails that Israel had already made on the board within the frame. Next, he kneaded the wet clay until he thought he could force it into the frame without disturbing the nails, working it until he thought the nails were completely engulfed. He then forced a piece of thin flat metal that was lying on the bench down through the clay but cross-wise of the nails at the center point.

"Now we wait," he said, looking at Israel for the first time since he had started.

"I understood all but that last little bit. Why did you push that piece of metal into the clay cross-wise?"

"Since the nails are tapered, maybe we won't have to break the mold if it's already split. At least that's what I'm hoping. I've got to get back to the mill, but I'll be back tomorrow to see if it's dry enough to work with."

Later that afternoon, he said to John, "Why is it that time seems to move so slowly when you're waiting for something to happen?"

"What are you awaiting?"

"I'm waiting for the clay to dry so I can try out the mold for the nails. It should be ready tomorrow, but I won't know until I test it."

"Does Israel think this will work?"

"He seemed to. He said he would buy my mold if it did. Why would he want to buy it when I would gladly give it to him?"

"That's how things work here. People buy ideas as well as goods." John smiled at Seamus' impatience and added, "You know, it's getting on toward dark, anyway. Why don't you go back over to the smithy and check on that mold? Whether it's ready or not, at least you can relax a little."

"Thank you, I believe I will."

Israel looked up from the forge when Seamus walked in. "There you are. I had an idea from something that I saw back home. I watched as they were firing bricks to make them harder. I slid the cast you made onto a piece of flat metal stock I had, took the frame off and slipped the whole thing in over the forge for a while. It should be just about cool enough to handle by now."

"What a good idea. Between us we might just make this work."

They tested it to see if it was cool to the touch. It was still warm, but cool enough to handle, so Seamus flipped it over, exposing the nails that were laid out on the other side just as he had hoped to see them. He held the mold so that the slit he had created with the thin metal was over the corner of the flat stock of the bench and pressed down until the thin layer of clay between the nails cracked apart. With a little more pressure, the points of the nails were freed from one half of the mold. He set the two halves face up and removed the nails. The hard part was getting the widened heads free without damaging the mold. He then put the two halves back together, exposing the nail shaped slots.

"If I had known it was going to be this quick, I'd have smelted some iron. It'll take a little while," Israel said with excitement.

"That's alright. I'm a might peckish anyway. I think I'll go over to the Preemption House and see if I can get a bite of supper. Have you eaten yet?"

"Let me get this started and I'll join you."

As they ate, Israel said, "Yes, I can make some smaller nails for the trim boards. Are you thinking about making another mold for those?"

"Yes, I am." Seamus chewed silently for a moment before adding, "We might have a good thing going with this. Maybe we should think about all the goods you have to hammer out on a regular basis and make molds for all of them, if it's practical, of course."

"I'll give it some thought. Let's make sure that this is going to work first."

As they walked into the smithy a young voice said, "I kept the bellows going just like you showed me, Mr. Blodgett."

"Thanks Charley. Here's two bits for your troubles. Run along home, now."

"You folks have some funny ideas about money," Seamus said, after the nine-year-old boy had left.

"What do you mean?"

"I saw what you gave the boy. It looked like a quarter of a dollar. Yet, you called it two bits."

"That's correct. Have you never been over at Paw Paw when the mail arrived?"

"I'm afraid not. What's a Paw Paw?"

"That's what we call our post office, after the paw paw trees growing around it. Paw paw fruit makes mighty fine pies, by the way. Anyway, you asked about the two bits. Let me explain. You pay for your mail when you get it. You give the postmaster a dollar, and he takes his chisel and cuts it in half. Then he cuts that into halves making quarters. If the mail cost less, he'll split that into two bits. It can be split one more time into picayunes."

"Like I said, you folks have some funny ideas and some even funnier names."

By this time, they had reassembled the mold and were pouring the molten metal into the slots. Smoke and steam rose off the clay from whatever organic materials and moisture were previously protected by the cold nails from the direct heat of the forge. After the metal had cooled, they again split the mold apart and removed the new nails.

Seamus picked one up, examined it closely, and then drove it into a board with the hammer.

"That seems to work pretty well. I can build the tavern with these. There is a little burr where the crack is, though."

"A touch on the grind stone and that'll be gone. I could even have Charley in to do that, since it's an easy task. That's a lot easier than pounding out each nail by hand. Maybe you might want to make a few more molds so I can pour in larger batches."

"I can do that."

They worked by lantern light well into the night. As Seamus made frames and put clay over nails, Israel began making smaller nails to use to create more molds. They chatted during the quieter moments and got to know each other as friends.

The next morning Seamus stumbled into the sawmill and John did a double take.

"You look like you were on an all-night binge," he said somewhat alarmed.

"Israel and I have been working all night on the nails. It works, John. It really works."

"That's good news. But are you going to be able to work today? I don't want either of us to get hurt because you're not alert around the saw." He took an even closer look at Seamus' haggard face and added, "Maybe you should get some rest today and I'll see you tomorrow."

"That is a good idea. I am pretty tired."

As time passed, the lumber was finished, the nails were poured, the tavern was built, and life continued.

Captain Naper went to the Illinois congress where he served with such men as Robert McMillan, with whom he butted heads over the Whole

License Law, and a young upstart called Abraham Lincoln, with whom he agreed that the law should be reduced. The Whole License Law dealt with taxing liquor.

"After all," Mr. Lincoln had argued, "the legislature has no right to interfere with a man's appetites; public opinion should regulate these matters."

Having finished with the construction of the tavern, Seamus was suddenly out of work. He had moved into a finished room as he was completing the work on the tavern. He rode home with Harry Boardman in the opposite direction from what had already become known as Naperville because of its spurt of growth.

"With your talents, I have no doubt that you can find work in Naperville. But if you want to get back to farming, you might want to talk to John Barber," Harry said as they tucked into one of Mrs. Boardman's famous fried chicken dinners. "It's just a mile or two on down the road to Barber's Corner. You stay the night with us and I'll run you over in the morning."

"That's very kind of you, John. Thank you."

III

"I sure can use the help," John Barber said as Seamus took his bag from the back of Harry's wagon. They stood at the crest of a hill with ripening fields of crops dropping away in three directions. "It's harvest time and we're stretched to the limit now."

Seamus waved as Harry turned back toward the ford over the east branch of the DuPage River. He was finally beginning to understand how this east and west branch thing worked now that he had seen more of it. The many twists and turns had confused him for a while. He still could not get over how beautiful and lush this area was.

"It seems like almost anything will grow here," he said to his new employer.

"That it does," John Barber said.

"But I understand that you have trouble with potatoes."

"I think it's the soil."

"My Da' and I grew potatoes in Ireland. Maybe I can help next year."

"We'll see to that next year. Right now, we need to get this year's crops in before the hard frost comes."

Seamus was glad that he had learned how to wield a scythe when he was a lad. He worked up a whole new set of calluses on his hands and could feel muscles he had forgotten existed. It all began to ease back to normal after a few days, and he started to enjoy the rhythm of the work again.

"I've never seen anyone work as hard as you do from sunup to sundown," John Barber said to him one evening, as they watched the cheese being made in the Barber dairy. "It's surely been a pleasure working alongside you," he added.

"Thank you for the kind words. I just do what needs doing."

The days were growing shorter and the work of harvesting was drawing to a close. When the last field was cut and John Barber had paid him his wages, Seamus agreed to return in the spring and plant potatoes, as they had discussed. He turned and followed the river as it flowed west and joined the other branch. Soon he would be with Bright Moon's people again, where he would spend the winter with Robin, Tall Grass, and Sinago.

Once again, he marveled at the height of the prairie grass and the color of the wild flowers when he broke out of the forested areas into the sunlight. How could nature be so abundant with no man's hand there to do the planting? *God in Heaven, this is beautiful,* he thought as he plodded along.

When he finally arrived at the village, he found nothing but emptiness. The lodges echoed when he asked where everyone was. The ashes in the fire pits had long ago washed away from numerous rain showers. He felt an icy chill as he went from dwelling to dwelling, calling out names of different tribesmen and receiving no answering voice. He wondered if they too had succumbed to the white man's greed and moved on westward.

He continued his journey west and south along the riverbank until he reached the little settlement of Plainfield. He had to quiz several people before someone could tell him that the people of the Potawatomi village had moved on to make room for the whites. And didn't he think that was fair, after all?

"Do you know where they have gone?"

"No, I'm afraid I don't. I'm just glad they're gone. They made me nervous."

"Why?"

"Well, the only good Injun is a dead one. After all, they are savages, aren't they?"

With chagrin, Seamus recalled Mayfair's identical comment about Irishmen.

"No, they most assuredly are not," Seamus responded vehemently. "They are probably more civilized then most white people I know."

"What are you, an Indian lover?"

"As a matter of fact, I am. My wife was of their tribe, and my son is with them," he said as he turned and stomped away. "Indian lover, indeed," he muttered to himself as he went on toward the Fox River in hopes of finding Half Day's People. Maybe they would know where Sinago was.

He came across the town of Oswego and once again asked about the Potawatomi.

"Yeah, I know who Half Day is. He and his folks are good people. They were finally crowded out though. I was somewhat sorry to see them go. Last I heard, they were headed down the river toward Ottawa."

"Thanks," Seamus said in dismay. Would he never catch up with anyone who knew where Robin and Tall Grass were? As he continued down the river, he spied a canoe drawn up into the undergrowth but poorly concealed. It was covered with a summer's worth of dust but appeared to be intact. He called out to the four winds in Potawatomi and English but got no answer. Finally, assuming that it was abandoned, he flipped it upright, stowed his bag in the bow, found the paddle and pushed off, letting the current carry him south. He seldom had to dip the paddle except to steer around occasional boulders, for like the DuPage, the Fox was not a deep river but it moved swiftly enough.

There were a few small white settlements along the way, but no place he wanted to stop and visit. He knew that he would find Ottawa where the Fox River met the larger Illinois River. As he came around another bend, he spotted it up ahead. He saw brick buildings for the first time since coming west from New York. As he stared ahead, he heard his name called from the embankment to his right. He looked over and saw Sinago standing on the bank, waving to him. He steered the canoe toward shore and came up a little downstream. In anticipation, Sinago had begun walking toward his landing point. He grabbed the prow of the canoe and pulled it from the grasp of the current. Seamus stepped ashore and the two men embraced each other.

"I knew you would find us before we moved on. My old Shaman told it to me."

"Before you moved on?"

"We have decided to see about those reservations the white man has promised us beyond the Great River."

"I've heard that it is quite a ways."

"As long as there is water, good soil, and hunting, what does it matter where we go?"

"I guess it really doesn't matter. How are the boys?"

"They are boys. They are mischievous just as you and I were as boys. They are healthy and growing. Come."

Seamus followed him into the temporary encampment. None of the comforts of home had been unpacked.

"How long have you been here?"

"Two days. We will go on tomorrow now that you are here."

Seamus stopped in his tracks. He had just found them. He wasn't prepared to go with them into unknown country so far away, and he wasn't going to say good bye to the boys again so soon. Sinago looked back and saw that he had stopped.

"What?" He walked back to Seamus.

"I'm not prepared to go where you are going and I don't want the boys to be that far away from me."

"I knew this already. You will rest with us tonight and take the boys to Chicago. It has been foreseen."

"The Shaman," Seamus said with resignation. "Of course you knew."

Sinago just smiled and turned back toward the encampment, leaving Seamus to follow.

Two small boys came tearing around the side of a temporary shelter, the smaller one growling and chasing the taller. The larger boy was looking back at his attacker and did not see Sinago in his path. As he crashed into him, Sinago grabbed him by the waist and hefted him up onto his shoulder, putting his open palm on the top of the other boy's head to stop him.

"Grandfather, you saved Tall Grass from the bear," complained Robin.

Seamus looked a question at Sinago.

"I thought he should know about his father, no matter who he is."

Seamus nodded.

"Who he," asked Robin.

"He is your father, Robin. Do you remember when I told you he would be back?" He then added, "You ask 'who-is-he' not 'who he.'"

Robin nodded and walked over to Seamus, putting both arms around his thighs. Seamus dropped to one knee and took him into his arms. "You are growing so big," he said. He lifted him off the ground, laid a gentle hand on Tall Grass' cheek and followed Sinago to the center of the camp. People began to gather around and greet him as a long lost relative, just as he was.

"You are also getting heavy," he said to his son as he set him on the ground.

"This one is even heavier," Sinago said as he put down his burden. "He eats more. He is not greedy; he is just bigger and needs more."

As they sat down on a fallen log, Seamus looked at his father-in-law a moment then sighed. "I was afraid he would inherit his father's greed for a moment. Thank you for making that clear to me."

"We have been careful to be as generous with one as the other. He is a good boy. You should not have trouble with either of them."

As they talked about the past few months and the changes taking place, Robin leaned on Seamus knee and watched his face as though trying to memorize him. Finally, he shifted to get his father's attention and said, "You talk funny."

They were silent for a brief moment before both men broke into laughter.

"Aye, that he does, laddy," Sinago mimicked in a mock Irish brogue, at which they laughed again.

Robin and Tall Grass stared first at one then the other, at a loss for what was so funny. They were too young to understand how unusual Sinago's vast knowledge of languages was. They thought it was normal to speak several languages, since that is what they learned from Sinago.

"I will go to Kinzie's at Fort Dearborn and see what work I can find there for the

winter. In the spring, I am going to Barber's Corners to help John Barber plant potatoes."

"I know of John Barber. You will do well with him."

"I already have done well with him. I helped him harvest his crops this past two months. He is a good man. He found a burial site on his farm near Lily Cache Creek. He thought it belonged to your people and told his sons to never disturb that piece of ground, as it probably was sacred."

"I know those grounds, and they *are* sacred to my people. I will speak of this with my council so they will feel better about the white men we left our home to. First, I have something for the boys." He reached behind the log he was sitting on and lifted two small, hand-carved paddles from their hiding place. He handed one to each of them. He smiled at Robin and said, "Your father can use some help paddling upstream to Chicago."

Both boys trotted down to the river's edge and began paddling and splashing. *This should be great fun,* thought Seamus, *I hope we don't get too wet before we travel the first mile.*

Sinago laughed and said, "You are going to get very wet, my young friend."

"That's what I was just thinking. This should be interesting."

"It will be good for them to learn how to stay dry—and warm."

"When I was a lad, I tipped a coracle on Lough Ree back home in Ireland. I thought my da' would never stop laughing. But I learned from that how to stay dry. I guess they need this."

"Don't be afraid to splash them back when they gang up on you with the paddles, which they will do."

"Oh, I won't. This may be more fun than I've had in a while. I look forward to the trip."

"I wish I could go with you. But we must go on." He thought for a moment then asked, "What about your saw and axe and other tools?"

"Have your people made good use of them?"

"Yes, they have. Just look at those paddles."

"Then take them with you. I can replace them if I need to cut down trees again."

A pall settled over them at the thought that their paths would separate forever in the morning. Sinago finally broke the spell when he said, "Be careful of the rivers. There are many streams flowing into the Illinois as you go east. The big ones are the Kankakee, the DuPage, and the Des Plaines—or Au Plaines as some call it. You take the Des Plaines to Mud Lake. You have been there before with Bright Moon."

"Yes I have, and it seems like a lifetime ago. I think I can remember the way."

They fell silent until one of Sinago's daughters brought them a meal.

I have to think of this as a new beginning, not an ending, Seamus thought as he ate. Otherwise the boys will start to wonder what is wrong. This must become a new adventure for them. After all, isn't life one long adventure anyway?

"You will do alright," Sinago said, watching the change of expressions on his face.

Chapter 17

Once adventures start to come
They seem to grow quite on their own.
The small canoe becomes the ship
Like a good tale that is self-grown.

The intrepid trio splashed their way up the last stretch of the Chicago River, under a newly built span of bridge, and up to the dock across from Fort Dearborn. Seamus tied the stern of the canoe to the pier and lifted the boys onto the dock.

An old man sat on a piling, whittling and singing a song from back in the war days. They stopped to listen.

"Oh, we camped in the sand
In the wild, wild land
At a place they call Chicago.
We work all day
Still a-wait'n for our pay . . ."

Seamus led the way for the wide-eyed boys up to the door of Kinzie's and inside. They had seen white men's buildings before but never been inside one. James Kinzie looked up from his writing as they entered.

"Now that's what I call perfect timing," he said. "Your friend Kyle has asked about you every time he's landed. This time he can finally see you himself."

"Kyle is here?"

"You just missed him. But he'll be in town a few days while they unload their cargo." James told him where Kyle always stayed.

"Maybe my business can wait," Seamus said. "I was going to draw out the money you've held for me and set up permanently out in Barber's Corners or Naperville. But I think I'll wait until I talk to Kyle."

"You can leave your canoe tied to my pier and cross over on the bridge."

"I saw that. It's new since my last trip here."

"It was masterminded by this new fellow in town from back east. His name's William Ogden. He's got a lot of good ideas going, including a railroad."

"Has he now? This town has grown a lot in a short time."

"Yup, it has. There are a lot of land speculators and investors coming here now." James Kinzie looked down at the boys and asked, "And who are these fine boys that followed you in my door?"

"This little fellow is my son with Bright Moon. His name is Robin," he said, ruffling his red hair.

"I remember her. How is she?"

"She was killed by an arrow meant for me."

"I'm sorry to hear that." After a respectable pause, he went on, "And who is the tall one?"

"This is my adopted son, Tall Grass. They are the same age."

"That's an appropriate name, then."

"His father is Bear Claw. I'm sure you remember him."

"Oh, I do," he said with chagrin. "He stole my survey map."

"I saw it later when we stopped at the Michigan Road Inn. He stole a good part of my share of pelts the next spring."

"I thought so when you came in with so few. And as to the map, I have it back thanks to your friend, Kyle."

"You don't say. By the way, is he still sailing on the *Western Lady*?"

"You have been away for a while. He bought the *Telegraph* a while back. Now he's Captain Kyle."

"He bought Captain Naper's ship? This is too odd."

"How do you mean?"

"I worked for the Napers for a while, cutting lumber in their mill."

"Did you, now. I got to know them pretty well when the whole settlement came here for their safety during the Blackhawk Wars. This is a very small world, indeed."

"I must go find Kyle, but I'll be back."

He led the boys down to the river and across Mister Ogden's new bridge, past the new lighthouse, following the directions James Kinzie had given him. As they turned the last corner, he saw his friend walking toward them.

"There you are, my friend," Kyle said as they approached each other. They embraced as old friends do before pulling apart for that I-can't-believe-it's-you look, and another embrace.

Robin tugged on Seamus' trouser leg, and when he looked down asked, just as Sinago told him to do, "Who-is-he," using the same hand gestures, not knowing that they were instructional.

"He is my closest friend in this part of the world, Robin. His name is Kyle." He smiled at his friend and said, "Kyle, this is my son, Robin, and my adopted son, Tall Grass."

Kyle offered his hand to the two and said, "It's good to meet you both. You can call me Uncle Kyle." He looked back at Seamus and said, "Mister Kinzie told me you were married. I can't wait to meet her."

Seamus had gotten past the point of tearing when he thought of the loss of Bright Moon, but he still had to look away, unable to speak for a moment. This was his best friend and it bothered him more than he thought it would that he couldn't introduce them. Finally in control of his emotions, he said, "I would like nothing better than for my best friend to meet my wife. But it's not possible. She is no longer among the living."

Once again, Kyle gathered his friend into his embrace, patting him on the back. "Tell me," he said as they turned toward a Sauganash Tavern for a meal for the four of them.

The boys were getting restless as the two friends remembered old times and Kyle talked about having the ship of his dreams. They were beginning to nudge each other and push back and forth. Seamus was beginning to lose his ability to concentrate on what Kyle was saying because of the distraction they were creating.

"Like most schooners, she handles beautifully, Seamus. You and the boys should join me for the run over to New York. I'll have you back in time for the spring planting, if that's where your heart is, lad."

"To be honest, with Bright Moon gone, I no longer know where my heart is. I can do almost anything I set my mind to, but it's no fun without her. Although, we did have a pretty good time getting here in the canoe, didn't we boys?"

They nodded their heads and settled down some, now that they were being included in the conversation.

"Let me show you the *Telegraph* before you decide."

"I've seen her. She was at anchor here when Bright Moon and I sailed north on the *Western Lady*."

"Then you know her size and what she can do."

"What do you think, boys? Do you want to sail on a real ship?"

Not knowing what a real ship was or what he was blathering about, they looked at each other and shrugged.

"Let's go. We'll show them the ship and let them look her over from the inside out and stem to stern," Kyle said as he rose. He didn't believe in delaying and allowing the other person to change his mind.

"Have you ever paddled a canoe?"

"No, I haven't."

"Now is your chance. Mine is tied up at Kinzie's. We'll take that out to the *Telegraph*."

"Why not. Seeing a canoe coming at them should make my crew raise their eyebrows"

II

The canoe was secured on deck, the cargo had been unloaded, and the grain going back east was loaded. The boys were still excited as they weighed anchor two days later and set a northerly course up Lake Michigan. It was earlier in the year than the last time Seamus had sailed this route, and the turn near St Martin's Island was much smoother than he recalled.

"This is where we saw each other last. I've paused every time I've come this way since and wondered if we would ever meet again," Kyle said at his friend's elbow.

"I've wondered the same thing so many times. I didn't leave things right between us all that time ago in the canals, and it has bothered me since."

"A lot of water has passed, literally, since then. We are here together, with a new opportunity. That's all that matters."

"Aye, that is true, my friend," Seamus said as he patted Kyle on the back. "And once again we have the wind at our backs and a sail above us. We have gone back to the beginning."

"You're still the poet, aren't you?"

"I try to keep my hand in. I don't want to become rusty. Bright Moon said that she liked the way my verses bounced."

They were silent as Seamus thought again about the wonder he had known as Bright Moon; and Kyle, knowing his friend's moods, respected his reverie.

"The crew knows the way. Do you feel the ship turning?" Kyle asked.

Seamus nodded and looked at the endless expanse of water in every direction.

"There," Kyle said, pointing to a tiny speck on the horizon. "And there."

Seamus squinted and finally saw the two points Kyle indicated.

"The one on the left is the Upper Peninsula of Michigan and on the right is Michigan. The space in the middle is the Straits of Mackinac. That is the most dangerous part of the trip. After we dropped you off, we nearly grounded on the rocks because of the gale-force winds that sprang up."

"I remember fighting the wheel in those winds before we were lowered. I'm glad we're not putting the boys through that now or they would never want to sail again."

Just then there were a series of whoops and screeches from the stern and both boys came racing forward, one after the other with one hand aloft, holding something. As they neared, Seamus saw what looked like miniature ships in their hands. Robin crashed into his thigh and held his up for inspection.

"I win!"

Seamus took the ship and held it up for a closer look. It was roughly carved but not a bad likeness of the very ship they were aboard.

"Where did you get this?"

Robin pointed at the stern where one of the sailors was reefing a sail in preparation for the upcoming turn to the south.

"That would be Jacob," Kyle said. "He has seven children of his own and misses them when we're away from port. I think he's glad to have the boys aboard to dote on this trip."

"He's not a bad carver," Seamus said as he examined the boat more closely.

"By the looks of that," Kyle said, pointing at the ship Seamus held, "he carved it in about ten minutes. He can do much better when he has time. He used to work the whalers out of Nantucket and did a lot of very good scrimshaw from the whale teeth he collected. I've seen some of it and it's beautiful."

They made the turn to the south and kept the coastline in sight as they sailed down Lake Huron. As they neared the port of Sarnia, Kyle got busy with the wheel and Seamus took the boys forward to the bow to watch as they entered the St. Clair River for the passage to Lake Erie. Robin and Tall Grass were silent as they watched in wonder all the traffic going both directions.

They cleared the mouth of the river and Seamus asked, "Is this Lake Erie?"

"Nay, my friend, this is Lake St. Clair. We cross this and sail the Detroit River before we reach Erie."

Kyle adjusted the wheel for the south-southwest course needed for the Detroit River entrance. It was a small lake and they were across it in a short time compared to Michigan and Huron.

"That on the right is the town of Detroit. It's a busy town," Kyle said as they approached the mouth of the river. "On the left is Richmond, Canada. No, that isn't right. They changed the name recently to Windsor in honor of Windsor Castle in England."

"I'm afraid we just can't get away from the British no matter where in the world we go, can we?"

"No. But the ones I've met here don't seem to be as British as the ones in England. Maybe it's the close proximity to the Colonies. Somehow, they seem more tolerant. At least that has been my experience."

"Forgive me for changing the subject, but you have been doing a lot of reading, haven't you?"

"Yes, I have. Why do you ask?"

"Your vocabulary has become much larger, my friend. Proximity and tolerant are not words you would once have used."

"Is it that obvious?"

"Only to those of us who knew you before."

"A very good friend of mine taught me the importance of reading and becoming more knowledgeable. Can you guess who that friend was?"

"I'm glad to have been of service. You have come a long way."

At Amherstberg the river began to widen out, and they could see the broadness of Lake Erie before them.

"That, my friend, is Lake Erie," Kyle said as he steered to port and headed for the middle of the lake.

"It's funny, but it looks like so much more water. These lakes all look the same."

"They certainly don't act the same. They're all at different depths and the wind does different things to them. This one is the shallowest and the warmest and probably the calmest of these Great Lakes. Do you see those islands far over to the right?" He nodded with his head.

"I do."

"Those are the North, Middle and South Bass Islands. There is a place in among them called Put-In-Bay. That is where Oliver Perry defeated the British in September of 1813. It was a decisive battle for the colonies."

"You have been studying history, too, I see."

"Mostly naval history. It's very interesting."

Darkness was settling around them as they chatted and Kyle turned the wheel over to Jacob. They went below for their evening meal and found that the boys had fallen asleep on sacks of the grain stowed below.

"They have worn themselves out again," Seamus said as he threw blankets over them. They ate and talked for a while before they, too, fell asleep.

III

"Buffalo ahead," the lookout shouted.

Seamus and Kyle led the boys forward to watch as the town came fully into view. She seemed to sprawl across the waterfront like a lazy lady being waited upon in the privacy of her boudoir.

"It's such a big town," Seamus said.

"It's grown considerably because of the Erie Canal. Goods are brought here from New York City on barges, loaded onto ships like mine, and hauled to Chicago. Chicago is growing the same way. If they ever finish that canal from Chicago to the Illinois River, those goods will go all the way to Saint Louis, then on to New Orleans by way of the Mississippi River. In the meantime, small towns are growing into big cities, my friend."

"Maybe this is the time to buy land."

"That's what I've been doing. You should spend some of your farmhand money on ground around Chicago before it goes crazy."

"According to James Kinzie, the speculators have already moved in and started buying up huge parcels."

They put into port and after the *Telegraph* was secured and orders given, Kyle turned again to his friend and said, "I have something to show you and the boys. Come with me."

They trailed after him, across the dock and down a side street to a stable. He rented a carriage and team and, once they were aboard, pointed the horses' heads north.

"This is the Niagara River," he said as though he were a tour guide. "In a little while it will be very hard to hear each other, so I thought I would warn you now."

"Warn us," Seamus said in alarm. "You wouldn't put the boys in danger, would you?"

Kyle looked at his friend in disbelief. "I thought you knew me better than that. Why would I ever do such a thing? No, I'm warning you because it will be louder than anything you could ever imagine."

"What will be?"

"You'll see."

The road along the river was well traveled and wide enough for two carriages to pass without mishap. The farther they went the louder became the distant rumble.

"What is that?" Seamus looked at the boys in the rear seat. They were silent with a look of dread on their faces. He had never seen them look that way.

"You are sure this is safe?"

Kyle's smile grew larger but he avoided making eye contact with his friend. He knew that if he looked at Seamus, he would have to tell him where they were going. As the sound became almost deafening, he brought the horses around a forested curve and to a halt at the edge of a precipice.

Seamus and the boys stared in awe at the sight of Niagara Falls. After a small eternity had passed, he turned to his friend and smiled. Words were useless; they would never be heard. He looked back at the boys, who, hanging over the back of the front seat, were mesmerized by the sheer size of the cataracts. Seamus felt the carriage shift and saw Kyle stepping to the ground. He joined him and they lifted the boys down. They walked to the edge for a better look and were even more amazed. Finally, Seamus felt a tap on his shoulder, and they led the boys back to the carriage. Kyle drove them a short way along the edge, back to the road and into the small town.

There was a tavern on the main street that had windows overlooking the falls. They found a table and ordered a meal to go with their view. It was both the quietest and the loudest meal Seamus had spent with Robin and Tall Grass. They were so enthralled, they had to be reminded for the first time to eat.

The trip back to Buffalo was anticlimactic at best. For the first few miles, the boys talked about the falls as if the adults hadn't been there and seen them for themselves, then they quieted and fell asleep with the swaying of the carriage. Seamus and Kyle occasionally discussed one thing or another but nothing of importance. The sun had set long before they reached the stable and they had to carry the sleeping boys back to the *Telegraph*.

"Pretty rainbows," Robin muttered in his sleep as Seamus laid him down for the night.

"Aye lad, they were," Seamus said softly as he brushed the hair back from Robin's forehead. He turned to see Kyle watching him. "He's all I have left of her now."

"Then, my friend, he will have to do, won't he?"

"Oh, he'll do nicely, I think. He has her eyes. That is what captivated me in the first place, you know. And he has her quick wit. I could show her something one time and she would master it on the spot."

Kyle studied him quietly for a moment, then said, "Seamus, my friend, you have been blessed more than most men are in their entire lives."

"I know that. There isn't a day that goes by that I don't say thanks; first for having known Bright Moon, and now for Robin."

"Let's get out of here before we wake them up," Kyle whispered, nodding toward the sleeping forms.

They found a couple of firewood logs that hadn't been split and set them up next to a pair of pilings on the wharf. They sat and leaned back to stare at the star strewn sky.

"I've been thinking about buying another ship," Kyle said.

"This has been lucrative for you, then?"

"I would say so, my friend. I have a house here in Buffalo and I'm having one built in Chicago. I'm also one of those speculators that you spoke of earlier."

"I'm happy for you."

"I want you to captain this ship for me so I can take command of the new one."

Seamus stared at Kyle in stunned silence. Kyle stared at the stars, pretending that he didn't know the effect his words had had on his friend. Finally, Seamus rose and paced back and forth for a moment.

"I will compensate you far better than if you were a farmer," Kyle said. "You will also receive a percentage of the profits from each run you make."

"You are making this very difficult. I have to think about the boys first."

"I would never ask you to do otherwise. Think about how well you can provide for them. We don't sail at all for three months out of the year. The waters are either frozen or too treacherous. You would be home for a few days every few weeks. You could afford a nanny to look after them and teach them in the meantime."

"I'm going to have to think about this. I just reacquired them, you know."

"No, I didn't know."

"I left them with Bright Moon's people while I went to Naper Settlement and Barber's Corner. When the work ended, I tracked them down. Her people were moving on to the reservations out west of the Mississippi."

"This may be better for them, then. They wouldn't be moving around. They could go to school in Chicago. And they could sail with you when they weren't in school."

"It all sounds logical. Let me consider it all before I give you my answer."

"Take your time. I'm not offering the captaincy to anyone else just yet, although I did ask Jacob if he was interested. I haven't even bought another ship yet. When I do, she'll be another schooner. I like the way they handle."

"She has nice lines," Seamus said, nodding toward the *Telegraph*. "I wouldn't mind sailing her," he said more to himself than to Kyle.

He had begun the justification process in his own mind and Kyle kept quiet. He knew that he could never force Seamus to make a decision. He had seen the heel-digging stubbornness of his friend before, and this was no time to give him cause for pause. He would wait him out and then plead if Seamus said no.

After some minor repairs to the *Telegraph,* and a couple of day's rest for the crew, they set sail back to Chicago. Kyle had dropped a hint that Jacob would be Seamus' first mate if he took him up on his offer, and that most of the crew would stay with the ship. Seamus observed the actions of the crew more closely than on the outbound cruise and paid particular attention to Jacob, not because he had made his decision, but in case he chose to take the offer.

Jacob not only understood the ship and her quirks, but he was lithe and capable with the rigging. He could command the crew as easily as luff a sail. Seamus suspected Kyle of turning control of the ship over to Jacob so that Seamus would develop confidence in him. If that was the case, it worked well, for by the time they reached Chicago, Seamus had nearly reached his decision.

"I need to see to a few things before I make my final decision, Kyle. But I'm leaning hard a-starboard in your favor right now."

"I can't ask for better than that for the time being. I will await your decision. By the by, would you like to see the house I'm having built?"

"I would, indeed."

Once again, Kyle hired a carriage and they headed north across the new bridge and out of the city. They came to a forested area a little way north of the river and followed the wagon ruts through the trees. There stood a large structure with several men working on various portions of the construction. Two were setting a large mullioned bay window in place while another tuck-pointed the stone work around the carved oak double doors. Plasterers were working on both levels inside, covering the lathe in layers of white plaster. The smell of the plaster permeated the building.

"This isn't a house, Kyle. It's a bloody mansion."

"I told you shipping has been good to me," Kyle said. "I also once told you that I wanted to live like a king."

"I didn't imagine it had been this good."

"It's a good life, my friend."

All this time, the boys had been watching the tradesman at their various tasks, and silently storing information in their heads. They were almost to the point of bothering the workers and asking them questions when Seamus called them to him and said that it was time to go back to the town.

"Would you like to leave the boys with me for a couple of days while you see to whatever it is that needs your attention?"

"Would you mind if I did?"

"I wouldn't have made the offer if I minded."

"You truly are a friend."

"Not at all. It's to my advantage, you know."

"Come now, you don't have a greedy bone in your body."

"Actually, I do. I just keep them well hidden."

"I may be a few days. I need to go back out to Barber's Corner and Naper Settlement, and that's a bit of a hike."

"Rent a horse at the stable where we got the carriage. You'll be there and back in no time."

"Maybe I will."

Chapter 18

Shall I till the land or plow the waves,
To plant the seeds of things to come?
Shall I reap the crops or crop the sails,
For these lads to make a home.

M*y Dear Father,*

I haven't written to you since I was digging the canals in Ohio a lifetime ago. I'm sure that by now you think I've gone on to the other side, too. I haven't. A lot has happened and after you read to the end of this letter, you will better understand why I haven't written. Part of it is not being near a post office or even a town for long stretches of time. I think I am about to settle down with a solid home for the first time since arriving in the New World. I think I must in order to give the boys a good home. Yes, I said the boys. One is my son. The other is adopted.

This is how the story goes . . .

. . . and now they are my responsibility.

By the by, tell my friend Robin that Bright Moon and I named our son for him. He would be proud. Little Robin is very smart.

Do you remember my mention of my good friend, Kyle? He has his own ship now and is about to buy another. He has asked me if I would take over command of one of them, and I've since been in a quandary whether to take his offer. I think I should for the sake of the boys. My whole life seems to revolve around them now. I consider them and their wellbeing before I make every decision.

If I do this, they will get a good education and they can sail with me in the summer. I could afford to do many things better than I can as a farm hand. Please don't misunderstand. Thanks to you I am a good farmer and I respect those who are. But I think I can do better for the boys as a sailor and ship's captain.

Thank you so much for helping me make that decision, father. I couldn't have done it alone. I will close now so that I can get this off to you. Give my best to Robin.

Your loving son,

Seamus

Dear son,

I was relieved to hear from you at last. It sounds like a lot has happened and I do understand. I am sorry for your loss and proud to be a grandfather at the same time. Hug our boys for me.

I'm glad to have been of assistance in your decision-making. Sometimes, in writing to someone, we think like they do for a brief time, and that is as good as hearing them say the words. I love you son. And anything you do will be the right thing.

Nothing has changed here. I let Robin read your last letter and now he is excited about America. He wants to come over for a visit. I don't think he has the concept of how far away you really are. Don't be surprised to see him on your doorstep someday. You make it sound so exciting that I would like to come myself. But I'm afraid I am a bit too frail now.

When I said that nothing had changed here, I wasn't exactly truthful. The new Lord of the Manor seems to be more concerned with his tenants' welfare than Mayfair was. He has repaired many of the cottages and crofts. Maybe there is hope for us yet.

You sound as if your hands are full. Take care of those boys and go sail your ship.

I love you son,

Fahey

By the time his father's letter arrived and he had paid his one bit to receive it, he had bought a house, hired a nanny, and taken command of the

Telegraph. He had previously visited the Napers and told them that he would be captaining their old ship. They gave him some advice about some of her quirks. He had visited the Barbers. There, he not only explained about the ship but gave them a few of his ideas about the soil conditions needed for raising potatoes, such as adding some sand to make the soil looser. "After all," he had told them, "potatoes need to expand as deep as a foot and if the soil is too tight, they won't grow."

He stood at the helm with the sun glowing in a clear sky and a hearty wind moving them along, thinking how good fortune had finally settled on him.

"Jacob, I'm glad to have you as first mate."

"It's a pleasure to sail with you, Captain. Before you met up with the boss, he asked me to take command. I told him I wasn't interested. I like being first mate."

"He did tell me he made you the offer of captaincy and that you turned him down. I was a bit surprised. Your experience on these waters will be of great value, though. We'll do fine together, I think."

"Aye Captain, we will."

"Captain; that has a nice ring to it. I can get to like that title."

"'Tis yours by rights, Captain. And make no mistake, if any man Jack has an argument with that, he'll be answering to me. I saw how you handled yourself when we sailed with Captain Owens. You know your stuff, Captain."

"I don't foresee any problems; do you?"

"There've been none, nor will there be, Sir."

Jacob was a bull of a man with a neck as thick as the main mast. That was the thought that ran through Seamus' mind as he looked at his first mate from the corner of his eye, thinking how fervent a follower he had already become. He wondered at Jacob's shyness at taking command when he was clearly capable. He had seen him handle himself, and there was no reason he couldn't have done the job. He chose not to press the issue just now. Maybe Jacob would let something slip along the way. Not that it mattered; he would trust him anyway. It was mere curiosity that made him want to know.

"We should have sight of the Port of Cleveland soon, Captain."

"That will be half our load ashore, and with a trailing wind we should make good time from there to Buffalo."

"Aye, Captain."

"When it's just the two of us, why don't you call me Seamus?"

"I could do that, but I may forget around the crew. I best stick with Captain, if you don't mind."

Seamus nodded and Jacob's salt and pepper whiskers parted in a grin. Seamus thought that he had an odd set of personal rules that he lived by, but who was he to judge?

They had been following the shoreline and now Jacob spotted the port up ahead.

"There she lies," he said calmly. "I'll get the crew ready."

"Then come back and take the helm for docking if you would," Seamus said. He had never docked a ship and was a bit nervous about doing so. Especially on his first outing as captain with the weight of a full cargo. Maybe he would give it a try in Buffalo. He didn't want this crew to know about his trepidation. That would not endear him to them. He needed this crew to respect him or there would be no future for him in this business. Word got around quickly about incompetence.

"Aye, Captain."

They slipped into place, as cleanly as could be wanted with Seamus studying Jacob's every move and command. "I can do this." he thought. "It's all common sense anyway." He would definitely give it a try at Buffalo.

They unloaded the cargo destined for Cleveland and gave the crew a few hours' shore leave before proceeding. Seamus and Jacob stepped into a port side tavern to feed themselves.

"Ain't that Cap'n Naper's old ship, the *Telegraph*?" The voice by the window belonged to another salt-and-pepper faced sailor type.

"Aye, 'tis that," replied Jacob.

"Is Cap'n Joseph aboard?"

"He sold her a while back. This here," he said, indicating his new boss, "is her captain. This be Captain Seamus."

"What happened to Cap'n Naper?"

"He settled a town in Illinois," Seamus interjected. "I worked for him and his brother, John, for a while in their saw mill."

"You don't say." He thought quietly for a moment than added,

"They built that ship from the keel up, you know. Yup, and I helped them every step o' the way."

"She's a beauty and she handles well," Seamus said.

"Kind words, thank'e."

"Have you ever sailed aboard her?"

"Nay, I don't go nearer the water than I have to t' build them. I can't swim and I don't like the water. But I do like to build ships."

"I understand that the Napers came from around here."

"Aye. Over in Astabula County," he said pointing in an easterly direction.

After they ate, they shoved off and finished the run to Buffalo in good time. Seamus docked the ship like an old hand though he was sweating the whole time. The rest of the grain was unloaded and the lumber was loaded and stowed for the return trip to Chicago. Seamus had already ceased to think of it as Fort Dearborn, as had most of her inhabitants. It was destined to become the City of Chicago from the day duSable had settled there in the latter half of the 1700's. It had grown so fast that it had already spread west beyond the south branch of the Chicago River. And that would be their destination when they returned, because that is where most of the lumber dealers had set up businesses.

His greatest concern was navigating the river around the bridges. Chicago had built floating bridges that could be moved out of the way when a ship approached with her high masts, but there were frequent accidents anyway. When they arrived, he managed the feat with silent fortitude, as he had the landing in Buffalo. They were secured to the lumberyard's pier and the crew was busy unloading.

"Captain, I have to say something," Jacob whispered next to him.

"What is it, Jacob?"

"I knew you had never docked a ship when you turned the helm over to me at Cleveland. I watched in Buffalo as you handled her like a seasoned sailor. And again, coming down the river and docking here. If you were the least bit concerned, you didn't show it. The crew never knew. And Captain, you truly are the Captain."

"Thank you, Jacob. That means a lot coming from you. Tell my nerves, would you?"

"That'll go away, the more you do this."

"I hope so." He paused before adding, "Give the crew a few days' rest before we load up again. I'm going to go see the boys."

"Aye, Captain."

II

". . . and Tall Grass got into a fight because of his name," Robin concluded.

"They were teasing me," the subject of the discussion said quietly in his own defense.

"It's alright," Seamus said in an attempt to calm him. Tall Grass wasn't aggressive, as Bear Claw had been. He had inherited his mother's passive nature. "I have had to deal with bullies myself, and they were usually bigger than I was. Though, I doubt there are too many here who are bigger than you are. Here is what we will do. We will change your name to sound more like a white man's name. How does Clement sound?"

"I guess it's okay."

"What does this 'okay' mean," Seamus asked.

"It's what the kids say for alright," Robin proudly offered.

Seamus thought about that for a moment then said, "Okay, Clement Tallgrass it shall be from now on."

"What does Clement mean?"

"It means to be calm or merciful. That fits you well. But more importantly, it was the first name of my village priest and mentor in Ireland."

After a pause for thought he added, "Then you will change schools for a fresh start."

"Can I change schools, too?" Robin asked.

"Why?"

"I popped the one who was teasing Tall Grass. He has some big friends."

"That was very brave of you."

"He's my brother."

Seamus smiled inwardly. Here again was that Indian use of the term brother, and in one so young. To see such spunk in his son gratified him. This was a serious matter, but at the same time, reassuring to him in a family way. They would look out for each other when he was not around.

"I don't see why we can't arrange that. You should stay together."

"Thanks, Papa," they said in unison.

"My goodness. Captain and Papa in the same day," he said with a smile. The boys looked at him as if he was daffy. "Now show me what you have learned."

They went through their entire school experience since he had set sail. It seemed a shame to have to move them to a new school; they were learning so fast. Maybe the new one would be as good.

He asked the nanny about the other schools and she agreed that a change or two would be advisable. She told him where the next closest one was and he went off to see the head of the school about enrolling the boys. He explained what had happened at the last one and what he was prepared to do to prevent a recurrence at this one. The principal agreed to the plan and said the boys could start the next week.

His next visit was to his employer and friend.

"You only just caught me at home, Seamus. I'm setting sail tomorrow for the maiden voyage of my new ship, the *Irish Lass*. I borrowed the name from the *Irish Lassie* we sailed over here on. Do you want to see her?"

"I would like that very much. And by the by, here are the earnings from the *Telegraph's* last voyage."

"You take ninety percent of the earnings, pay the crew, refit the *Telegraph* as needed and buy the next load. Whatever is left is yours to keep. Just give me ten percent. She is paid for, you know."

As they traveled back to the river, Kyle described the *Irish Lass* to Seamus in as much detail as time allowed. ". . . and she has four masts for more speed and larger loads. Well, you'll see. There she is. What do you think?" Kyle was like a lad with a new toy.

"She's beautiful is what I think."

"She's been around for a few years. This is only her maiden voyage as the *Irish Lass*. I didn't like the name *Wanderer* very much."

"I can't say that I blame you. What businessman would trust his goods to a ship called *Wanderer*? He might wonder where his goods would wander."

"Oh har, har," Kyle interjected.

Seamus admired the sleek lines of the vessel and the intricacy of the rigging. He had no doubt she would outrun the *Telegraph* if it came down to a race. He could almost hear her wake as he looked her over from the dock.

"She's a fine one, Kyle."

"Thank you. We'll see how she handles, but I've heard good reports."

"Did you keep any of her crew?"

"Most of them. Some of them grumbled about changing the name. They liked the *Wanderer*. But, they don't like to change ships once they get used to their quirks. It makes my life easier. That's how I got the crew you have now. They came with the *Telegraph*."

"There is no question as to the *Telegraph* crew's abilities. And Jacob was a Godsend on that first voyage. He was very understanding and helpful."

"He's a good man. They are all good men. I have yet to get to know this new crew . . . I have an idea. None of them know you. One or two are eyeing us now and wondering about you—let them think you're a new hire. Why don't we let Jacob take your next load, and you sail with me as one of my crew? You can find out firsthand for me just how this crew feels."

"You're the boss. I'll let Jacob know and be back in the morning, ready to shove off."

Jacob was writing a letter when Seamus found him aboard the *Telegraph*. He had never seen him write anything, and hadn't been sure he knew how.

"Jacob, the boss wants me to sail with him tomorrow. I need you to load the *Telegraph* and take command for the next trip. Would you do that for me to keep Kyle happy?"

"I'm not sure that's a good idea, Captain."

"Why would that be?"

"I'm not sure the crew would trust me again so soon."

"So soon after what?"

"I'm afraid that the last time I commanded a ship, I panicked in a storm and lost a few of the crew on the rocks. The survivors all said there wasn't anything I could have done different, but I know they won't trust me."

"Let me have a talk with them and see how they feel. How long ago was that?"

"Maybe seven, eight years ago."

"A lot has changed since then. You're more mature now. Where is the crew?"

"Most of them prefer Miller's Tavern, but some may be at the Sauganash. They're both near the post office. Let me finish this letter so I can mail it and I'll go with you. I can drop it off on the way."

"Go ahead. I'm going to my cabin for a couple of things anyway. I'll see you on deck when you're ready."

"Aye, Captain."

"And don't call me Captain while we're talking to the crew this time. Trust me, I have my reasons."

"Aye, Captain."

"Start now."

"Aye . . . Seamus." He shook his head. "That's not easy."

While he was in his cabin, he made notes for Jacob about the loads at each end and about the money part of the business. He wrapped the notepaper around the money for the crew and the loads and gave it to Jacob for safe keeping before they went ashore.

III

"But you said you would be here for a while," Robin said with a little whine in his voice.

"Sometimes plans change. Uncle Kyle wants me to go with him this time. And you know better than to whine like that."

"I'm sorry," he said as he hung his head. He picked up his fork and played with his food for a moment. "When you get back, can we do something special?"

"This is probably the last voyage of the season. When I get back, we'll have the whole winter to do a lot of special things."

He marveled at the improvement in both boys' vocabularies. Not only were they multilingual, but they could hold up their end of a conversation. He thought he might read to them later that evening as a special treat. But first he would pack different clothes than he was accustomed to wearing so the crew of the *Irish Lass* would see him as one of their own. He needed to be at the dock early to become part of the crew. He found the bag he had used when he left Ireland and began stuffing it with the appropriate gear. With that done, he called the boys into the parlor.

"This is the story of Rip Van Winkle, as told by Washington Irving . . ."

IV

The *Irish Lass* made the eastward turn at Saint Marten's Island under similar conditions as Seamus recalled from the trip with Bright Moon and Bear Claw. The *Irish Lass* didn't pitch as much as the *Western Lady* had, because she was a larger ship. But it was still a rough passage through the Straits of Mackinac, worse than Seamus recalled during the warmer months. The temperature was still above freezing, but he wondered how it would be during the return trip. He saw the rocky point, closer than he would have liked, and wondered if that was where Jacob's ship had floundered. It was easy to imagine the panic he spoke of if a ship were sucked into that mess. He made a mental note to speak to him about it on his return.

"This isn't normal," a voice shouted over the crashing waves. "It's too soon for the winter storms to start!"

"Do you think it'll ease up," Seamus yelled back.

"Yah, I do!"

The wind made it difficult to speak normally, so both men stood braced at the railing and quietly watched the waves crash around them and on the nearby shore. Seamus' thoughts went again to Jacob, who would be coming this way in a few days. He could imagine the fear that this storm would cause him after what he confessed about his last command. He fervently hoped it would subside before then.

As they passed Nine Mile Point, Kyle turned to port to put more distance between them and the rocks. As they moved away from shore, the sailing became smoother and the crew's nerves relaxed some.

"He knows what he's doing. I'll give him that," came the same voice at his shoulder.

"Who?"

"Captain Owens."

"Oh. Did you have doubts? Haven't you sailed with him before?"

"Nah! He just took over the ship. This is our first time out with him, and yah, you always have doubts about a new Captain. There's tales, of course, but that ain't always the truth of it, is it?"

"No, I guess not."

"But he showed good sense there. To turn out too soon at Nine Mile Point is dangerous because of the hidden rocks below. He's sailed these waters before. By the way, I'm Tom Pritchard."

"Good to know you. I'm Seamus."

Seamus found it hard to not defend Kyle. He trusted his friend with his life, but he understood how strangers might not feel the same. That didn't make it any easier to play dumb, and he had to keep his promise to Kyle to get a true feeling of the crew's concerns. He admired his friend's desire to correct what needed correcting and leave all else alone.

The storm was a distant memory by the time they reached Port Huron and the Clair River. Nowhere was the weather more unpredictable than on these Great Lakes. Few other places could exhibit summer and winter in a seven day stretch, especially when the fall changes were beginning. By the time they had cleared the Detroit River and entered Lake Erie, they had landed in the doldrums. The crew fished and lolled around waiting for a breeze to move them on their way.

Kyle took the time to inspect every inch of his vessel and find out what would need attention when they returned to Chicago, and what to leave alone. He didn't mind the time lost for it was time he would have had to otherwise borrow later. He wouldn't want this to happen every trip, but this was his get-acquainted voyage and it worked out well.

It also gave Seamus time to chat idly with his fellow crewmen and get a feel for their moods. Of course, he couldn't report directly to Captain Owens, but he did give him an occasional wink to let him know all was well. He knew that there would be plenty of time for a detailed report, in private, after the voyage.

"She blows," came a shout from amid ship. All the hands on deck looked up to see the sails flutter and begin to fill, and they cheered. To a man, they would rather be moving than sitting idle.

"I'd like to see those Fulton paddle wheelers come to these lakes. Then we wouldn't be stuck when the wind died," Tom said.

"Have you seen one yet?"

"Yah. I was over by the Erie Canal once when one went by. Nice steady pace, no mules, and no worries about the wind. I don't know why there aren't more of them."

"I'd like to see one someday. It's a good idea, from what I've heard," offered another crewmember.

Seamus didn't know if he was expected to learn all the crew's names. If so, he was failing miserably.

"Jake, this here is Seamus."

"Good to meet you," they said simultaneously.

"Jake's been with the ship the longest, and probably knows where every loose peg is better than anyone."

"Are there a lot of them," Seamus asked in mock horror.

"Figure of speech, friend. She's as solid as they come. Now some of the crew have a few loose boards, if you know what I mean."

"Should I worry about them?"

"Not too much. Mostly, they just spend too much time away from real people, and don't know how to act when we're in port. They're harmless otherwise."

"What's your opinion of the new captain, Jake?"

"So far, he seems alright. But it's been my experience that Irishmen are short tempered."

"I'm Irish, Jake. Didn't you hear Tom introduce me as Seamus?"

"I thought he said James," Jake said with a blush.

"No matter." Seamus shrugged. "Most Irishmen are more fun loving than they are short tempered, though. I think we should give Captain Owens time to show us what he's made of before we judge him too harshly. What do you think, Tom?" He thought he needed to keep them both in the conversation to steer any suspicion away from himself as Kyle's co-conspirator.

"So far, I don't see any reason not to trust him. Time will tell."

V

The voyage included stops in Cleveland, Ohio; Erie, Pennsylvania; and Buffalo, New York. They unloaded goods at each port but only loaded lumber aboard at the last. With three stops, the doldrums, and larger loads both ways, they still made better time on the overall trip than the *Telegraph* had ever made.

Seamus sat with Kyle in his study in Chicago, giving him his report on the crew as he had observed them.

"And they never suspected you of spying for me?"

"If they did, no one let on that he knew."

"So, other than a couple of hot heads when they get drunk in the bars, I don't have to worry about them?"

"I don't think so. Now I have a question for you, my old friend."

Kyle smiled generously at Seamus and asked, "What would that be?"

"When are you going to get married and have a family of your own?"

Shocked by such an unexpected question, Kyle sat still and stared at Seamus with a stunned expression. He stuttered but remained silent.

"Have I stepped onto soft ground?"

"No, no. It's just that I never gave it any thought after that awful experience I had in New York." He looked imploringly at his friend before adding, "It's hard to trust another woman."

"But you have built this huge manor house and have no one to help you fill it. There is no sound of children laughing and chasing down the stairs, no wonderful smells emanating from the kitchen. You must miss those things."

"I never told you this, Seamus, but I lived in an orphanage until I was ten years old. I couldn't take the workhouse type of atmosphere anymore so I ran away. I don't miss home because I never had one."

"I am so sorry to have brought it up then."

"It's alright, my friend. You have raised a valid question. I have not spent time around women and haven't had the chance to meet one I liked. Perhaps I should put myself in the right gatherings so that I can."

"I don't want to seem like a match maker, but I know the right woman for you. Of course, the boys and I shall be sorry to lose her, but she is a wonderful cook, and she's Irish."

"That doesn't matter. Being Irish never did me any good. What I am is an American."

Seamus thought about that for a moment then said, "It never occurred to me, but I guess I am, too. Anyway, you've never been to my home. Why don't you come to supper tomorrow night, and meet Jean and sample her cooking? She need not know why you're there unless you choose to tell her."

"I don't know that I'm in any hurry, but it can't hurt. Besides, I'd like to see the boys again."

"Then it's settled. Supper will be at eight o'clock. You know the address on South State Street even though you've never been there."

"Eight o'clock it is then."

Having become an avid reader, thanks to Seamus, he showed up the following night at seven o'clock with an armload of books for the boys. They, in turn, disappeared into the library to explore the pages while the two men discussed business in the study. It was a man's room with walnut half paneling and matching mantle over the hearth.

"No, the *Telegraph* hasn't returned, yet," Seamus said. "But I don't expect her back for another week or two at the earliest. Jacob will contact me as soon as they arrive."

"I have no doubt he will. I was just curious."

The cook entered the study at that moment to announce that supper was on the table. Seamus took the opportunity as it presented itself.

"Kyle Owens," he said, "this is the most wonderful cook this side of Killarney, Jean O'Malley. Jean, Kyle is my boss and very good friend of many years."

Jean blushed at the complement, curtsied as she had been taught in Ireland, and said in a voice that captivated Kyle, "I'm very pleased to make your acquaintance, Mr. Owens."

"Please, call me Kyle."

"That I will, if you insist, Sir."

"And please," he stressed the *please*, "don't call me Sir."

She bobbed another silent curtsy and went to retrieve the boys from the library.

"I like her already," Kyle said to his friend. "And that voice! Ach, it sounds like an angel singing."

"I thought you'd fall for her right off."

"Let's not be rushing things, but do you mind if I call upon her from time to time?"

"Mind? I'd be insulted if you didn't. After all, didn't I say she would be perfect for you?"

"Aye, that you did, Lad. That you did."

Kyle and Jean smiled at each other a lot over dinner. Seamus insisted that the hired help dine at the same table as the family, for after all, hadn't they all come from the same poor roots? There was no discussion about business, but plenty about sailing. The boys were always curious about what the men did for a living and the adventures they had aboard ship. Seamus told of the dangers on the last voyage and the comments made by Tom as they moved away from Nine Mile Point. Jean kept watching Kyle's face with a look of adoration in her own eyes for his bravery.

"The ocean crossing was the scariest time of my life," she finally blurted. "I would never do that again."

"It's not so bad once you get used to it," Kyle said in reassurance.

"No, thank you," she said. "Once was enough!"

"I have some port in the study if you would care to join me," Seamus said to Kyle as they finished dining. "And I'm sure the boys want to get back to the books you brought them."

"Thank you, Uncle Kyle," they remembered to say as they raced down the hall.

"Uncle Kyle," Kyle said. "I kind of like that."

They settled into the royal blue wingback chairs on either side of the fire, each with a glass of sipping port.

"She really is a wonderful cook, just as you said."

"I would never lie to you, my friend."

"I know. You're too honest."

"And that is why you have to promise me, that if you ever buy another ship, you won't ask me to spy on the crew for you. I hated that. I just don't like being deceitful."

"I give you my solemn vow to never put you in that position again; and I thank you from the bottom of my heart for being open with me."

"What else can I be? We are old friends."

"When you say it like that, I feel ancient."

"I mean old friends as having experienced much together, not how old we are."

"I know what you really mean, my friend."

They sat quietly enjoying the port, the crackling fire and the comradery of each other's presence for a while, each wrapped in his own thoughts.

"I really must be going," Kyle finally said, "But I do mean to call on Jean. You have once again pointed me in the right direction, my friend."

"I'm glad to be of service. Boys," he called down the hall, "Uncle Kyle is leaving."

Jean, trying to not appear too eager, arrived at the study door before the boys with a parcel carefully wrapped in brown paper and tied up with string. "Here is something for your dinner tomorrow, Si . . . Kyle."

"Thank you, Jean, I'm certain I will enjoy it as much as I did tonight's feast."

Jean blushed and curtsied her way back to the kitchen, too overcome to say anymore.

"She is a gem, Seamus."

"I know. Why do you think I said I would be sorry to lose her?"

The boys skidded around the corner from the hall and came to a stop.

"Thank you again for the books, Uncle Kyle," Robin said.

"Yes, thank you," Clement echoed.

"You are very welcome, both of you," he said, as he made his exit.

Chapter 19

A road is more than just a way
For one to get from place to place.
A road is man's ingenious way
For all his people to interlace

PLANK WANTED—We will take any amount of white or burr oak plank from those indebted to us, if delivered at Naperville, or any other place on the line of the Naperville-Oswego plank road, before the first day of April, in payment of their account, or will pay goods for them. The planks to be eight feet long, three inches thick, and not more than thirteen inches wide. 500,000 feet wanted for the stock of the company,—Naper & Skinner; Lyman and Company; W. Scott and Son; A.H. Howard & Company; A. Kieth; H.L. Peaslee and Company, George Martin." [4]

"That's a lot of lumber," Robin said to Seamus and Clement. As usual on Sunday morning after mass, they were lazing around the front parlor

---

[4]Actual advertisement posted in the DuPage County Recorder, on January 3, 1850

reading the papers from all the surrounding towns. Robin had picked the DuPage County Recorder of January 3rd, 1850.

"On my last visit out to the folks in Naperville," Seamus said,

"John said they were going to build a better road than that dusty track we always take."

"You mean the one that starts at Ogden Avenue?" Clement asked.

"That's the one," Seamus said as he lowered the paper he was holding. "Anyway, their plan is to lay down two parallel stringers, dug down into the earth, then lay the planks crosswise over them, pretty much like Chicago is doing with her streets. It sounds good, although it will be a noisy road to travel, just as the streets of Chicago are now."

"I imagine it might be just as slippery when it rains or after a night's hard frost," Robin interjected.

Clement chimed in with, "Here is something I've always wondered. What about when it floods? Won't the planks float away?"

"They'll be nailed down, of course. Our streets don't float away. We'll just have to wait and see how well it works," Seamus added sagely.

Robin changed the subject and said, "Well, it was good to see the first bridge re-open over the river. Taking the ferry was becoming more difficult with the number of people trying to get from this side of Chicago to the other."

"You have to admit, brother, that it was a pretty spectacular flood that washed all the bridges out at once. I've never seen the Chicago River that full of water."

"They will eventually all be rebuilt," Seamus interjected. "We can only hope they're designed better for the ships to get past them with fewer wrecks. Now there is a problem that can snarl traffic on the river for days. I see it all too frequently when I come back with a load of lumber."

"Papa, what do you think about all these railroads," Robin asked as he shook open a new page of his paper. "Should we invest in them?"

"They're here to stay," Seamus replied, "and yes, you should buy in if you've got extra money."

"I've got about three thousand I saved up," Clement said. "Maybe I'll buy into the Galena and Chicago Union Railroad."

"Chicago ships grain and cured pork all around the country. The lumber I bring in is milled here and shipped west on railroads. I can't see how you could go wrong. Just please promise me that you'll never forget where we came from and how little we had in the beginning."

"We would never forget, Papa," Robin said. "Besides, working in Cyrus McMormick's reaper factory will keep anybody from becoming too egotistical. That's hard work."

"Yeah, but at least we're close enough to the new college to take classes," Clement added.

"I told you boys I would pay for your tuition and books."

"And we appreciate the offer, Papa. We talked about this and decided that it would mean more to us if we paid our own way at Saint Xavier's," Robin said.

"Okay, to use one of your own favorite words. But remember that I can help you if you need it."

"Thanks, Papa."

Seamus folded his paper and set it aside. As he rose, he said, "I feel like a ride in the country. Would you two like to join me?"

"No thanks, Papa," They said in chorus.

"Isn't it a little cold for a ride in the country, Papa?" Robin added.

"This isn't bad. I recall some winters that were a lot worse. They tell me that the people in Naper Settlement were snowed in and frozen for days back in '32. Besides, I've wanted to have a chat with some of my friends out in Naperville for some time now. The article you read out loud from the Recorder makes it even more important now."

II

"My son, Robin, was the one who read the article this morning. I think I can get a good-sized load of planks for you in the spring, but, as you know, we shut down in the winter," Seamus said as he and John Naper sat in front of John's flagstone fireplace, warming their fingers. John had been outside, splitting firewood when Seamus rode up.

"I remember those straits when they were relatively calm," John Naper said. "I don't blame you for shutting down. It's just that I don't know how much plank we'll still need in the spring. We already have wagonloads coming in every couple of days. I'm buying it and Willard Scott is buying it and a whole lot of other people as well."

"What if I come see you when we refit the *Telegraph* for our first run of the year?"

"That might be best. Now tell me about those boys of yours."

"That's just how I'll always think of them," Seamus said with a sigh, "as boys. But they're men now. They both work for Cyrus McCormick and they're going to college. They're attending Saint Xavier, that new college that opened three years ago."

"Any romantic attractions, yet?"

"No. They don't have time for that as far as I can tell. They seem to be more interested in their studies than they are in the ladies."

"No matter. They are young, yet. They kind of remind me of someone else I knew. I think it was a young man named Seamus." John grinned at his friend. "You were a hard-working fellow when you were here. You've taught them well."

"Thank you. And thank you for the opportunity all those years ago," Seamus added. "By the way, how is Joseph doing?"

"He's up to his neck in politics still. Although, I must say he's doing a lot of good for the community and for the state."

"Speaking of the community, I hear there are a lot of people leaving from here for the California gold."

"Yeah, and a lot passing through, too. Willard Scott moved his family into town and built the Naperville Hotel a few years back. Now it's a favorite gathering place for folks with the gold fever."

"I suppose it's better to have the gold fever than the cholera epidemic you had last year. I read about that just before I left on one of my voyages."

"We lost quite a few. Believe me when I say we're glad that it's gone."

"Oh, I believe you. It was scary enough just to read about."

After John told Seamus the names of some of people lost to the epidemic and a moment of reverent silence in their honor, Seamus surprised John when he said, "Now tell me about this Underground Railroad I've only heard rumors of recently."

John gave a little start. "How did you hear about that?"

"I'm always listening, John. I don't always believe what I hear, but I do hear what's being said. I know that the good people of this town are involved somehow," he said, to reassure John of his faithfulness.

"You won't say anything to the authorities, I hope," John said.

"I think you know my feelings better than that, John."

John proceeded to fill Seamus in on the details of how the railroad worked up to this point and what they hoped to accomplish in the future.

"I have an idea of how I can help," Seamus said after a little thought. "It will take a little time to set up and some changes in shipping routes, though."

"We'll take all the help we can get," John said with new excitement in his voice. Any ally in their efforts was appreciated. "And . . ." he added conspiratorially, "we're not the only ones who need to move these people along, you know."

"How many more are there, John?"

"Oh, my good Lord, we are all over the northern part of the state."

"Are you in contact with any of them?"

"We are in touch with most of the others."

"I'll get back to you as soon as I can," Seamus said as the two old friends shook hands and parted.

III

"I've recently heard the stories, too," Kyle said as he ushered Seamus into his parlor. "How long has this been going on?"

"Apparently, since the seventeen eighties or so," Seamus said.

"Why have we never heard about it, then?"

"Obviously, the fewer people who know, the better, don't you think? I'm only telling you because I need your blessing as president of the company for what I'm about to do."

"And what might that be," Kyle said as he led the way to the warm fire, "if I may be so bold as to ask?"

"I would like to use the *Telegraph* to provide a final link in the 'Freedom Line,' as it is lovingly called."

"Why would you want to stick your neck out for people you don't know?"

"Come now, Kyle," Seamus barked. "You of all people know my history. You know how I feel about repression. Look what our own people suffered at the hands of the British. Look what they tried to do to the people of this land before the Colonies rebelled. How can you ask such a question?"

"First of all, I know all that, and I think you know my own feelings, Seamus. Secondly, I wasn't questioning what you wanted to do so much as how badly you wanted to do it. I see a passion that I haven't seen since Kicker killed the old man in Ohio. Now that I've seen that passion, I know your plan will work. What are you going to do?"

"I want to use the *Telegraph* for the final leg to get these people to Canada."

"Where are you going to load her to keep the prying eyes away?"

"A while back I bought a piece of farm land down past Lumber Street, after the river makes the bend to the west. It's pretty secluded there and there's a barn on it next to the river. Nobody pays much attention to the *Telegraph* going down there because she's usually hauling lumber to the mills down that way. So we slip on down the river a little farther, load up after dark, and leave before sunup."

"I like the concept. But you might want to haul a little cargo to cover yourself in case you're searched. You said yourself that getting caught could mean imprisonment."

"Good point. We can haul the minimum to allow the most passenger space."

Kyle got up and poked at the fire to liven it up. "What condition is the barn in?"

"It needs some work, but I know a couple of young men who are pretty good with their hands," he said with a wink.

"Aren't they working for Cyrus?"

"Yes, but I think they'll work on this in their free time. They are my boys, after all."

"You tell them that I will personally pay them what they are making now from McCormick for the time it takes to do this, and I'll talk to Cyrus myself about keeping their jobs open for them when they're done."

"That's awfully generous, Kyle, but I think we, the company, should pay them, not just you."

"Done!"

IV

Clement looked Seamus in the eye with concern and said, "You do know the risks, don't you, Papa?"

"Well, of course I know the risks. The biggest one is having too many people find out about it, so keep it mum, okay?"

Robin piped up, "Who are we going to tell, Papa? We don't want to be caught any more than you do, and yes we'll do this, even without pay if we have to. It's too important to ignore."

Seamus hugged each of the boys in turn before as he said, "You truly are your mother's sons."

"No, Papa, we're your sons," Clement said.

"Is this a result of your ride in the country, Papa?" Robin asked.

"Yes, it is, partly. I've been listening and thinking about this for a little while. When I found out that the good people of Naperville were involved, it rather put the cap on it. I found out while talking to John that there are a number of depots in the towns west of Chicago. The *Telegraph* will haul many souls. She's certainly earned us enough money. Now she can repay her debt to society and make freedom possible for a lot of people."

"What is it you want us to do, Papa?"

"I showed you the property I bought out past Lumber Street, didn't I?" After they nodded, he continued, "There is a barn on that property that is kind of dirty and drafty. I want to make it livable for as many people as will sail on the *Telegraph*. Put a reverse batten over the chinks, see if you can put a stove in there to ward off the chill on spring and autumn nights, and I want places up off the ground for people to sleep, kind of like we had in Sinago's lodge."

"I remember those," Robin said happily. "I always thought those ledges were the neatest place to play."

"Yeah, they were, weren't they," Clement added with a grin. "We can do all this, Papa. We'll work every weekend."

"We need to have it ready by spring. Kyle and I will pay you the same wages you're getting from the reaper factory, and Uncle Kyle will ensure that your jobs are there when you're done with the barn."

"We'll head out there tomorrow and take a look around. We'll see what we need to get the job done."

"I would bring the lumber in on the *Telegraph,* but we're done for the season. You know that I have standing accounts at several of the lumber yards. What I don't want you to do is buy too much in any one place so that it raises suspicions. Also, don't have any of it delivered. You don't know who you can trust. Take a wagon and haul the lumber yourselves."

V

The excitement was growing as the winter snows melted and the ground began to thaw. Seamus made the trip to the barn with the boys. He laughed to himself every time that term went through his mind. They weren't boys, any more. As a matter of fact, Clement towered over him by a good eight inches. He liked to kid him about having to look up twice to see his face just once, because it was so far away.

"I remembered something else from Grandfather Sinago's lodge," Robin said, as he pulled open the small utility door they had cut into the big door of the barn. He didn't have to say a word because the aroma of freshly cut cedar wafted over them at that moment. Seamus felt the joy of memory as his senses took in the aroma.

"That should make them feel welcome, if nothing else does," he said. "Were you planning to replace them after each group?"

"I hadn't thought that far ahead, I guess, but I don't see why not. Do you?"

"Do we have that much cedar on the property?"

"I'll have to take a closer look."

"After all, you are setting a precedence. Don't think that word doesn't filter back to the ones who haven't come yet. Otherwise, how would they know where to come in the first place?"

"We'll look later on as we're going back home."

"I've hired someone to see to their needs on a daily basis and keep some kind of order between voyages," Seamus said. "John recommended him, so he should be trustworthy. He should be along any . . ."

The door scraped open.

"I'll fix that before we leave," Clement said as they all looked up to welcome the newcomer, a thin Negro man about Robin's height with thinning hair and shining eyes.

"Is you Seamus?"

"Yes, I am. You must be Isaac."

"Yessah, I is."

"Welcome, Isaac. These are my sons, Robin and Clement."

"You shure is a biggun'," he said, squinting up at Clement.

Clement smiled and stuck out his hand. "But friendly," he said.

"Isaac, you do know what we aim to do already, so the plan is this. The people will be sent here from the surrounding towns, and when we have enough to fill the ship, we'll load them up at night and take them over into Canada."

"I know all that. I done been there, freed, and come back to help. What I wants to know is what you want me to do here."

"Look around at what the boys have done here and try to keep it in that order. See that the people stay inside, out of sight, and quiet enough that anyone walking by won't hear them. Keep them fed. My boys will bring certain foods out regularly. And keep them warm when the weather changes." Seamus looked around, thinking of what he might have missed. He remembered and pointed, "Oh, yes, the privies are connected to the barn by that short hallway. They never need to go out once they're inside. There's a bag of lime and a scoop at the end of the hall. Sprinkle that over the privies now and then to keep the stink down."

"Das all I gots to do?" Isaac looked back and forth between the three and said, "Das easy nuff."

"Also, we won't take any travelers in the winter because the lakes are too rough," Seamus added. "I'm riding out to see some people this afternoon so our passengers should start showing up soon."

"Yessah, I'll be here."

"Thank you, Isaac. If we all do our jobs right, we shouldn't have any problems. The boys will show you what they've done to make this place livable. Right now, I need to go see those people I talked about."

"You shure is a good man to be doin' this."

"Thanks, I do what I can," Seamus said as he turned and left the barn.

Robin and Clement showed Isaac around and answered the few questions he posed. The stage was set, and the cast assembled, for their new venture.

Chapter 20

Why must there be people
Who only bring the rest grief?
Why are they not the ones
Whose lives are but brief?

"hy, if it ain't my old partner, Seamus," came the gruff voice
from behind the heavy beard.

Seamus looked up from his musings as he approached
Bear Claw, who was leaning against the frame building on the corner of
Clark and South Water Streets. It was all he could do to not cover his nose
from the smell. He shied away as he replied, "What are you doing in town?"

"Now, there's a genteel welcome," Bear Claw said with a sneer. "I'm
still collectin' on hides." He paused and grinned before adding, "Only now I
gotta deliver 'em alive on account o' their owners wants 'em back that way.
Don't know why, they're all lazy good fer nothins anyway."

I could certainly say the same about you, Seamus thought to himself. "I can't
help you there," is what he actually said. God help him but, he wanted to say
so much more. He wanted even more to get as far away from his smell as
possible.

"If you see any of them 'scaped niggers, you let me know for old times'
sake. I'm staying here," he said, indicating the building he was propping up.

"Right," Seamus said as he walked away. He couldn't believe how bad luck had a way of showing up when he least expected it. The gall of the man to try to cash in on his good will after the way he left things so many years before. Did he think Seamus had forgotten, or was he just ignorant about his own character? Seamus opted for the latter choice. He would have to warn Isaac and the boys about Bear Claw before any damage could be done.

II

He told the boys that evening as they were sitting down to supper.

"I want to see him," Clement said. "I want to see what a man looks like who doesn't want his own son."

"That might not be a good idea, Clement. You might do something you will be sorry for later," Seamus warned.

"He doesn't have to know who I am. I'll just go to the South Water Street Arms and watch for him. You have described him so well, I'm sure I'll recognize him."

"Just don't go near him, okay? I've always wondered if he didn't kill that whole Chippewa family up north. His tale about the fever was a little too contrived to believe. I've told you before how vile he is, and he cares about no one, not even himself by the smell of him."

"I'm going with you," Robin said. "I need to know what he looks like, too."

"You're the hot head if there is one," Seamus said. "Keep him out of trouble, will you Clement? I going out to the barn after supper to warn Isaac. If Bear Claw goes snooping around out there, there's no telling what might happen."

III

"Yessah, I think I'll know him if'n I sees him nosin' around. Heavy whiskers, bit off nose and scarred face, right?"

"Right. Scarred this way," Seamus said, dragging two fingers down across his eye. He turned to look at their current guests. They were dressed so sparsely; he wondered how they would survive in the cold climate of the Canadian north once winter arrived. He walked among them and began shaking hands. A tear crept into his eye as he looked at the scars across some of their shoulders and backs. How could anyone inflict these wounds and look at himself in the mirror? *Probably the same kind of person as Bear Claw,* he thought. He sincerely hoped that man would go away soon and never return. He couldn't think of anyone he had met in his forty-nine years of life who was more onerous. God help him, he almost wished the man dead.

IV

"He's been asking a lot of questions around town, Papa. I don't think he's learned anything though," Robin said as they gathered later in the parlor.

"He certainly is filthy," Clement added as he screwed up his face in disgust. "We could smell him clear across the Arms lobby."

"He probably hasn't bathed since I last saw him. That's when you two were newborn babes."

"Classes are out for a few days," Clement said. "I'm going to take some time off from McCormick's and follow him around discreetly. I want to find out what he knows."

"What if he spots you?"

"I'll tell him that someone told me he was my father and I was curious. That should throw him off the trail, don't you think?"

"It might. Don't use it if you don't have to, though. He'll try to get something out of you as sure as we're sitting here. Or worse, he'll try to enlist your aid in tracking down escaped slaves, thinking you're of a like mind just because he's your father."

"I won't, Papa."

"May I come with you?" Robin asked.

"I don't think that would be a good idea."

"But I . . ."

"No, Robin. I can be less conspicuous alone. I know a few tricks if I get into trouble, so don't worry about me."

"Okay. But I want to see you at supper tomorrow tonight," Robin said.

"So do I," Seamus added.

V

Clement sat on the bench in front of the hardware store and watched the front door of the Arms Hotel, waiting for Bear Claw to put in an appearance. He slouched down with his hat pulled low over his brow, trying to look inconspicuous, as he promised Robin he would. He had shifted a couple of times on the hard bench, looking for a comfortable way to wait.

Bear Claw finally came out, picking his teeth, and turned down the street. Clement wondered where he was going. There wasn't much that way but the shanties where the free black folks lived. He waited until his quarry turned a corner before getting up to follow. He raced to the same corner and peered around. He waited again until Bear Claw was around another corner before following.

Bear Claw finally stopped and spoke with one of the people before moving on. Once he was out of sight, Clement approached the same person and asked what the bearded man had wanted.

"He says he be lookin' to help the escaped slaves and wants to know where they is."

"What did you tell him?"

"Why you wants to know dat?"

"Because he really wants to know where he can capture them."

"It be a good thing I didn't tell him nothin', then."

"Thank you," Clement said as he patted the man on the shoulder.

"Why you so interested in all dis?"

"I am trying to help and I want to make sure he doesn't spoil it. I've got to go."

He trailed after Bear Claw half the day. Suddenly, Bear Claw went off at a faster pace toward the west. Clement approached the last person he talked to and asked what he had told the bearded man.

"I says dat I hear of a place out by the river das helpin' folks get to freedom."

Clement didn't even thank the man. He took off at a dead run for the nearest bridge over the Chicago River. The skin on the back of his neck was prickling. He got to the barn out of breath and sweating and gave the signal rap at the door. When Isaac unbarred it and swung it open, he dove through and said, "Bar it quick," through clenched teeth.

"What be da' matter?"

Clement put a finger to his lips in the universal sign of silence and they waited. Soon, there was a rattling of the door latch followed by a fist banging on the door planks. They waited and listened. A twig snapped and then another. They could hear the progress of someone going around the barn.

Finally, a small shaft of light that no one had paid attention to was broken and Clement knew they had been discovered.

"Re-bar the door behind me, Isaac. I have to stop this man."

He raced around the barn, stopping long enough to pick up a large piece of dead limb that had fallen from the oak tree. He came around the corner in time to find Bear Claw backing away from the knot hole with a look of triumph in his eye.

Clement swung the heavy end of the branch at that shaggy head and heard bone crunch as Bear Claw raised his arm in time to ward off the blow.

"Ow," he bellowed as he cradled his broken arm. He looked Clement in the eye and asked, "Why in hell did you do that?"

"I'm not letting you spoil this, too."

Bear Claw winced from the pain in his arm and asked, "Damn you, what do you mean, you ain't lettin' me spoil this too?"

Clement remembered Seamus' words of caution and clammed up.

Still cradling his arm, Bear Claw began edging toward him and bellowed, "Well, what'd you mean, boy?"

"You hurt people everywhere you go."

"We've never met. How do you know anything about me?" He was nearly up to Clement, still cradling the broken arm with the other. Finally, he was close enough that he gave Clement a shove in the chest. Clement hooked a heel on a root and fell over backwards. Bear Claw sprang at him and Clement raised the limb in time to knock him sideways and roll away. They both got to their feet and began circling each other, moving closer to the river.

"I asked you a question boy, and I expect an answer." Bear Claw raised his voice in a show of anger. His arm was broken and this boy who was taller than him was putting up more of a fight than he was accustomed to dealing with. "Why, boy?"

"Why?" Clement continued to circle. The river was on his left now. He could no longer hold his anger in check and he said through barely parted lips, "Because you're my father and you deserted me?"

Bear Claw stopped and stared at him with a bewildered look on his face before asking, "What'd you say?"

Clement had not realized how much Bear Claw's desertion had really hurt him. "You heard me," Clement said as he swung the branch harder and faster than he thought himself capable. It connected with Bear Claw's skull, spattering blood and toppling him into the water with a mighty splash.

When bear Claw surfaced, he was not fighting for breath but floating face down. A trail of red water accompanied him and Clement watched him float away with the current. He felt a sudden twinge of conscience and that surprised him. He didn't think he would be able to feel anything but loathing for the man who had deserted him as an infant. Clement lowered his head and said an act of contrition for the deed he had done. He knew he would have to confess this to his priest for it was a mortal sin. He didn't have time for self-flagellation right at the moment, so he moved back to the barn and gave the knock so Isaac would open the door.

"Dat was close," Isaac said with widened eyes. "He be gone now?"

"Yes, Isaac, he's gone now. Everyone okay here?"

"Day be jes fine, Boss. What you say to dat man?"

"I just told him he wasn't welcome here," Clement lied. "I've got to get back to town, now. Take care of them, Isaac."

"I will, Boss."

VI

"Let us just say that he is no longer a threat and let it go at that, okay," Clement said to Robin and Seamus as they sat down to supper that night.

"Isaac and our guests are alright, then?" Seamus asked.

"They're fine. They stayed in the barn as far as I know, so they didn't see or hear a thing."

"How did Bear Claw go off down the river?" Robin asked. "I mean, did he have a canoe or a boat?"

"I mean he went off down the river. Can we please just drop the subject?"

"Okay. Enough said," Seamus said. "Robin, let it go. If he doesn't want to talk about it, then we won't."

Clement lowered his head to hide the expression on his face. He was afraid that the shame welling up inside him would show and the other two would start to pry. He dug into his food to cover the real reason for lowering his head.

Why did he have to lose his temper and kill another human being, let alone his birth father? Of course there was no love between them; that was evident with the desertion years before, but, why did it have to result in murder? There, he said it; he had murdered his father. Murder, murder,

murder. What a loathsome word. He was capable of it even though he always tried to control his feelings when he was around other people. He had to control those feelings better from now on since he now knew what he was capable of doing to someone who really got to him.

"Clement, are you alright?" Seamus asked as he sat with his knife and fork poised over his plate, forearms resting on the edge of the table.

Clement looked up and realized that his vision was slightly distorted from the tears trying to form in his eyes. He thought fast and said, "I just don't want to ever become the uncaring individual who sired me." Phew, he had covered that well.

"You could never be like him," Robin said softly.

"Thanks, Brother."

Chapter 21

It is not right for men to own men,
To take their humanity and give naught back.
It is not right to let this occur,
For then, don't we all something lack?

The Owens and O'Flarity Shipping Company had grown into a large enterprise by the fall of eighteen sixty. They had several small warehouses along the Chicago River, and a number of ships of different sizes plying the waters of the Great Lakes from Duluth to Buffalo. They hauled almost any product that needed to be moved from one port to another. Therefore, taking one ship from the main part of the fleet to haul special cargo did not hurt the company. Of course, it docked in a place where few other people ever came. It was usually loaded late at night and left the Chicago River into the vaster waters of Lake Michigan before daybreak to avoid detection.

These were the years of high risk to anyone who was caught aiding escaped slaves. Not only was the shipping line and the Captain at risk, but the entire crew could be jailed for aiding fugitives. It was a chance that each and every crewmember freely chose to take. Every man aboard agreed to keep quiet about what they were doing, not even letting their family members know what that they were involved in freeing slaves. The entire venture could be jeopardized by the slip of just one child's tongue or one wife's gossip to a friend.

This ship left from the last depot on the underground railroad but never with a schedule that could be worked out by those who hunted the runaways. It was only fitting that the *Telegraph*, built by Captain Joseph Naper and his brother John so many years before, should help deliver this precious cargo that often times came through the depot of Naperville.

This particular cargo was bound for Goderich on the western shore of Ontario, Canada. There were so many coming and so many destinations for them, that it was an almost endless stream. For many people in Illinois, it was not happening fast enough. But detection could mean imprisonment, so caution was far more important than speed.

Seamus, now white haired from all the worry, stood next to Jacob at the bottom of the gangplank. They shook the hand of each of the newly freed people as they reached solid ground. Seamus almost wept when the last one came ashore and kissed the ground before being escorted away.

"Oh, how I wish I could do more," he said as he and Jacob returned up the gangplank.

"I know, Captain. I do too. But right now, we had better put in an appearance in Detroit where the spies are watching. Otherwise, they will start to suspect."

"Cast off," Seamus called to the crew on shore and they were underway.

"Captain, what do you think of this fellow Lincoln that's running for president?"

"I heard him speak from the porch roof of the Preemption House in Naperville a number of years ago. He was running against Douglas for the senate then. I think he's very intelligent and he's morally opposed to slavery. I think that if we elect him president, he will find a way to end slavery once and for all. Are you going to vote for him?"

"You're darned right I am," Jacob said. "I like what I've heard about him and I want this to be over, too. That's why I'm still sailing even though I'm getting old. Right now, we have to get these people to Canada where they can be safe. They shouldn't have to go to another country to be free."

They later docked in Cleveland and unloaded the goods that were brought along to cover their real reason for the trip. There were the usual spies lurking around the dock who ignored them, since they seemed to have legitimate business there.

Later still, they sailed eastward to Geneva-on-the-Lake, where they received their signal and put in after dark to take on a fresh load of special cargo for Canada. This cargo was delivered to the port of Colchester on the south coast of Ontario. Once again, Seamus and Jacob shook the hand of each man, woman, and child as they left the ship. By making this kind of run, they could account for their time between departing and returning to Chicago, in case anyone was keeping track of their movements.

The army had asked the Owens and O'Flarity partners repeatedly to haul cannons and powder for them but they had steadfastly refused. Their thinking was that if they didn't have the armaments, they simply wouldn't have a war no matter what the rumors said. Helping slaves escape was a good and noble cause, but helping people kill people was an entirely different matter.

They knew relations between the North and the South were heating up, but they continued to hope that feelings would mellow and peace would prevail. Seamus hoped that Lincoln would win the presidency and solve the problem the way he had his own wrestling match with Jack Armstrong many years before. He seemed like a wise man who could do a lot of good for many people.

As they approached Nine Mile Point, the weather turned nasty. Seamus noticed that Jacob kept eyeing the rocks along the southern shoreline with a look of trepidation.

"Would you like me to take the helm," he asked quietly.

"If you wouldn't mind, Captain."

"Is this the place where it happened?"

"Aye, it is."

"It was an awfully long time ago."

"Some things you never get over, Captain. It was this time of year, almost to the day."

"I understand.

"'Course the storm was mightier, but not by much."

"Once we're through the Straits you can relax. This is the last run of the year."

"Thank the Lord for that."

They soon made the southward turn toward Chicago and the winds and Jacob calmed at about the same pace. When they reached Chicago, they had to wait their turn to enter the river. Chicago had become such a busy port since the opening of the Illinois and Michigan canal that the lines of ships waiting to unload their goods onto canal barges for the trip to the Mississippi, and ultimately New Orleans, was a long line of masts, bobbing in the current.

Seamus thought back to the day that he, Bear Claw, and Bright Moon had waded through the slime that was Mud Lake to make the same crossing. *What a marvelous feat of engineering*, he thought to himself again. He was constantly amazed at what mankind could devise, and wondered again why they were even considering another war. Did they never learn? Was greed that powerful an elixir that they have to kill for it? And in his mind, it *was* greed. When people wanted to own other people, what else could you call it but greed?

Once they were into the river, they were able to pass the other ships, since they weren't awaiting a berth among the various loading docks. The destination of the *Telegraph* was elsewhere as usual, even though there were no more scheduled loads this sailing season.

They rounded the bend and docked in the barely adequate cove where the barn sheltered his horse and carriage while he was away. It also served as a staging area for future passengers.

Isaac, his 'stable master,' was in an agitated state when he ran out of the barn to greet him.

"Captain, I know you said dat was da' last load for da' season, but a lot more has showed up in da' last two weeks."

"The Straits are already getting dangerous."

"But Captain, what are we goin' do wid dem?"

"Show me." And they went into the barn. There was almost a full complement, and he knew more would be showing up before they could take these away.

"One more trip," he finally said to his Isaac. "Any more that show up will have to go the alternate route. You must be firm; gentle, but firm. Do you understand?"

"Yessah."

While he hitched the horse to the carriage, he said, "*The Telegraph* has to be reprovisioned, so it will be a couple of days before we can shove off. Feed them and keep them quiet. I'll be back." He smiled at the throng in his barn to reassure them, then climbed aboard the carriage and left.

II

"It's too risky, Papa," Robin said.

"I'm inclined to agree with the boys," Kyle stated matter-of-factly before Seamus could get a word in edgewise.

"We are talking about human beings who have already risked their lives enormously to get this far. I am not going to deny them that last sprint for freedom. A freedom they have only dreamt of since the day they were born into this cruel world of greedy men," Seamus said vehemently.

"But Papa," Clement chimed in, "what if you don't make it back? What about future travelers? How will they get to freedom?"

"That's a valid argument, son, but I cannot put these people's lives in jeopardy on a 'what if.'" Seamus was almost angry that his sons and his partner were putting his safety before that of so many other people. He understood their concern, but didn't see why they couldn't understand how important this was. He added, "I need someone to go out to the Napers and have them spread the word to the other depots not to send anymore travelers."

"I'll go right after supper, Papa," Robin volunteered.

The atmosphere in the O'Flarity study eased as Jean opened the door and announced that supper was ready. She always came with Kyle to help the current cook with meals, for which Seamus was grateful since no one could cook the way she did.

As they walked down the hall to the dining room, Seamus added, "And look at you two, talking to me about taking risks. Here you are dressed in Union officer uniforms. What if there is a war and you have to go fight? Isn't there any risk that you might be killed?"

"It's not the same, Papa," Robin said.

"Oh? And just how is it not the same? Because you're younger, it's okay?"

"But you're our Papa. What if something happened to you?"

"How would that be any different than if something happened to you? Son, my point is that I taught you to be firm in what you thought was right. I think I taught the two of you some good lessons. But what kind of lesson would I be teaching you if I turned my back on these people when they most needed me?"

"You've made your point," Robin said grudgingly.

Clement nodded his agreement and the subject was suspended as they joined the ladies in the dining room.

"Don't they look handsome in their uniforms," Jean said as Robin helped her into her seat. "And such gentlemen."

"They had better be if they know what's good for them," Seamus said with a wink. "I may be getting older, but I can still lick 'em."

Grace was said and the meal was eaten with the usual chat and laughter that filled the O'Flarity household.

Afterward, over the requisite glass of port in the study, talk turned to the upcoming election and what effects it might have on the mood of the nation. There had already been much made of the threat by the Southern states to secede from the Northern states if Lincoln was elected. No one wanted there to be a division in this country, at least not in that room at that moment.

When the ladies came in, Robin got out his fiddle and Clement sat down at the piano, and the rest of the evening was devoted to music.

III

The wind howled and the sheets hummed as they were tossed from the top of one wave to the crest of the next. "Thank you, God for letting us get the passengers to safe ground before you threw this at us, but did you have to make it so rough?" These and many other prayers were going up from Seamus, Jacob, and the rest of the crew as they attempted to get past Nine Mile Point on one of the darkest nights of the year.

Seamus steered to starboard, trying to put some distance between the *Telegraph* and the rocks as they rounded the point. The Straits seemed to have different plans for them, for it seemed to keep sucking them back toward the rocks. It was a battle of wills, waged by the elements and the incautious Captain who sailed this time of year.

His Da' had told him years ago how he had entered the world amidst a flurry of prayer. He wondered, as he peered into the darkness for signs of the rocks, if this was how he was to leave this earth. They were suddenly whipped to port so hard that Seamus was hanging from the wheel, then snapped upright on the next wave.

"Captain, we're not going to make it," Jacob shouted. "Shouldn't we turn back?"

"I've got it, Jacob. Lash yourself down."

The sheets on the starboard side chose that moment to snap from the strain and the foremast cracked from the force of the wind. Jacob and a crew member leapt to cut the remaining sheets to ease the strain on the hull.

"It doesn't look good, Captain," Jacob shouted at Seamus. Seamus waved his agreement and swung the wheel in an attempt to turn the *Telegraph* around, but at that moment a wave much greater than any before picked them up and threw them mast-side-down on the waiting rocks, in the very spot that Jacob had floundered so many years before.

IV

The funeral for the Captain and crew of the *Telegraph* was one of the best attended that the city of Chicago had seen. Every free descendant of a slave who lived in Chicago came to pay his or her respects. They knew what the Captain and crew of the *Telegraph* had done and why they had risked their lives. Every descendent of an Irishman was there because they also knew about the hardships of the repressed and, of course, Captain O'Flarity was Irish. Every descendent of the Potawatomi who still lingered in the area came because they knew what a good and wise man Seamus had been as, by extension, were those who kept company with him. All the members who worked the Freedom Train attended, for the Captain and crew of the

Telegraph had given their lives after taking so many to the promise and hope of a new and better life.

The crowd spilled out into the street and down the block. They all looked up at a sunset that was the most glorious anyone had seen in months. It was a shame that Seamus wasn't there to see the skyfire that seemed to be dedicated to him and his crew, but then, he probably did see it, just from a different vantage point.

Once they were back at the O'Flarity home, Kyle said to Robin and Clement, "He just quietly did what had to be done, as always, and you two will carry on by quietly doing what you have to do, just as he would expect of you."

"I feel bad," Clement, the thoughtful one said, "that he didn't live to see Mr. Lincoln elected. He must have died about the same time the last ballots were being counted."

"It's up to us, now," Robin said as he patted Clement's shoulder. "We know best what was in his heart; and since he's no longer here to carry it out, we need to finish the job."

"Your father would be proud of both of you," Kyle said with a sad smile.

Post Script

Dear Reader,

My wife and I have been residents of Bolingbrook, Illinois for over fifty years. We raised five daughters in this town and can't think of another place we would rather live.

In the 1830s, this was known as Barber's Corners. You saw the name in this tale. The Barber family did own a dairy farm near what is now known as Boughton Road and Illinois Rte. 53. They were friends of the Naper family, who settled what is now called Naperville.

The Scotts did reside at what is now the south end of Naperville on a farm called Fountaindale, which includes the confluence of the east and west branches of the DuPage River.

The River is named for the French fur trader DuPage. The DuPage trading post was said to be on the south bank at the confluence, consequently allowing easy access for the Native Americans traveling by shallow canoe.

Bailey Hobson's name shows up on many streets in the area, as he was an important part of the area, especially to the farmers who needed to get their grain ground. He set up a horse-operated grist mill along the west bank of the river where farmers could bring grain and, using their own horses, grind it and bag it. It didn't take long before the line of waiting farmers grew to the point that Hobson erected an inn and tavern, where the farmers could rent rooms and get meals and libations while they awaited their turn at the mill.

I have always felt that research and familiarity with one's topic lends authenticity to any tale; therefore, I have tramped the banks of the DuPage River, tangling my feet in the tall grasses washed flat by the spring floods. I have been trapped under a tree in a downpour, with a small herd of deer under an adjacent tree while we eyed each other for possible danger. The buck did lower his head and chuff at me several times in warning before determining that I was no threat.

Many of the people, places and events in this tale were very real. Many were the result of my vivid imagination. Your task as the reader is to determine which is which or to at least enjoy the tale. I sincerely hope you have as there are at least three more volumes to follow before the tale is told. Welcome to my imaginary world.

—Art

About the Author

Arthur W. Johnson and his wife June live in the Chicago suburb which, had it survived continuously, would today be called Barber's Corners. They raised five wonderful daughters in the town of Bolingbrook and now have eight grandchildren. Art plays a number of musical instruments, has played in two Air Force bands, and is currently a member of the West Suburban Concert Band, performing a number of free concerts each year. Art's experiences in construction and the many other positions he has held over the years have contributed greatly to his storytelling. He is also fascinated with history, and will incorporate as much fact in his stories as possible in the hope of his reader becoming as avid as he. He has recently finished writing his second script for a musical. He and his partner hope to have both produced before long. Art also hopes that his first collection of poetry, *Kindly Fool And Other Poems*, will be well received when it is released by Big World Network. *Skyfire* is the first in this series, and he is nearing completion of the fourth book.

www.ingramcontent.com/pod-product-compliance
Lightning Source LLC
Chambersburg PA
CBHW070533260626
47161CB00002B/360

* 9 7 8 0 5 7 8 6 8 1 7 5 7 *